Nevada Blue

John Tilsley is 50 and lives in Crewe. After serving in the Royal Marines he spent a number of years living in Las Vegas. His first novel, *Be A Good Boy Johnny*, was published in 1995 and was widely praised by the critics.

Nevada Blue

JOHN TILSLEY

PHŒNIX

This one's for you, Sharon. Thanks. Thanks also to my agent, Robert Kirby, and to Simon Spanton of Orion for their guidance and encouragement.

A PHOENIX PAPERBACK ORIGINAL

First published in Great Britain in 1997 by Phoenix,
a division of Orion Books Ltd,
Orion House, 5 Upper St Martin's Lane,
London WC2H 9EA

Copyright © 1997 John Tilsley

The right of John Tilsley to be identified as the author of
this work has been asserted by him in accordance with the
Copyright, Designs and Patents Act 1988.

A CIP catalogue record for this book
is available from the British Library.

ISBN: 0 75380 031 4

Typeset at
The Spartan Press Ltd,
Lymington, Hants
Printed and bound in Great Britain by
Clays Ltd, St Ives plc.

I

Ruby Goldstein parts the blind and looks down from her third-floor window. Below her a shadowy figure steps off the sidewalk and scans building frontage. The guy hesitates for a moment, snaps his fingers, then moves along; he's found what he's looking for. Ruby shakes her head and thinks this guy has got to be crazy to step from the safety of street lighting to find a joint like this.

Tommy Mace is neither crazy nor lost. Having walked cautiously five blocks from downtown, Tommy's eyes have slowly adjusted from neon to darkness. Just ahead a porno parlour sneaks a puddle of light across the sidewalk, but not enough to ease the chill that hangs like an ice-pick over this run-down district. There's not enough security in that muddy lighting to slow his pace or dismiss a long hard look at the dead-beat Negro leaning in the parlour doorway. The shuffle of sneakers somewhere behind him – Tommy snaps his head around – nothing there; just the back-drop of downtown casino glitz.

Next door to the parlour sits a skin-flick picture house. Tommy takes a long look into the small entrance. Inside a cracked glass case, a poster shows two blondes sporting huge breasts, baring the film's XXX-rated narrative. In appearance, this movie house seems a million miles from the one he passed not ten minutes ago on 6th. There they have near enough the same show, but the seven-buck entrance fee came with carpeted foyer and working candy machine.

He steps inside the shadowy entrance. A turnstile to the left. Beside it, built into a recess, a Plexiglas fronted booth. The bulb brightening the booth barely reaching the doorway. He freezes – somewhere close those sneakers are back treading sidewalk. Tommy makes his move. Six strides into the foyer and he's looking through the single light at the upturned face behind smeared glass. It's the kind of face Tommy knows from instinct could read back a story; a brutal story. Heavy scar tissue around the eyes says a one-time fighter – he wants to look a little longer but the face tells him to move it some. Taking the hint, he fishes around in his back pocket for the five-buck entrance.

The bill is quickly slid under the glass. The deadpan face nods, then slants towards the turnstile. Tommy stops in his tracks, trying to remember where he's seen that knock-about face before. He walks through the turnstile, squinting into the darkness, looking for room to sit alone. Taking a seat on the back row, he settles his flab into torn seating, eight-wide pink pussy and Dolby sound, this is Tommy's kind of joint. His eyes now fix to the screen, savouring the action, never missing detail. After a minute they close briefly. Where's he seen that face before?

Joey O'Sullivan rocks back in his chair and checks his watch: 10.20. Just forty minutes before the show ends and what the hell is that guy doin' coming in this time of night? There's one sucker that sure ain't going to get his money's worth. Reaching forward, he turns the dial on a small television tucked underneath the counter. He bangs its top, the black and white screen flickers into life; showing the movie action in the auditorium. Joey yawns and stretches his arms out wide. He knows the drill, he sees all the main players in the movie coming together for a group scene and knows soon he'll have to walk the aisle, flex some muscle and make his presence felt. Fridays and Tuesdays the picture house puts on a new two picture show. Tonight being Friday the place is pretty packed and he knows they'll be guys in there slung low in their seats, beating their meat like there's no tomorrow.

The turnstile being a one way deal, all Joey sees is one way traffic; everyone leaves by a rear exit door. For this reason an alarm sounds in the booth every time the exit door is opened. If it sounds off when a movie is running, Joey takes a peep through a small aperture in the wall studding to his left. A bulkhead light over the exit doorway shows him who's going out but, more important, who's coming in. Over the past six months he must have caught the same crew a dozen times now. They open the door and let their friends in and this don't sit good with Joey. Then he's got to wade in amongst them, sort them out and pitch them into the alley out back. They never give him real trouble, just a chase around the seating; it's a pisser all the same.

Sometimes he'd like to say fuck it, what's the big deal here? But the guy turning the projector would soon be talking with the owner and Joey too would be out in the alley looking for another place of employment. Joey pulls a heavy duty rubber flashlight from a shelf and releases the turnstile lock. No need to turn the key on the main door, this won't take too long. Before threading his way amongst paying customers, he walks to the doorway and sucks in the night air. Next door, Moe, the parlour manager, is leaning against the window taking a long pull on a filter.

The butt spins from Moe's hand and showers the sidewalk.

'You doin' any good tonight, Joey?'

Joey looks across. Moe must be all of sixty years and plenty past it for this kind of business, in this kind of neighbourhood.

'We're doin' good, Moe. Yourself?'

'Jack shit. It's a fuckin' joke. Thirty bucks is all the take. I guess Maurice must be makin' the payroll in your joint.'

'Guess so,' said Joey, looking up and down the street.

'Watch my back, Moe. I'm needin' to chase 'em around some.'

3

'OK, Joey.'

As Joey brushes through the wheel, Moe calls after him.

'That same nigger been hanging around again. I'll be watchin' the door, don't you worry none.'

Moe hears the dull thud as the rubber flashlight thumps a beat into the flesh of Joey's palm.

The first thing to hit Joey is the stench. Drunks piss on the threadbare carpet. Guys jerking off on to seats and mixing it with the piss. Spilt beer and ground cigarette butts add spice and seeing this place doesn't get cleaned properly from one year to the next, it amazes Joey how anybody could sit through the entertainment. OK, an old guy breezes through mornings, sweeping empty beer cans and cigarette cartons into a black bin liner, but that's as thorough as the cleaning gets.

From the back row, Tommy's eyes shift from the screen to the shadowy figure making its way down the aisle. Since he took a seat, his mind has been running in and out of bars and night-clubs. Where the fuck does he know that face from? That guy's a dead ringer . . . The figure walks slowly down – stops – moves on some. The flashlight comes to life, burning yellow down a row of sunken heads. The figure cuts the beam then moves quickly down the row and yanks out a body, spinning it into the aisle. As the body is thrown against the wall, grabbed by the collar and frog-marched to the exit door, it suddenly dawns on Tommy where he's seen that face before.

Below yellow haze from the bulkhead light, he studies the angry face. He'd have figured it in time, sure he would. It's been an age since he seen Joey – nine years – maybe ten. Yeah, Boston back in '64. One day Joey blew town and no one knew where. Talk at the time had it Joey got whacked and was buried deep in the foundations of the Rockwell Savings and Loan Bank. Jesus! Has it been so long? Tommy slumps lower in uncomfortable seating, the images on the screen become blurred as his thoughts race back through the years. Okay, he can figure why Joey walked out on Boston and made this city, any city, his home. But man! What's a guy like Joey O'Sullivan doin' working in a dump like this?

The steel door slams shut behind the jerk-off. There's just garbled dialogue from the screen as Joey makes his way back up the aisle. This is the second time he's had to throw that same guy out this month. But you can bet he'll be back next week and dollar politics dictate Joey will let him back through the turnstile. This joint barely turns a buck mid-week, so Joey will give him the nod; like I'm on your ass buddy, and maybe that'll stop the guy creaming over the furniture.

Joey swings back by the booth, Moe leans around the doorway and gives Joey the thumbs-up. They could shut down the main doors now, twenty minutes to run and the chance of more business is zero. Still, he needs the door open to charge his lungs with fresh air after the reconnoitre in the main hall. Signalling a thank you to Moe, he sees the jerk-off scooting past the entrance.

He settles back to count the evening take: 250 bucks. A fair take. He peels off a ten and five singles and slides them into his side pocket. Hell, no one's gonna know the difference. That turnstile don't clock shit anyway. He rolls the bills in an elastic band, then places the coin box alongside the television set. This money he'll hand over to the projectionist when they close up. Freddy's been on the payroll two years now, so he's the senior hand in this shit hole. He takes it on himself to handle the money for Maurice and this is the way Joey likes it; a little insurance: let that weasel take the responsibility, and God knows what Freddy skims off the top. Joey reckons more than his fifteen, so he makes the guy sign for the daily take just to be on the safe side.

His watch hand sweeps the half-hour – ten minutes to go, and at that moment Joey hears the bell warning him the rear exit door has opened. Perhaps it's some guy wanting to clear the joint before he hits the main lighting. Some guys are like that, they don't want to be seen shuffling outside with the rest of the crap. He won't inconvenience himself looking through the hole this time of night. The whole damn street could pile in for all he cares, in a short while he'll be flushing out the building anyway.

Joey turns off the set and ponders on where to stop for a beer before he meets up with Abilene. Someplace with a decent restroom so he can strip to his waist and soap this place clean out of him before Abilene finishes her shift at the Mint come midnight. Joey's thoughts are interrupted by a long shadow casting the passageway. His hand feels into a drawer. His eyes dart for the doorway, his grip tightens on the butt of a short barrel .38. It could easily be a stick-up artist this time of night. His eyes dance to the end of the shadow and his grip slackens on the cold steel. Joey read this face earlier tonight – standing there is the fat guy – yeah, the last one through the turnstile. Joey gets to his feet.

'We're lookin' to lock up any moment, sir. Come back tomorrow. The first show begins at two.'

The guy doesn't look like backing off. Joey plants his feet and spreads his hands, 'You don't hear so fuckin' good, buddy?'

Tommy takes one step back, raising a defensive hand.

'Joey O'Sullivan?' said Tommy, cautiously.

'There ain't no one by that name here, mister. You swing by at eight tomorrow an' I'll have you a seat reserved,' Joey said, dismissing Tommy, reaching for door keys.

'You're a likeness, that's for sure.'

'A bad likeness is what you see, mister – but who the fuck would be askin'?' Joey barks, his hand resting on the revolver.

'Tommy Mace. Out of Boston an' the name might mean a thing to Joey. I used to work for the *Globe*.' He pauses, waiting for a reaction. Joey's eyes remain ice cold. 'I seen him workin' out with a kid in Sammy Wathco's place on East 25th. The kid went on to good things. What was his name now? Boom Boom–'

6

Joey cuts in, 'Biello? Even *I* heard that fighter's name before.'

Tommy remembers the workout and Boom Boom's surname all too well. Biello went on to bigger things. Joey's career slipped away, but his out-of-the-ring activities became well documented for other reasons. Joey was a loose cannon back then with an Irish gang. And Tommy knows that's the reason Joey hitched a ride to be holed up in a dump like this.

'That's the guy. He was some fighter, yeah?'

'I remember some of his fights. Listen, I'm gonna get busy soon . . . real soon,' said Joey, flipping the keys.

Tommy nervously rotates a pinkie ring on his small finger.

'Hey! I'm only passin' time. What'd you say we go for a drink once you get outta here?'

The keys hang the air, then snap into Joey's clenched fist.

'You some kinda faggot?'

'Hell, no!'

'Beat it, mister. Now ain't the time. Like I said, I'm gonna get busy an' I have someone to meet right after the show.'

'Some other time, eh Joey? It'll be my pleasure.'

'Are you completely fuckin' deaf! There ain't no Joey, now take a walk before I bust your head.'

Tommy turns and shuffles out of the door. Joey's right behind him ready to throw bolts and hit the lights for the main room.

All those years, and sure Joey remembers the night back in Sammy's. That wop kid Biello went on to make boxing history, but the name Tommy Mace doesn't spring to mind. Tommy's sports coat fades into darkness, and Joey feels a shiver run along his back. Where the fuck did he come from? All these years, and nobody's got close. He feels the hair stand up on the back of his neck as he watches the stumpy figure cross 5th and turn a corner. Jesus!

Moe presses his face to the window and wonders what in the world the fat guy could have said for Joey to follow his progress with such sombre interest. Joey buries his hands deep into his pockets and bunches his shoulders. Moe's never seen Joey like this before. Their eyes meet briefly. Moe turns quickly away, embarrassed that he's somehow trespassed on Joey's thoughts.

Time's running on. Joey heads inside the auditorium to flush out the sleepers. There are only a few stragglers left, mainly the ones holding too much booze. They're easy, a dig in the ribs, a slap around the head and in no time they are on their way. While he's doing this, he's got to keep the rear exit locked; just in case someone sneaks back inside when his back is turned. Freddy, the guy who feeds the film, has come down from the projection room to give Joey a hand.

Freddy is a real puzzle to Joey. Fortyish and neat in appearance, Freddy looks the kind of guy who should be schooling college kids instead of projecting porno flicks. His scrawny frame now scooting between rows of seating, his eyes darting this way and that. Freddy's not looking for bodies, he's got his hopes set on a dropped wallet, a full cigarette pack or Zippo lighter. Freddy gets lucky most evenings, it's surprising how much the movie crowd jettison when they're tugging at their pants when Joey does a walk about. If it's cash, Joey takes the split. Cigarettes and lighters, Freddy pockets, and Joey figures Freddy must have the best Zippo collection in the state of Nevada.

For a second, Freddy freezes, then swoops low between seating.

'Joey! Got me a wallet.'

Joey looks over. Now Freddy's thumbing through the wallet with the greed of a kid locked in a candy store.

'Eighteen bucks – out of state drivin' licence. Aw, shit man! That's it.'

'Put the licence back and pitch the wallet in the drawer,' Joey calls over his shoulder, kicking open the door to the john.

The guy who lost the wallet might miss the dough some, but getting back his licence will be a paper-work pain in the ass for him. If the guy should come back, Joey will tell him they found the wallet in front of the picture house. 'What the fuck do'ya expect,' he'll tell the guy, 'be grateful you got the licence back, at least.'

There's no one in the john. Joey stoops over the single cracked urinal and takes a leak, thinking why this place smells fresher than the rest of the building. Perhaps it's down to neat bleach that's splashed about the floor and tiles each morning? Perhaps it's the fact that customers spill their urine in the auditorium and never make it back here? His thoughts are broken as Freddy walks through the doorway.

'How we do tonight, Joey?'

'Two hundred and ten,' Joey calls over his shoulder.

'We done OK. You walkin' downtown?' asks Freddy, propping grey-white wall tiles.

'Yeah. I'm walkin' that way.'

Joey always walks that way, and Freddy knows it. Thing is, Freddy's shit scared to walk by himself the six blocks to the cab stand. No cabs will stick around waiting a fare this time of night because three nights ago a cab driver got his head blown away, right outside the cinema. Lucky for Joey it happened after they had closed for the night, otherwise he'd have had all the rigmarole with the cops. It'll be a couple of weeks before the cab companies settle back into their old routine, then Freddy can call and order and as soon as he's searched the place for loot he'll be out the door faster than an express train, leaving Joey to secure the building.

They are just about done. Joey hands over the dollar wrap, makes sure Freddy counts the cash box and scratches out a receipt. The lights are left on to keep the rats from settling, and Joey slams the steel door tight and turns the key. Some nights the odd stray stumblebum hangs the alley; usually winos not too good on their feet and easy to step over. But they have to be careful. These bozos round here wouldn't know the takings are stashed along with the revolver in a floor safe. Joey takes the lead out of the dark alleyway and on to Fremont.

Moe's tucked inside the parlour doorway waiting. Out they come, the old man shuffles in behind and they walk towards the casino end of the street. The night has chilled, Joey pulls his old three-quarter coat tight around him and they gather pace. They walk against on-coming traffic so no fink can cruise along side and bushwhack them. Keeping centre sidewalk, away from store doorways and kerbside. Just a block gone, and Freddy gets lucky.

'Hey fellas, there's a cab up the street aways. I'm gonna run over an' get me a ride. You'll be OK now?'

'No problem, Freddy, see you tomorrow.'

Freddy got lucky. The cab won't hang about too long. He hotfoots at an angle across Fremont and after a brief exchange of words with the driver climbs in the rear door. The cab makes a U-turn, its headlights stirring cold grey store fronts and graffiti-sprayed plywood, then comes on towards Joey and Moe. Freddy's waving out the side window like Joey just done him one big favour. Then, perhaps he did. Because what Joey didn't see was what the cab off-loaded on the sidewalk. Now he sees them, and it's like the lights have gone out at the far end of Fremont.

Three black dudes mosey across the street to cut down distance on Joey's sidewalk. They walk like they're about to fall apart; arms swinging loose, legs weaving like they're ready to knit a pattern or take off quickly in any direction. Joey hears their mumbo jumbo. He knows these bastards could mean business. Just me and the old man, we must look sent from heaven for these guys.

They stop ten feet short. Moe moves in tight alongside the fighter. Joey grips the switch blade in his coat pocket, his thumb ready to press the button and snap the blade. Joey takes a step closer – eyes dart over the three hooded faces. His initiative has thrown them, now these guys ain't too sure, but still they bob, the middle kid straining hard to size Joey. What's slowed them?

The middle kid steps forward. 'Ain't you the guy that works the porno palace?'

Joey nods and the kid nudges his friends. Joey knows it's all over. Maybe it's not Joey that carries the weight around this neighbourhood, but the owner of the movie house. If the word got out that Joey or Moe suffered street hassle, Maurice would call in the heavy mob and those guys would have a crowd around them in quick time. The gang about turn and amble off with heads bouncing in tune to a monster coon box. Joey eases his grip on the blade and they follow the racket for three blocks down Fremont.

Moe nudges Joey playfully in the ribs.

'Those bastards! If I were thirty years younger, Joey, I'da torn their fuckin' heads off.'

'I bet you woulda. Forget it, Moe, you gonna join me in a beer?'

'Depends. What you got in mind?'

'The Roxy.'

Moe grunts an OK and jumps in step with Joey. They walk in silence, the cloud-wrapped sky pulling the tall cold buildings in on top of them.

They make a left at the intersection on 8th, and head for Joey's favourite watering hole. The Roxy is on the edge of the downtown area. Close enough to draw some vacation trade but far enough to discourage out-of-town mainstream gamblers. Everywhere in this city the clatter of slots is the norm in any casino hotel or bar, but here it's different. The bar area sings the city tune but the lounge is free of machinery and tonight there'll be cabaret. The Roxy is also a good place to clean up and wind down before meeting Abilene in the machine gun rattle of the Mint.

Ten minutes later Joey's washed and sat the furthermost

table from the crooner. Refreshed, he pulls on ice cold beer. On their walk and during the wash-down, his thoughts have drifted momentarily back to that guy, Tommy Mace. In and out he's come and gone, like some bad dream. Moe's sat opposite, slumped in red vinyl soaking in the singer, tapping his fingers on the table top as the crooner closes a Tony Bennett number.

'He's a singer all right. Ain't he something'?' said Moe, draining his glass. 'I'd bet you'd pay cover charge to hear this act any place but this city.'

'Sure you would,' said Joey, dream-like. He's sat this lounge, in fact this very seat, with Moe several times over the past months. Moe's a regular guy, he'll down three beers max then head home to his wife and trailer park some place on the south side. Problem is; more than three beers and Moe starts getting philosophical and inquisitive. Joey knows this old guy must be kinda street-wise. After all, working that parlour ain't your regular nine-to-five. Look at the neighbourhood? Jesus! Joey can't imagine his old man riding such a district, never mind working in it. He looks across at Moe, who's standing, waiting for Joey to empty his glass.

'C'mon Joey, what're you takin' your time over? You wanna a chaser?'

'Naw. I'm fine with the beer. Make it a bottle, Moe. It don't matter which.'

As Moe props the bar, Joey gets to thinking on this Mace guy. Thing is; he says he's from Boston and the more Joey rolls that old city through his mind, the more bitter the taste in his mouth. Too many memories, mostly bad, flood back to Joey as he waits for Moe to return with the beer. His mind twisting this way and that, the singer's cottony voice a million miles away. The chance of somebody sliding in off the street and recognising him in a dump like that? All the fuckin' way from Massachusetts? Man! Even this city wouldn't make a book.

Waiting for service, Moe takes a stool, tinkers with a beer mat and glances round the room. The room is pretty packed, its mood easy, the singer doing his job. His eyes settle on Joey. Now there's a dark horse if ever he saw one. You take Joey out of the picture house, walk him six blocks and you've got one nice guy. But back there he's all business. Moe's seen him go to town on guys and it wasn't a pretty picture. No sir! He went ballistic, moved in like lightning and wham-bam thank you ma'am, that's it – all over. He knows Joey was a fighter, not just the shape of his bust-up nose and the way he carries himself, but his speed and co-ordination. After a few beers he tried to draw a story out of Joey. Some chance, Joey clams up tighter than a crab's ass every time the past is mentioned. The bartender leans in his ear.

They sit in silence. Moe lights up a large cigar, in between puffs, hums softly in tune with the singer. Joey stares vacantly into space, he can't shake the fat guy out of his head. The *Boston Globe*? He don't remember no Tommy Mace, that's for sure. But this Mace remembers him. He never had the time of day for newspaper hacks anyhow. They know the phraseology of boxing, but none of them ever felt the sting and thunder of hooks and jabs, or the loneliness and rejection after a loss. How many times has he sat alone in a changing room? His head bent, his body racked with pain. Sweat dripping like an open tap, handwraps hanging loose, trailing the floor, soaking up dust and sweat. His trainer now too busy preparing the next fighter into the ring. This Tommy guy won't be any different.

Joey sinks down in the booth and thinks back on his last professional fight. It's like slo-mo black and white flickering images now, but boy! Did he take a beating; counted out in the fifth and he knew that was it. He hung the gloves, then hung out at Sammy's gym for a couple of years, picking up the odd buck sparring, letting younger kids like Biello take the piss and knock the shit clean out of him. But things had began to go wrong well before that last fight. The discipline that was once there as an up-and-coming had slipped into late nights and hard liquor.

OK, the training shook off most of the liquor but his sharpness and timing had slipped by the time he climbed through the ropes for his last fight. Where once it was a bedside clock that kept him company, now other things ticked the night away, like Irish mob guys and their broads who got it off around the fight scene. Although never anything more than a good journeyman fighter, Joey had been a somebody and was paraded around bars like some big celebrity. Out of his depth he was soon sucker punched into a 2000 dollar loan from an Irish mobster called George McLaughlin. The fights weren't coming Joey's way and he was struggling to make payments. No big shakes, says McLaughlin, but suddenly it's 'Joey take care of this, take care of that, will ya'. No big shakes indeed. All of a sudden a war kicks off between McLaughlin and the Italian New England mob. Now Joey's owing more favours than money, and that was the beginning of the end.

He allows the singer back inside his head for a moment or two . . . 'I left my heart, in San Francisco'. Unconsciously his hand runs over his belly and pinches at excess poundage, must be carrying an extra stone these days. Those were the days, but just how much does this Tommy fella know about them? A newspaper hack? You bet he knows the whole fuckin' story!

2

Tommy Mace kicks his shoes across the room and plods over to the bedside cabinet, pours a large neat vodka and settles into the easy chair. He looks around the room and nods his head with approval; the Starburst looks after him royally. He was here this time last year, liked its position on the Strip and already he's making plans to book in advance for the Fall. It's too damn hot come summertime in Vegas. It's early March now, the temperature just about right for Tommy. He slumps on the end of the bed, massaging his aching feet. Boy! That was some walk tonight. Through the patio window fairy lights swing to and fro over the kidney-shaped pool, glimmering and rippling in the pool's deep blue water. He watches the lights float against the coal black sky. It couldn't be better.

Tommy slowly unbuttons his white cotton shirt. He looks down at his huge belly: fifty-five years of neglect, thirty of those due to exaggerated expense account returns with various New England newspapers. If Tommy was to stand up and look into a full length mirror he'd be looking at a small, near to balding, round as a billiard ball, Irish-Italian. Tommy has certainly let himself go, and wasn't it he who not too many years back scribed, and knocked back finely tuned fighters in their prime years.

Tommy slaps his gut. Appearances can be deceptive, no way he's a soft touch. Walking the streets tonight, in a district he hardly knows, didn't phase him none. Most of his working life he'd been round the fight game. Most of that time he'd spent leaning through dusty ropes in broken-down gymnasiums. Watching the hopefuls and has-beens. Listening to endless freeloader spiel and wiseguy speech. The fact that most of these gyms were situated mainly on the wrong side of the tracks got Tommy street-wise early on in his journalistic career.

The other side of the tracks brought other fascinations for Tommy. From coast to coast, Tommy has made his sordid pilgrimage. Red light districts from Times Square to San Francisco's Tenderloin have been his Mecca. Tommy knows them all; for thirty years he's savoured their rancid odour and sloped lustfully in their slimy under-bellies.

Tommy pours another shot and skins cellophane wrap off his favourite cigar. He slowly plays the flame around its tip then sucks at the King Edward. His watch shows 11.10 and he's thinking, after his smoke, he might take a shower, a change of clothes, and step down the Strip to a casino and try his luck at the tables. He raises the glass slowly to his lips, the vodka tastes good and he sees the bottle being smarter company than some casino wanting to rip his money. Tommy swings and rests his legs on the king-size, his mind spinning back to Joey the middleweight. Although the guy in the flick show was denying all, Tommy knew it had to be him.

Tommy first saw Joey back in '58. The *Globe* had sent him across town to write a piece on Sammy Whatcho, an old time Negro fighter of no repute, but now training a couple of decent hopefuls. The story-line was to take on the struggles and aspirations of trainer and fighter. Tommy had been around the fight scene too long; nothing new in that cast of players. The narrative was so weak it never made copy. But that was the night Joey caught Tommy's eye. The kid had terrific timing, jabs and crosses slicing air like lightning. Man! Was that kid sharp. That night Joey was working down his poundage to make welterweight for a match the following Saturday.

16

Tommy could see Sammy's rising star making the middle weight division pretty soon and noted the name Joey O'Sullivan in his diary.

Joey made his next fight with an easy point's win. Moving up to middleweight he struggled against bigger fighters for a while, but by the end of the year had chalked up three victories by KO. It looked like many years of hard work and patience had paid off for Joey O'Sullivan and Sammy Watchow. Tommy reaches over and grinds the cigar into an ashtray. Dates and venues begin to bang about in Tommy's head; abruptly interrupted by a ringing tone from the bedside telephone. It can only be one of two people calling Tommy.

'Hey Tommy, how'ya doin' down there? You havin' any luck, buddy?'

The caller is an old friend, Jack Bones. Jack's a retired bookmaker of sorts. He still practises, but on the QT, away from the long arm of the IRS. His hoarse voice sounds unusually tense.

'What time you got there, Jack? . . . One p.m. . . . Jesus! . . . Naw, gamblin' ain't my bag, you know that. Anyway, Jack, it's good to hear from you. What's on yer mind?'

Jack wouldn't be calling unless it was important.

'You remember Frankie Francione . . . That's him. Clipped me for two grand last year?'

Wow, thinks Tommy, we're straight into business. What's goin' on?

'I got word today he's in Vegas. How about that, Tommy? D'ya fuckin' believe that?' Jack blurted, between breaths.

There's a moment's silence. Tommy's not too sure why Jack should be mouthing on about this guy, Francione. Sure, Tommy met him a couple of times, but what's the beef? What's the story?

'So what you gettin' at, Jack? Am I a fuckin' mind reader all of a sudden?'

There's a long silence, and Tommy senses Jack's hand over the mouth piece, as if he's cross-talking with someone else in the room.

'OK – OK, here's the deal. Francione stuck me for nine grand three nights ago–'

'What'd mean, stuck you?'

'What the hell do ya think I mean, Tommy. The guy stuck a piece in my ribs, and took off–'

'Nah. C'mon, Jack, he wouldn't do that. Frankie's been doin' business with you for years . . .OK, I believe you. Go see Carlo, why dontcha. He'll straighten things out.'

'I got a meet with the old man tomorrow mornin', but it ain't lookin' too good.'

'You fell out with Carlo! Jesus, Jack . . . OK, I ain't goin' to rub it in, but what help can *I* possibly be?'

'Go see him. Tell him some story–'

'Go see Francione! What fuckin' story! Go see him yourself, Jack. That guy's a fuckin' animal – is this some kinda joke?'

'It's no joke, Tommy.'

'I'm down here on vacation - you know? Kicking back my sixteen stone, relaxing and that kinda thing. Maybe tomorrow I'll enrol in a work-out class and knock myself in shape. Then I should start walkin' through hotel lobbies? Maybe I'll get lucky an' bump into him before the next millennium–'

'Sorry to bother you, Tommy. I only thought – you know I wouldn't ask if I wasn't up a fuckin' tree. Perhaps I'm gettin' too old for all this shit . . . Yeah, right, we're all getting too old. You have a good one, Tommy.'

'It's late your end, Jack. Call me back in the mornin'. Before ten o'clock my time.'

The line goes dead. Tommy stares in bewilderment at the telephone. What the fuck is going on? Never in a million years would Jack Bones call Tommy Mace over such business. OK, they go back forever, but what the hell was that all about? What's the *real* reason behind the call? It don't make sense.

Jack would only have to call one of a dozen guys that would take off right now, pay their own airline ticket even, for a forty per cent kick-back on the debt. So why the call, Jack? Have I suddenly turned into Superman? He closes his eyes, shutting out the pool-side lights to concentrate his mind. It just don't make sense. Jack must have flipped.

Minutes later his eyes pop open. The outside lighting no longer attractive, he pulls on a purple dressing gown and walks over to the window to draw the drapes. Looking out he hears the intermittent drum of night-time traffic stirring along the Strip. He presses his face tight to the glass, up the road some, he sees the bright lights of Caesars as they arc into black desert sky. His thoughts on stepping out have abated. Legs tired after treading the streets, his body sore after being cramped into poor cinema seating and the Vodka now beginning its rush, Tommy leans against the glass.

His fingers play around the business card in the gown pocket. Tired and dog-eared, the card has been in and out of wallets and drawers since his last visit to Vegas. Suddenly Tommy feels invigorated, the aches and pains falling aside as he lifts out the card and strains his eyes over the escort agency number. It's been a while since he was last in town. Will the agency still be in business? He hesitates for a moment, wondering if he should wait until tomorrow night, give his batteries time to charge.

Tommy draws the drapes and strides over to the bed-side telephone. Just on the off chance he'll call the number – see if they are still in business – maybe make a date for tomorrow night. The card shaking in his hand, he hurriedly lifts the handset.

'Hi there. Glamorous Escorts. My name's Sherr-ie. How can I help you, sir?' said a sexy, silky voice.

'How you doin', Sherry? I've used your agency before, and I was–'

'What's your Christian name, sir?'

'Tommy, the name's Tommy.'

'Hi Tommy, nice hearing from you again. This is just procedure, so don't take offence. Give me your number and I'll call you straight back. Are you staying in a hotel?'

'Yeah, the Starburst, on the Strip. Listen Sherry, I'm only calling to–'

'I'll call you straight back.'

The line goes dead. Tommy stares into the handset. What the hell, he says to himself.

Twenty minutes later, refreshed after a long hot shower, and sprinkled with cheap deodorant, Tommy opens the door to a tall brunette. Sherry had told him Doreen wasn't available, she'd left town in January. Doreen had been a favourite with Tommy. She knew his likes and dislikes, they had struck up such a friendship they once took in a show at the Tropicana. He ushers Susie into the room. She's mid-thirties, looks good and smells good too. She smiles down at him, and without a word brushes past his huge belly. Tommy attempts to rein in his stomach, rubs his hands with glee and follows her to the king-size.

Moe clenches his hands together, rings his knuckles white and yawns. He's tired. The singer has been replaced by a three-piece band and people have drifted out into other rooms to play the slots or try their hand at the blackjack tables. Moe glances down at his watch. He'd better be calling Mary soon, or she'll be getting worried. It's time to be going anyway, Joey's in a pensive mood tonight. Several times Moe has tried to open up a conversation but Joey stayed shtum.

'I'm gonna call Mary.'

Moe takes off, leaving Joey looking round the half empty room, glancing at a couple sat at the next table. The guy's heavy and bald, very much like that reporter fella that came by tonight. The woman is young and pretty. They touch and tease, like it's a fresh date. The guy looks out-of-town and loaded. Heavy gold around the neck and fingers stand off against dark expensively cut cloth. The guy's obviously mob connected, Joey thinks on what might have been if the Irish–Italian war had gone the other way for him. If he'd taken sides with McLean instead of McLaughlin.

Back in the late fifties, Bernard McLaughlin's Charlestown mob and Buddy McLean's Winter Hill mob, Boston's Irish Mafia, were as one, skilfully brought together by the New England Mafia boss Raymond Patriaca. The Italians had all but wiped out the power of the Irish mobs years back, but these two groups were reckless and territorial, so Patriaca figured, give 'em some room; there's plenty for everyone. Let the Italians take the cake; the Irish a slice. It's June 1960, Joey, realising his fighting days are coming to a close and looking to future pay-days, slides into McLaughlin's gang.

It all kicked off at Salisbury beach, a resort north of Boston, in May '61. Joey had been with Bernie a year now, and on this day he's chauffeuring his brother George McLaughlin around the resort bars. Joey has problems parking the Buick, George loses patience, kicks open the car door and heads for the beach. He's pissed with McLaughlin's attitude, it's always the same old crap when George takes to the sauce. So Joey takes his time finding a parking space. This kind of thing happens all the time when George is on the bottle; he knows he'll find him later in one of the beach bars.

One hour later he found George, the shit beaten out of him. It had all started when George got fresh with a girl in the company of a guy called Andy Petricone, an all right guy who was a friend of Buddy McLean. Andy and a friend gave George the beating. Over the next months there's friction between McLaughlin's Charlestown mob and McLean's outfit. Nothing too serious until Buddy finds a package of dynamite strapped to his car engine. McLean couldn't let that pass. In October he catches Bernie McLaughlin and, in broad daylight, lets go with a .45 automatic. Bernie's dead and the shit is about to hit the fan.

That was the beginning of a war that lasted into '65. During this time, scores of bodies are turning up, old scores are being settled, but worst of all it's making newspaper headlines. The public demand action. The police chiefs in the payoff of the Italian mob put the hammer down and the mobs are losing millions of dollars each week. Patriaca, who till now had thought these Micks would kill each other off and leave more room for the Italians, saw it backfire. McLaughlin's rackets begin to run dry in South Boston, so he starts shaking down bookmakers and night-clubs all over the city. Bookmakers – like Jack – have only one man to run to, Raymond Patriaca. The New England crime boss decides enough is enough and brings the two Irish mobs together to negotiate their differences.

Albert Tameleo, Patriaca's number two, is to table the meeting. George McLaughlin and his boys turn up armed to the teeth and Tameleo hits the ceiling and fires them out the door. This act of stupidity showed lack of respect for Patriaca, the very man who tried to broker the peace. That's it. Patriaca sides with McLean and all hell breaks loose.

In October '65, McLean's top gun, Joseph Barboza, whacked out Punchy McLaughlin in West Roxbury. Barboza was a cold killer who hated everyone, even himself. He was feared by all sides, including the Italians, who paid him weekly, year-in year-out, as a standby assassin. Joey was still driving, but the Buick had gone. Cars were changed every week to throw the opposition. It didn't cost, they were all stolen anyway. This was a tough assignment. If he was spotted on the street he'd have been blown away instantly. Worse still, he was driving a head case by the name of Steve Hughes, and sometimes Connie, Steve's brother.

Ten days after Punchy takes the count, Joey drops Steve off on Broadway, Somerville. He's told to move along the block and wait. Connie waits in the car with Joey. Ten minutes later, BOOM! – BOOM! – BOOM! Shit! Joey hits the gas pedal, swings the corner, barely misses a couple of people running for cover. Steve meets the car as it breaks to a halt, throws a shotgun through the opened rear window and walks coolly down Broadway.

Joey has just enough time to see three bodies lying on the sidewalk before he eases out into slowing traffic. Before they hit the end of Broadway, sirens are howling. Beside him, Connie hasn't said a word, just threw his coat over the shotgun and turned on the radio. Steve got Buddy McLean, the other two were wounded. The cold winter months rolled on. All sides hit the mattress. No money was being made and this war was hurting everyone. No one could be trusted, one minute a guy was on your side – next, he's crossed over and sleeping with the enemy.

After the shooting, Joey got so close to Steve Hughes he could almost read his mind. Steve wanted to take over McLaughlin's mob, and the way things were going, Joey could see that happening. Everyone was terrified of the guy, even when his brother Connie got killed on the Northeast Expressway in May '66, Steve kept up the pressure. Here was one guy the Italians just had to whack out, and Joey was stuck to him like glue. Everywhere Steve went, Joey was by his side. Joey was more than a driver now. He was bodyguard to the most wanted man in Boston.

Joey changed too. Sure, he'd been toe-to-toe with some tough mothers in his time, but this lot were different. Cruising the streets late one night they caught a guy by the name of Billy Bell escorting his girlfriend home from the movies. They drove them both to the basement of an empty tenement block and tied them back-to-back to a post. Joey sat guard in the lead car, the engine idling for a quick get away. The guys' clothing reeked of gasoline as they jumped aboard. He heard the fate of Bill and his girlfriend in excited cross-talk as they pulled away.

Both their heads had been doused in gasoline – then set alight – that's the way it was.

Hit – whack out – wiseguy spiel. Soon he was high on the adrenaline rush that came cruising the streets with Hughes searching for targets. On a hot sticky day in July, riding downtown, outside a barber's shop Steve recognises the plate on a '64 Lincoln. It belongs to Patriaca and in no time they are parked and running through the barber shop doors. That's how fast everything happened with Steve Hughes. Inside they open up with shotguns and left a trail of horror. They read later that the fire service was called in to hose the place. They also read they'd killed the manager of a body shop; he had been taking the car back to Patriaca after minor repairs and had stopped off for a haircut. The other three were customers waiting in line, sat there reading the papers. It didn't make a bit of difference to Hughes. 'At least,' he said, 'it's made the front page, and that'll keep those wop guineas on their fuckin' toes.'

The Italians imported a top gun from New York to assist Barboza. His name was Angelo Persaci. The heat was on.

This senseless shooting brought it all home to Joey. He was now as crazy as the rest of them. The Italians had the same dollar price on his head as Hughes. The contract was out – Barboza, Persaci and an army of guns were out day and night looking for them. One day Joey called George and said his father had taken ill. He had a trusted friend from the fight days to drive him to a Greyhound terminal. That was the end of the war for Joey. Barboza caught up with Hughes on 26 September 1966 on a Massachusetts freeway. There was another guy with him at the time, and both were killed. Joey read about it in the *Phoenix Gazette*.

Moe walks back into the lounge and stops short of the table.

'What're ya thinkin', Joey? You were a million miles away – hey, do ya need a ride anyplace? Mary will be pickin' me up in fifteen minutes.'

Joey bolts upright in his chair like he's been stung by a bee.

'Don't be doin' that! You nearly gave me a fuckin' heart attack.'

Moe looks apologetic, almost hurt, and moves back to his seat. 'Sorry pal. So – do you need a ride to the Mint? Mary will be happy to–'

Joey looks at his watch and scratches his thick head of hair. 'Naw, it's OK. Twenty minutes an' Abilene will be off her shift, but we'll walk out together. Can you manage a quick one?'

Moe springs to his feet.

'I'll get 'em. You want ice – or straight up?'

'Straight up. Tell you what. Bring me back one of those big cigars you're always tellin' me are the best thing since the Maguire Sisters.'

Moe winks an eye, smiles down at Joey and ambles off to the bar.

Joey's eyes close, memories flooding back. Funny thing – he went to a real picture house last Tuesday daytime to see the movie, *The Godfather*. It's like he's back in Boston for half the movie. Guess who's playing Sonny – he couldn't believe his eyes. That same kid that inadvertently kicked off the war – Andy Petricone.

If Petricone came out of the war OK, Joey didn't. After stepping off the Greyhound, he spent the next four and a half years flitting between Arizona and California. Doing any kind of work that didn't require a college diploma: digging ditches, laying pipe and just about anything manual around the construction industry. All the time he had to be aware of the long arm of the Boston Mafia. The contract on him stays forever, so he stays clear of union work, doctors and dental surgeries or anyplace he's got to show ID. He never owns a vehicle and never applies for a state driving licence.

He roomed in cheap accommodation, boarding houses where the landlady don't give a rat's ass about names so long as the rent is paid. The mob can trace anybody. Their hands are in every government agency. Apply for that driving licence and, before you know it, there'll be someone visiting as you step out the boarding house. Down at the picture house he uses the name Burke. No one asks any questions and he's paid in cash. That's just as well, because he couldn't open a bank account anyway, not being a Nevada resident. But who the fuck should turn up tonight – right out the blue – that fat guy, Mace. Where's he staying again? The Stardust? Star – something. Got it! The Starburst. Joey figures he's got to get to this guy before his journalistic nose tees off cheap copy for some New England newspaper.

There you go again, Joey. Fallin' asleep on me.'

'Must be all the excitement. Man! Sat in that dump, it's been a long day.'

Joey unwraps the cigar and lights up. A pretty Filipino cocktail waitress sweeps past the table. She glances over, her shitty smile tells the story. Him and Moe always buy their drinks at the bar to save on the tip. They wouldn't dream of tipping the bartender either; after all, no bastard tips then down at the porno joints.

'Tell me this, Moe. Is Mary still OK you workin' in a place like that?'

Moe pops the cigar between his teeth and locks his hands behind his head.

'She's OK with it,' he said, between clenched teeth. 'After all, what's a guy at my age got goin' for him? Not too much I can tell you. Perhaps if I'd gotten into casino work early on things would be different. They keep old timers till they drop. Still, I got a military pension to fall back on.'

Joey recoils at the words military. His Vietnam war didn't go too good. He never made it. And this is another ID crisis as far as Joey's concerned. He, like everyone else with half a brain, has dodged the draft. Too many cripples hobbling about on crutches for Joey's liking. There's one war Uncle Sam can shove sideways up his ass. Where's it all leading to anyway?

Stick a squeaky-clean Californian college kid alongside Private Slipinshit from an Alabama backwater, and what have you got? A fighting machine? A fucking disaster is how Joey sees it. Moe swings in his chair. Cigar ash tumbling down his shirt front as he points towards the stage. He leans forward, flapping ash from his jacket.

'Wouldn't you know. Just when we're about to leave, here comes the darn singer,' he said, easing down in his seat, resting the cigar in the ashtray.

'I ain't seen Abilene in a long while. How's she doin', Joey? Still enjoyin' workin' down at the Mint?'

Joey glances down at his watch again.

'Yeah. She's still there, but whether she likes it or not is another story. We better be moving it, you don't want to be keeping Mary waiting.'

They step outside into the cool night air, taking shelter from the biting wind behind a billboard. They'd have stayed inside the lobby and waited in the warmth, but Moe doesn't like Mary parking up. This CAB KILLER, as the *Las Vegas Journal* headlines him, has got the entire population of downtown Las Vegas on tenter-hooks. A guy sick enough to fire into cab windows for no apparent motive is crazy enough to fire into Mary's car. Several times Moe has told Joey to take off, he's going to be late for Abilene. Joey takes no notice, sticking by his side.

It's a little after twelve when Mary's station wagon turns on to 8th Street. She stops a while and exchanges pleasantries through the rolled window with Joey. Moe gives him a fatherly hug, then slides in alongside Mary. Standing on the edge of the sidewalk, he watches the car disappear down 8th. Yeah, Moe and Mary are an all right couple, he thinks as he foots pavestone for Fremont Street.

3

Abilene walks unsteadily towards the bar. Her feet aching like crazy, her head crowded with customers' cocktail orders. She should be in the staff room right now changing into street clothing, but for the second time this week her shift relief is ten minutes adrift. The management will give Masie a final warning, but that won't be nothing to what Abilene will lash at her after eight hours of hustling tips, and putting up with that cruel bastard pit boss, Jimmy Jinks.

She looks around the bar area. Joey's late, Masie's late. What's going on around here! Where the fuck have they got to? The bartender moves along the bar, stops to light a filter and hands it over to Abilene. She pulls hard on the cigarette.

'What you got, Abilene?'

'Jesus, Mike. Ain't the management heard of air conditioning? This place is as hot as hell.'

Mike looks at her impatiently. He sees another two waitresses making their way toward him.

'What you got for me, sweetheart?'

'Holy Moses, Mike! Hang on to your hat, will ya?'

She looks over the list in her hand and peels off the cocktail order.

Inhaling deeply, she watches Mike make a big deal out of the order. Pouring and shaking mixes like he's some kind of movie star.

'Hurry it, Mike,' shouts another waitress, slapping her order tab down on the bar. Mike looks up, blows a kiss, and carries on mixing for Abilene.

'I thought you'd finished your shift, Abilene? You like it here so much? I'd have had my ass outta here faster than a rattlesnake,' said Karen, gingerly lifting a sodden tab out of the liquor tray.

Abilene hisses, stubbing the butt into the ashtray, 'That bitch Masie is late again. Do you fuckin' believe that? Twice this week already.'

Abilene's about ready to lift the drinks tray from the counter when she sees Joey stepping between slot machines at the far end of the room.

'Just look what walked in, girls. What time you got, Mike?'

His eyes shoot to Joey.

'Fifteen after twelve. Give the guy a break, for chrissakes.'

Karen begins to call her order out to Mike. Abilene steadies the loaded tray then weaves her way through tables and gamblers, slapping her rump as she side-steps Joey. In Abilene's line of work, broad smiles are reserved for the best customers – the ones with luck running for them at that moment in time. She can spot a local hero a mile away; doesn't matter what they win, you can be sure they'll be checking in the chips and taking it home to mamma. She can easily spot the ones that just stepped off the Greyhound bus; dusty boots and grubby finger nails. These guys get service every thirty minutes. She's on the look for tippers with deep pockets, sharp cut suits and manicured nails.

Now and again it's more than a tip that's squeezed into her palm. Sometimes the nod of a head, the slow wink of an eye, and scratched in pencil, the telephone number of some hotel-casino. Depending on her mood, or if the guy is trim and handsome, she'll shack up with him the night. It's always worth a twenty-dollar note, plus a free steak if the guy is hungry. These affairs only happen if Joey says he's staying out all night. A card game, whatever, she don't give a shit.

But if Joey was to know *she'd* been out all night, he'd go apeshit.

As she passes a table near the front entrance, she feels someone pinch her backside. She quickly looks around, then down at the guy with the hand trouble, sees dusty boots and grimy nails.

'Fuck off, cowboy, an' take the horse you rode in on.'

The cowboy cocks a smirk and taps his card on the table for another draw. She hangs there long enough to see him bust his hand with a six of spades. Abilene feels a little better as she makes her round.

Through flashing lights and the rat-tat-tat of dollar slots, Jimmy Jinks walks across.

'Hey! Abilene.'

Before she has time to place the tray on an empty table, Jimmy's close enough for her to smell his cheap hair oil.

'Masie's turned in. You can knock off now.'

She's quickly through the tables, drops the tray on the bar, snatches up Mike's lit cigarette and turns on Joey. He shrugs his shoulders, tips his head and throws her a blank look.

'Where the fuck have you been? I should buy you a goddamn street map,' she said on the turn, before shooting off in the direction of the staff room.

With thoughts on wringing Masie's neck, her feet aren't aching any more. Joey watched her all the way, stood back as the tray hit the bar top with a thud and watched in amusement as Mike rescued glasses from tumbling to the floor. Mike rolls his eyes and shakes his head.

'Jesus, Mike. What's got up her ass tonight?'

'Masie's late. Christ! She's a wild one, Joey. Is she like this at home?'

'All the time, Mike. Give me a beer, will ya.'

But for Masie, the staff room is empty. By now the girls on Masie's shift have changed and hit the floor. Masie's sat on a low bench seat, her left foot resting her right thigh, fixing her shoe strap – pondering her lot – she has a fair idea what's coming. How come she had to be the one to relieve such a crazy horse as Abilene Rimarmo? Why couldn't it have been some fresh-faced kid new to town? The thinking is over; the staff room door crashes open. In a flash she's on her feet and backing up against the wall.

Holy Mary!

'Right! You fuckin' bitch!'

Before Masie can blink an eye, Abilene's swarming all over her. There is no way she can retaliate against the action-packed Abilene. Masie's seen her brawl once before with a girl called Rosie Oats outside Binnion's Horseshoe. Rosie is as tough as they come, but took the beating of her life, right there on the sidewalk.

All of a sudden Masie's tangled in the rush of Abilene's anger. She feels herself being pulled to the ground by what seems a man's strength. Her eyes pinched tight, waiting for blows she knows are coming, her head hits the floor, her hair ripped from her skull by a powerful hand. Her breathing almost stops as Abilene's weight straddles her chest – the blows don't come – frightened eyes sneak a peep up at the raging face above her.

Mike's busy at the far end of the bar. Joey's leaning back against the bar-rail, watching faces and action at the tables, fiddling about with loose change in his trouser pocket, wondering if to try his luck on the nickel slots. Joey dismisses the idea and looks along the bar to Mike. They make instant eye contact, and both seem to be reading each others' thoughts. What's taking Masie so long?

'You think I should check back there, Joey? Just to make sure everything's OK?'

'Girls talk. Give 'em a minute will ya? You know how it is. Say, you got any decent cigars?'

Mike reaches back, pulls one from a tin and waves it in the air at Joey. Joey nods connoisseur approval. It'll do, he's not a regular smoker, so he wouldn't know a good smoke from bad. He peels off a match from a flip-top and lights up. What the hell is keeping Abilene?

Masie's eyes shoot open, Abilene's distorted face is a blur behind the glowing cigarette end that is inches from Masie's face. Momma!

'Listen to me, dog breath, and listen good. You pull that stroke on me one more time an' I'll burn your fuckin' eyes out – you got that?' screams Abilene.

Masie would nod her head in agreement, but she's still locked to the floor, her face twisted upwards. Abilene strenthens her grip, leans in close.

'You hearing this?'

Masie's speechless, she's trying to utter something but the words won't come out. Her eyes plead, and she feels the weight lifting off her arms and chest. But Abilene isn't the kind to let go easily. The cigarette flashes before her eyes and she smells burning as Abilene grinds the butt into Masie's hair splayed along the tiled floor.

'Don't fuck with me, Masie! Next time I'll go all the way. Got that?'

Masie stutters, then words begin to form.

'I'm sorry Abilene – it won't happen again, I promise – it's just that–'

Abilene's not listening now. She's on her feet, straightening her skirt and running her fingers through her hair. She walks over to the handbasin and washes ingrained cigarette ash from her fingers. Masie, shaking like a leaf, thinks it prudent to stay on the floor until Abilene's gone.

Masie crawls to the bench seat and drags herself upright. God Almighty! Ten minutes adrift on a lousy graveyard shift and I hit a shit storm. She makes her way slowly over to the mirror. The hair on one side of her head is singed and torn, her face stares back, worn and old. Thirty years of age and lines are showing through the make-up. Hands creep up to her face and she begins to sob. Fuck you, Abilene. Fuck this the goddamn city, and fuck you too, Mike Walker. You knew all along what Abilene was up to.

After a short while, Masie dries away the tears, and begins to patch up with make-up. Reddening her lips and brushing out with powder, her grey-white face staring back at her from the glass. She's been in town seven years now. The city that promised all as she danced nimbly off the bus those years back turned to shit in two summers.

Las Vegas was no place for a wide-eyed tenderfoot. Her father told her so, but would she listen? Every Fall she tries to make it back to Deadsville, Kentucky. Clean mountain air shaving golden-brown leaf from tall aspen, and sometimes that little old town doesn't look as bad as it did when she was younger. It's too late now to be thinking on going back. Unlike the old timber-framed town, she's changed. Hardened around casino fast talk and scum like Abilene. She smoothes her short skirt, ready to go. She looks back in the mirror one more time. Watch your back, Abilene. I got your number, and one day soon it's gonna be pay-back time.

Abilene swept out of the staffroom like nothing had happened, but Joey knew different. 'Ladies talk,' was all she muttered as she brushed past him. Joey stays a step or two behind on the walk out. Masie inches out of the staffroom, her eyes darting this way and that – making sure Abilene has left the casino. She sees Abilene standing by the main door, and picks up speed towards the bar.

Mike looks up from the glass-washer.

'You OK, Masie?'

Masie picks up a tray and looks him straight in the eye. She'd like to smash it into his patronising face.

'Fuck you, Mike. You knew what was going on back there, don't tell me you didn't. You know something? That Joey fella seems OK to me, and that's a cryin' shame 'cause you and that trashy animal Abilene would make a nice couple.'

'Oh yeah?'

'Yeah. A couple of sad lousy shits. You talk to me when your balls have dropped. Till then, piss off.'

All the time she keeps one eye on the main doorway, waiting for Abilene to leave. Almost through the door and Abilene screws a finger in the air behind Jimmy Jink's back. Masie sighs, slaps the tray against her thigh and breaks out in laughter.

They walked some, then Joey flagged a cab outside The Lucky Dollar. They both sat in silence during the ten-minute ride to their apartment on Main. Inside, Abilene's shoes are kicked off and left lying by the door as soon as she treads carpet. Joey's close behind her, stumbles over the shoes, swears, then kicks them in the direction of the television.

'Hey, Joey. You seen the filters anyplace?'

He watches Abilene rooting around the kitchen looking for coffee filters. He shakes his head, there are none, he looked this morning.

'We're fresh out, ain't got none,' he shouts from the lounge.

'You have to be jokin' me! Didn't we shop last week? What're we gonna do?'

'Drink tea.'

'Drink tea! What the hell are you talkin' about? I ain't drinking no tea.'

'Please yourself. I'm gonna take a shower.'

An hour passed. Joey kept a tolerable distance from Abilene. She'd spent most of that time in and out of cupboard drawers. Clothing now lies scattered over the bedroom floor and Joey's hoping she'll stick it all in a suitcase and leave town. How long have they been together now? He counts the months on his fingers. Six, and all that time it's been much the same story. They have no common interests. Now and again they seek each other out in night-time darkness and their bonding is wild and furious, but come daylight they begin to circle each other like two bruised fighters once again.

Abilene mutters a sleepy goodnight, turns off her bedside light and snuggles down on her side. Joey props himself on two pillows and opens the pages of Micky Spillane's, *My Gun Is Quick*. This is the first book Joey's read since he was a kid, and that was so long ago that he'd forgotten its title. So now, at the age of thirty-eight, he's struggling with the words. Slowly reading the pages, flipping back at names and places every so often so as not to lose its construction. He found the novel amongst a pile of stroke books in the picture house booth next to the black and white television. The cover now a faded yellow, its pages chafed and dog-eared. That didn't matter, he liked the title and is enjoying the book in his own unhurried way.

After forty minutes his eyes begin to ache. He looks around the room. Across to the double wardrobe. Inside it is all he owns; five shirts and three pairs of slacks. Draped over a chair, his jacket and raincoat. Under the bed, two pairs of shoes in need of repair. That's it. He could carry all he owns in an holdall.

He looks at her clothing, scattered around the carpet, then down at Abilene, sleeping peacefully; if only Las Vegas could see her now. He shakes his head, reflecting on how they came together.

Six months ago, Joey shared a ride into town with a couple of guys he was working alongside in Southern California. The construction site closed for the summer vacation and a couple of the guys had booked a motel room in Vegas. Joey thought: why not? The motel room had been squared months before, one guy dropped out. So Joey was invited along to make up the numbers. Joey packed, slinging a few clothes together, and tossed his case in the trunk. It was Joey's first time in Vegas, and he was immediately attracted to its bright lights and fast pace. On the second day they stopped by the Mint to shoot craps and liquor-up.

That's when he first saw Abilene. It was instant attraction. He found out later she'd been a peel-off artist back in Illinois. The strip joint let her go when she hit thirty. There was nothing really wrong; her tits were holding up, her ass was nice and tight, but her face was looking too danced out for the younger clientele the joint was drawing in. But to Joey she looked a picture. Some foxy lady, and pretty soon a generous tip and a slow smile clinched a date. He asked what time she was getting off the shift, and they arranged to meet at the bar afterwards.

Joey never made it back to California. He told his friends to trash whatever was his in the boarding house, and set up home with Abilene. Everything was fine to begin with – like it always is. But Joey found Las Vegas hard for work. There is plenty of it here, the fastest growing city in the Union. But this is a union town. Casinos, catering, construction, you name it, it's all tied up by the union. Now union reads mob to Joey, and thoughts of days gone by steer him clear. No money coming in and love soon goes out the window. Abilene's keeping both of them on her salary and tips, and don't she let him know it. All the time she's bitching and calling him a lazy bum, and Joey's losing self-respect and sinking deeper into psychological debt.

Other things had Joey on his toes when he first arrived. This being Mob City, every time he steps outside his eyes are darting this way and that. Although most of the guys involved in the Irish-Italian war are either in the bone yard or banged up in jail. Step by step, street by street, he loosens up. Then one day, sipping coffee from a polystyrene cup on a bench seat up by the courthouse, an old timer talks on about his job at the picture house and how he's got to leave and take care of his invalid wife. Joey's all ears.

He takes off down Fremont and makes enquiries. Two days later he gets to meet the owner, Maurice Turner, who first off tries to dissuade Joey. Telling him he's too young, the wages ain't so hot, and soon he'd move along and once again he'd be having the problem of finding another manager. Joey senses

Maurice has taken a shine to him. After all, doesn't Joey look the kinda guy who can bang heads and keep the place in order? If the truth was known, that old timer was older than baseball, and had let the place go to the dogs. Guys running in and out the back door like it's some easy-come easy-go theme park. 'OK,' he says to Joey, 'I'll give you a shot. But don't come around tellin' me I didn't warn yer.'

Now at least he's got some kind of income, but still Abilene keeps him poor. Every Friday she holds out her hand for half the rent, food and utilities. The weekly shop he hardly eats; the monthly rental on a telephone he never uses, a list of waste as long as his arm. She knows the more he's strapped, the less chance he has of finding a place of his own. Her motives bewilder Joey; if they lived an amicable existence he might understand. But the way things are, you'd think she'd be glad to see the back of him. Joey sees the day when that will happen, and he's making plans.

It's not every night he dips into the picture house takings, just weekends. Most of this money he hides under a loose board in the bedroom. Yeah, right there below Abilene's discarded underwear. There must be close to 200 bucks under there; enough to move out right now, but he needs to play along with Abilene a little longer.

Joey douses the bedside light and closes his eyes. He pictures a single trailer out in the desert, its paint-work a burning orange set against a blazing sunset. The freedom to walk out in the early morning light and fill his lungs with desert freshness. Watch the sun rise over distant mountains and feel the cool of the desert floor beneath his feet. He could do it, but he'd need transport. That would mean a driving licence and phoney ID. It's going to take a while yet. He settles down and feels the untouchable warmth of Abilene's body.

The dawn creeps in, kindling sage brush *terra firma*, releasing a canvas of blue sky over the Nevada desert. Tommy stirs out of a deep sleep, his hand padding the bed in search of Susie. She's not there. What the hell! His mind is put at ease as he hears the toilet flush. Eyes slowly open, then shut tight. His forearm clamps his forehead, shielding him from the light streaming in through the opened drapes. He hears her silky footsteps, then the shower pound the nylon curtain.

Jesus! What time is it? His hand sneaks out and gropes the top of the bedside cabinet, clinking the wrist watch against the half-empty vodka bottle. Clutched by the strap, the watch is dragged under the covers and brought close to his face. 8.45. Goddamn! I got Jack Bones calling me anytime now. Wrestling his roly-poly frame off the bed, he slopes into the bathroom.

Several times he cups cold running water to his face and lets it run over his naked body. Somewhat rejuvenated, he clenches the toothbrush in his mouth and gapes at the outline in the shower curtain. She was good – damned good. But it wouldn't have really mattered if she'd have walked in with a hare-lip and a hunched back. Tommy was in desperate need of company last night. He'd edged a little when his thoughts had turned to making that call to the agency. But he's sure glad he did. Another ten minutes later, another shot of vodka and you bet he'd have made the call anyway.

Susie parts the shower curtain and steps gingerly on to tiled floor. Tommy's toothbrush hangs in mid-air for a second or two, ogling at the bits that cost him twenty bucks last night. He throws her a bath towel. She smiles, but Tommy knows that smile don't count for a thing. She's showered, so a fuck is out of the question. He could ask, tell her she was the best thing since sliced bread, but that wouldn't work. Once she's showered and powdered that's it, buddy, the party's over. Tommy's been down this road too many times; he knows an extra five bucks will secure a blow job, even if she was about ready to race out the door. The toothbrush gets back to work and he's thinking on it when the phone rings.

Tommy wraps a bath towel around him; it's a good thing

the motel stocks extra large, and makes a beeline for the telephone.

'That you, Tommy?'

'Hi, Jack. Who else, what d'yer know?'

He winks at Susie standing in the doorway.

'You know I was tellin' ya about this no-good bastard Francione. Listen to this, will ya. I got word back he's throwing dough around Caesars like there's no tomorrow. Know what I mean Tommy? My dough, for chrissake!' blurts Jack, like he's about to explode.

'I've been thinking on this business, Jack, and it ain't makin' a lot of sense. I mean, what's happenin' up there? All you gotta do is give Baritsi a call. He'll call Carlo an' that's that.'

Tommy can almost feel Jack's irritation on the other end of the line.

'Weren't you listenin'? What did I tell you last night? I'm just about to meet with Carlo. I'm stood in a call box freezing my balls off, so don't *you* be givin' me a hard time.'

'If I could help you, Jack—'

His eyes roll to Susie, sat on the end of the bed pulling at her nylon stockings. She hooks up, then rubs her fingers.

'Pay-up time,' she whispers.

'Hold fire, will ya, Jack? Somebody's knocking the door.'

He opens the bed-side cabinet drawer and pulls a ready twenty bill. Susie pouts her lips and lowers her eyes. Is that all, Tommy? Wasn't I worth more? He waits until she raises her eyes, then tosses a five-spot on top of the twenty. She smiles and places her hand between his legs. He shrugs his shoulders, making out he's not interested. It don't amount to nothing keeping in with Susie. She was good all right, but it's the agency he's got to look good with. If it gets back he's tight-fisted, the next time around you bet they'll send him the hunchback.

She pockets the dough and skips the room. Tommy stares at the door long after she's gone.

'Sorry, Jack . . . yeah . . . changin' the linen.'

'Look, Tommy. There's got to be a way. Get word to Francione.'

'Me? That gorilla!'

'It's serious.'

Jack's voice trails off like Francione just got a hold on him. Tommy's thoughts run back to the picture house.

'Call me back tonight, I seen an old face in town.'

'Who the fuck are you talkin' about?'

'Joey O'Sullivan.'

'You shittin' me, Tommy? I thought that Irish pig was dead and buried. If word got back to Carlo.'

'Do yourself one big favour an' tell him, Jack. It might do you some good at the meet.'

'Thanks, Tommy. I owe yer. I'll call you later. Hey! Don't be doin' anything I wouldn't. Hear me?'

'I'm hearin' you.'

Tommy rests the handset and reflects on Jack's urgency. Though retired, Jack still takes bets from a few mob guys. But as Tommy knows, one minute those guys are in bed with you, the next they're out to kill you. His stomach starts to rumble. He looks at his watch. Breakfast is calling.

4

Rubbing sleep from his eyes, Joey ambles out on the veranda and leans against the handrail. He scans the courtyard below. Inactivity and calm, a radio somewhere below eases off a soft Johnny Mathis tune, along the veranda a baby cries for its early morning feed. It's early yet on this Saturday morning, its residents still at peace. Joey knows this will change as soon as the community is up and moving.

Negro men will roll out bare top and dive into car engine compartments. Later they'll sit amongst oily debris, drinking cheap thin beer and passing around cannabis smoke. Their wives will mope around, rocking an endless number of kids on their large wide hips, bitching and goading their menfolk into action. Hispanics will polish their cherry red pickups to a brilliant shine, all the time keeping a distrustful distance from the Negroes. Sometimes there's friction between the weekend mechanics, then the Hispanic women, who normally keep themselves to themselves, come out and join in the action. On these occasions, Joey watches from his grandstand pitch in great amusement. Those Hispanic chicks aren't to be fucked with, they can really turn up the heat.

Below in the courtyard a couple of months ago, a pretty young Hispanic girl slashed a Negro's cheek wide open with a paring knife. She was the girlfriend of some kid down the block. Anyway, the cops turned up and took her away, she was never seen again. Turns out she was a wetback from Old

Mexico, and he got to thinking how one single incident like that can turn your everyday world upside down.

How many times over the past years would he have liked to tell some jumped up construction supervisor to stick the job up his jacksie? Plenty. He couldn't because having no social security number limited his choice of employment. How many times has he held back smashing some fink who got his back up? He's lost count. All because of getting his name back in the system. But the days of apprehensively walking the streets, placing strangers' faces in daytime brightness or smoke-filled casinos have all but gone. These days Joey walks the streets sure of foot, and casinos no longer hold the bogey man.

Behind him he hears the television jump to life. Abilene's up and Joey's peace has been disturbed. Before he has a chance to turn and plan his entrance, he hears Abilene's voice. Turning slowly he sees her leaning the doorway, fingers running through dark shoulder length hair, her baby doll riding high on her thigh.

'You gonna run the store for filters, honey?'

To say no would cause a shit storm. She may be OK right now, thinks Joey. But one look in the mirror and she'll see the work needed to reconstruct her face back to something normal. It's obvious she hasn't looked yet, otherwise she'd be throwing make-up around the bathroom and telling the world what a bitch life is. Normally, Joey would tell her go get it herself. But is anything normal anymore?

'Yeah, I'll go. Put them on your list for the next shop, why don't you? All the time we're runnin' short.'

'Go fuck yourself, Joey. I ask a favour. Just one thing, an' look what happens. Straight away it's too much trouble. Who pays the fuckin' rent—'

With one leg in his flannels, Joey turns so quickly he stumbles against the sofa. His blood is boiling, the veins sticking out on his neck, he steadies and rounds on Abilene.

'Damn! Five blocks to the store. Too much trouble? You're the fuckin' trouble around here. An' am I hearin' right? Every week I tip up, so don't be givin' me this rent shit,' he said sharply, buckling up his belt, throwing on a T-shirt.

'What you gonna do about it then, Mr Tough Guy? If it don't suit. Check out.'

Joey slams the door behind him. Go take a look in the mirror, he mutters to himself as he skips down the flight of stairs. At least he'll get some peace for the next hour or so. He makes a left out of the complex and strides out for Fremont. He'll take coffee in the California Hotel on Stewart, maybe jaw a while with guys he's got to know since he's been in town. Then he'll walk to the Seven-Eleven on the corner of the Boulevard to buy coffee filters and razor blades.

The sun's heat has begun to scour downtown sidewalks. Joey keeps tight to building shadow, stopping briefly at a kiosk to buy a Coke to quench his thirst. There aren't too many people on the sidewalks this time of day. The casinos will still hold the die-hards; the kind that never know when to quit. But most of them will have retired to hotel bedrooms by now to recuperate before their next big roll of the dice.

As Joey expected, the California's bar is as quiet as the sidewalk outside. There is plenty of spare seating along its bar. Joey takes a stool, makes his order and looks around the walls. Across the room in a corner booth, he spots Jake Lassoto and Eddie Tonks. These two work the tables at the Mint, and they came across to Joey as OK kind of guys. It was Abilene that introduced them to him. He remembers the night; it was the night she tore some poor broad to pieces outside the Horseshoe.

The black coffee bites at his throat. He's facing the bartender who's trying his best to look busy when he hears Eddie's call.

'Hey, Joey. Why don't yer c'mon over an' join us?'

Joey raises his hand to say in a moment, and nods at the

bartender. His cup refilled, he walks over to the booth. Jake slides over some and Joey slips in beside him and pushes away cigarette smoke.

'How you doin', boys?'

'Fine, just fine. Yourself?'

'Couldn't be better, Jake. Kinda early, ain't it. You guys must be workin' the afternoon shift. Right?'

They both nod and share a look that tells Joey something's amiss.

'We've been playin' the table down the Tropicana. Eddie done real good.'

'What's happenin', Eddie? I missed somethin'?' puzzles Joey.

Eddie fumbles around the edge of a table mat. Jake nervously stubs out his cigarette, and both look childishly about them.

'C'mon, boys. Let me in, will ya?'

A thin-lipped smile forms below Eddie's narrow eyes. He sees Joey getting impatient, both his hands clenched on the table top like they're ready to strike.

'Just thought we'd tell yer – Abilene gave Masie a workin' over last night.'

'She did? Jesus! You sure about this? I didn't see nothin''

Eddie flips a table mat and throws Jake a knowing side-glance.

'It happened in the staff room, Joey. She's gonna be outta work–'

Joey sees Jake about to light up, slides the ashtray over and eyeballs Eddie.

'Hey! Masie's been around the block a time or two. She won't be sayin' fuck all, that's for sure.'

Jake cuts in. 'That won't count for beans. Jimmy Jinks is shafting Masie these days.'

Joey looks at him with genuine surprise. 'No kiddin'? I thought the guy was set square with his woman?'

'No kiddin', Joey. So, Abilene's out, believe me,' said Jake.

Joey shrugs. Eddie and Jake fake an astonished look that Joey never knew Jimmy was screwing Masie, and the three sit in silence. Joey knows why they appeared concerned. Hasn't Abilene told all of Clark County how she supports Joey? How he'd never make it without her salary and tips. But doesn't it come to something when three grown men have to walk around each other just because some maniac cocktail waitress loses her fuckin' job?

Joey knows Jake has reasons to rock the boat. Last year Jake had a three-week romance with Abilene and this tattle might have something to do with that fact.

'You sure about this?' enquired Joey, warily.

'Dead sure. We called in the casino on the way over an' that new floor manager, Jerry White, told us so,' said Eddie.

'Fuck her anyway, boys. How's Masie?'

They both laugh nervously.

'Masie's fine.'

There was some small talk, then Eddie and Jake took off. Joey waited a while then stepped out into the sunshine. His step along Stewart is slow; his thoughts in overdrive. Abilene losing her job will throw his game plan. He needs to hang in a few more weeks, but how's he going to cope with all the shit that's sure to fly. You bet within a day or two she'll be all over him for money he hasn't got.

'What money? I don't make a decent wage as it is,' he'll say.

It won't make any difference in that department to Joey. As far as he's concerned, even if he had, she wouldn't see a dime. She'll be moaning day-in day-out, never off his back. As he turns into the Boulevard for the Seven-Eleven, he's wondering if it's worth hanging in any longer. Should he go back to the apartment and pack his meagre belongings and leave her to moan alone?

5

Two thousand miles north, under a blanket of grey sky, two men sit beneath the Bunker Hill Monument. The park workhand sweeping litter twenty feet from them could easily think the two old timers are reputable business men. Both are smartly dressed and clean shaven. But as he sweeps closer to the bench a menacing side-glance from the smaller of the two tells him to leave and sweep the area later. Those piercing blue eyes once belonged to the front page of a *New York Times* he'd found in a trash can one Monday morning last summer. He'd propped himself against an oak and read the article. Something about a new commission into mob racketeering. He'd never forget those cruel eyes, set like stones in crumpled news print. The sweeper makes a beeline for another stretch of pathway. Grasano shrugs his heavy overcoat around his shoulders and looks up at clouds skimming low and fast from Massachusetts Bay.

Carlo Grasano shifts restlessly on the cold bench seat, trying to generate warmth from the wooden slats.

'It's gonna rain, Jack.'

'Tell me. You know, Carlo, we should be resting these old bones down in Florida. Sat by the pool. Cocktails, broads and the sun on our backs instead of this damp city. What you say?'

Carlo looks over at Jack like he's going crazy in his old age.

Broads? Where the fuck you comin' from? It took you all

46

your time to walk the park. Broads? This Francione thing? I think you're losin' it, Jack.'

Jack looks up at the clouds racing overhead. Just somewhere to look, avert his eyes from Carlo's stony scrutiny.

'Dreamin', Carlo. Just dreamin' is all.'

'Well dream on, Jack. This is Boston, an' the heavens are gonna open any minute.'

Carlo pauses, and waits for the sweeper to get out of earshot.

'Let's get to where we're goin' on this thing.'

Carlo leans forward, wringing his hands, staring up at Jack.

'What you gonna do about the money? Basto is breakin' my balls an' you know the guy is a fuckin' whacko. I need an answer now, Jack.'

Jack eases himself off the bench, digging his hands into his coat pocket. He knows that no way is Tony Basto breaking Carlo's balls. Carlo Grasano is number one in the New England mob, supreme boss; Basto's a mere soldier. Trouble is, both he and Francione are made men, they're family. Jack feels a chill run over his body, and it's not due to the inclement weather. Carlo stands, snaps the brim of his felt hat and stands shoulder to shoulder with Jack.

'How long we known each other, Jack? Forty years?'

'Must be. I sometimes wonder where all the years got to.'

'Yeah. Only last week I'm in Brockton to see my grandkids–'

'Laura's kids? It's been an age since I seen her. How's she doin' these days?'

'They're just fine, Jack. They got a lovely property down there. Six bedrooms, basement games room, double garage – the works. How much is yours worth these days, Jack? Twenty – thirty grand, maybe?'

Jack stops dead in his tracks and tugs at Carlo's sleeve. Carlo shakes him loose and carries on down the path. Jack shouts and catches up with him.

'Hey! Wait on, Carlo. Listen to me. I made a call to Vegas. In a day or two things will be straightened out, you'll see. I promise ya.'

Carlo reels and meets him square on. His right hand freeing his coat pocket, a diamond studded finger strokes the air in front of Jack.

'For you Jack, an' for old times' sake, I'll tell Basto to back off. You got one week – one week only. It's the best I can do.'

Jack's eyes plead for time, he's got to throw in his ace card. 'I got word Joey O'Sullivan is in Vegas.'

'Is that the guy who's gonna straighten things out for you? Forget it, Jack.'

In the space of fifteen minutes the meeting is over, but Jack did well to induce a meet in the first place. A man of Grasano's stature shouldn't be here at all. Grasano follows a slight turn in the path. Two heavies fold their newspapers and silently move alongside Carlo. As if by magic, a highly burnished limousine rolls to the foot of the pathway. The driver looks quickly into the rear-view. Satisfied, he nods to the three descending figures and they gather speed. For a seventy-year-old, Carlo Grasano pops through the opened rear door like a running quarter back.

Jack stands motionless for a couple of minutes. Watching the limo ease into slow-moving traffic. Treading slowly along the tree lined pathway, thoughts run through his head; he'd been set up on this one; but it had to be Grasano's doing. Basto might be a made man, but he's a fringe member and would have to have Carlo's blessing to pull a caper like this. Jack always found him an easy-going guy; he'd call by sometimes with stolen this and that from hijacked trucks running out of Logan Airport. After a while his face gets familiar to Jack and he lets him run a line of credit. Losing bets, Tony came good every time on payback. He came good until Jack credited him a big one; three thousand on a pony called Sassy Sally, running the 3.20 at Suffolk Downs. As long as he lives, he'll never forget the name of that fuckin' mule!

Sally bolted home a two-length winner at odds of three-to-one. Jack nearly had a coronary as he heard the result over the wire. Before the day is out, word has it Grasano put the fix into the race. Jack knew he'd have to eat this one; there's no enquiry into the running of Sassy Sally, the result stands and Jack's got to weigh in nine grand with Tony Basto.

This hurts Jack like hell. Not only in the pocket, but the fact he's been stitched by Grasano, who not ten minutes ago was preaching the old pals act. It was Carlo's money all along, so why use Tony to run up a line of credit? Jack figured these guys like to play games and they'll play 'em right down to the wire.

Basto calls Jack and tells him he'll pick up the cash between eight and eight-thirty the following evening at Jack's Sommerville address. In his bookmaking days, this kind of payout wouldn't have phased him. But now, repairs to the old detached house and Jessica's medical bills have eaten into his bankroll. The next night he's sat in a room at the back of the house he calls an office, waiting on Basto. Sitting in a captain's chair, the money lying in a suitcase at his feet, every now and then tapping the case with the toe of his shoe to assure himself this is for real; it's not one bad dream. Glancing up at the wall clock – shaking his head – wondering how the hell he got caught so green after forty years at the sharp end of the bookmaking business.

Five after eight. The rear door bell rings, Basto's early. He slowly uprights out of the chair and saunters over to the door. He figured Basto wouldn't be late, after all, this is a load of dough. As the door inches back, it isn't Tony Basto standing there, it's Frankie Francione. Straight away Jack knows he's in big trouble. Francione sticks a .44 in his face and Jack starts backing off. Francione didn't even shut the door behind him; that's how confident he was. It's obvious he wasn't expecting Basto to show.

Within minutes, Francione's out into the night with the suitcase, and seconds later Jack's making desperate calls all over the city to find Carlo Grasano. Grasano can't be found. Just when he's calling his sixth restaurant, the door bell rings. Jack drops the hand piece, and races to the door. Surely there's been some mistake.

Tony Basto stepped in and asked for his money. Jack explained Francione had taken the nine only minutes earlier. But Basto's having none of it. He threatened Jack with all manner of violence if the cash wasn't there when he returned. He didn't set a day or time. It was then that Jack knew he had been set up in grand style; Francione would turn over at least three grand to Grasano. Grasano comes out an outright winner. He skins the track. Collects the three from Frankie. Then, by way of Basto, comes after the nine he stole from Jack in the first place. If Jack doesn't tip up the nine, or a decent part payment, Grasano will be asking for the deeds to 15 Cromwell Gardens.

Grasano wants Jack finished. He's getting in the way of a mob book. It's come time for Jack to close *his* book.

The dark sky emptied before Jack made the roadway. The soaking didn't trouble him. It felt like the rain helped wash away the bullshit he'd just endured from Carlo. He had to take it on the chin, there's not a friggin' thing he could do about it. Worse still, he'd called that fat fuckin' pervert, Tommy Mace, last night for help. Jesus! What's the fuckin' world comin' to?

Inside the Starburst dining room, Tommy sprinkles Tabasco sauce on scrambled egg and hashbrowns. He'd have ordered bacon, but got spoiled once, remembering the time a friend flew in from Ireland with bacon so big and broad it looked like beef steak. His friend said they called them rashers; he wished he had rashers on his plate this very minute.

The breakfast over, he settles down in brown vinyl seating and chews busily on a toothpick. A young waitress sidles over and refills his coffee cup. The pot seems to hang forever as she bends forward, giving Tommy an eyeful of creamy cleavage. She sees the way his eyes are focused, but lingers a little longer before tossing her head and sidling back to the coffee station. This doesn't faze Tommy; it happens all the time. He watches her ass all the way back. Out of earshot words are spoken to fellow waitresses. Heads turn, all eyes level at Tommy as he discards the toothpick and lifts the cup to his lips.

They all knew the agency girl, she'd been before. They saw her leave his room. She breezed in twenty minutes before Tommy, like she owned the place, and made a call. There was laughter in her voice, and the girls got the gist of the conversation: Tommy's dick was the smallest darn thing she'd seen since she played doctors behind the Mickey Mouse house at pre-school.

Tommy can almost read the thoughts in their eyes, but it's like this with Tommy. Out there, there has to be a million guys with his problem. As he sees it, ninety-nine per cent of those guys are either consulting shrinks, jacking off into enlargement devices, or cursing their fathers. For what? In his world, you take a broad, pull her pants down and fuck the ass out of it, shoot, and heh! Who gives a shit what she thinks. At least *I've* had a good time. Tommy folds a five spot under the breakfast plate. This is a big tip in a place like this; tomorrow breakfast they'll be all over Tommy like flies on shit.

It's too hot outside for Tommy to walk more than forty paces. Thirty brought him smack bang on to the Strip, and this time of morning there's taxis passing by the score. Within seconds he's tucked low in the cab's rear seat heading downtown. His thoughts over breakfast were centred around the call from Jack. What the hell is going on with that guy? How can he be in so much trouble he's callin' me? Now his thoughts turn to Joey. That was definitely Joey he saw last night. Where can I find him to set him up for Jack? Or even Grasano, come to that. The picture house don't open till two. Will he be there? Could it be his day off? Before he has time to steady his breathing, the cab is drawing outside The Pioneer. The driver calling over his shoulder a buck-fifty fare.

Tommy steps out into eleven-o'clock glare. This isn't Tommy's scene, it's all too bright. There are no night-time shadows – no eerie streets to walk that final chapter. He shades the sun from his eyes and throws his wobbly frame across the street, side-stepping traffic, dancing the last few breathless steps to the kerbside.

Air conditioning blows dream-like cold at Tommy's sweaty head as he weaves slowly between card tables and roulette wheels. Thinking it might be too much effort to prop a stool, he takes a booth close to the bar. No sooner has he begun to mop sweat from his brow, a petite Anglo waitress named Brenda stands before him, placing a keno card and pencil on the table. She's young, she's pretty, and unlike the girls back at the Starburst restaurant, this girl gets paid to be looked at. Tommy can look all he wants, and that's one of the pluses in this city; all the girls that work the bigger establishments are young and pretty.

Tommy guesses this girl is new to town. Someone with her looks and body shape will soon be spotted by scouts from the big-time Strip casinos; places like Caesars, Flamingo, Tropicana. Then she'll tread plush carpet and pluck generous tips from serious players. But as she moves in, someone's got to move out. Brenda's fading beauty will move from Strip glamour to downtown glitz. But even this place won't last forever. It takes a couple of years, then, as Brenda's flesh begins to sag and her backside broadens, she has to take another walk. Just a short walk this time, to third-rate casinos that draw nickel and dimes and change their neon characters every six months to keep pace with new owners. If by this time Brenda isn't married or got the instincts of an alley cat, she's in big trouble. Age is a killer in this town and, at the ripe age of thirty-five, there's only one place that wants her: the kitchens.

Tommy orders iced-tea and tracks her fishnet stockings a booth or two. He loses concentration, his mind's not on the job today. The call from Jack is fragmenting deliberations on today's events. Normally he'd stay in the cool of the casinos, ogling attractive croupiers and, if she was something special, chancing a dollar or two at her table to get a little closer to her beauty. Once again, his thoughts are wrapped around a past journeyman boxer and a present day ageing bookmaker. What if he couldn't make contact with Joey? That would surely get Jack off his back. But Tommy feels a sense of artificial duty and a story building. His old purple nose smells copy and old habits die hard. He's beginning to warm to this intrigue. Maybe there's one big story left.

He nudges his specs to the tip of his nose and peers through smoke-filtered light at fat old ladies clutching twenty-five cent hot-dogs in one hand, while pulling furiously at nickel slots with the other. A fat lady whoops in genuine delight as the slot spews a rattle of coins. He somehow envisages her as Brenda, calling her nickels home in years to come.

The young waitress places the iced tea gently before him. Smiling down at Tommy, and he knows this girl is as green as grass. But give her time, and she'll be as hard as the rest of 'em, he thinks pressing a dollar bill into her finely boned hand. A broader smile now as Tommy indicates she can keep the small change. Just then, as she reads the change, her smile fades, her face hardens. Hey! Maybe she's learning already.

6

From the eighth floor of the Flamingo Hotel, Frankie watches traffic ease along the Strip. The autos below appear so small, they barely seem to be crawling past the radiant white frontage of Caesars Palace. Johnnie Walker is banging away inside his head, while hands tremble against the balcony guard rail. He recalls the thirteen-hundred he dropped in Caesars early this morning. He'd walked into a poker game after belting too much Scotch. A fatal mistake in a disciplined poker school such as the Palace. He recollects the redneck Texan throwing down a full house. He can still see the bastard's cheesy grin as he scooped the pot. What a fool he'd been; Frankie wiseguy Francione taken to the cleaners by some Archie Bunker? It's a fuckin' joke!

Scratching his balls, he delicately looks behind him. Is that one or two broads lying in the king-size? Willing his eyes to focus, he sees it's one and why he bothered, he doesn't know. Perhaps she was some kind of consolation after losing the dough. Whatever the reason, he might as well have slept alone. Yeah, they fooled around some, but within minutes he was sleepy, his eyes closing and his only sensation was the closeness of low-cost perfume.

The duvet is rolled high about her neck, all he sees is a shape beneath the covers and a mass of jet-black hair splaying the pillow. He can't rightly remember what she looks like. He can't even remember her name he was so tight. But he remembers the thirteen hundred! He ponders for a moment; should he nudge her awake? Ask her if she wants coffee or something? Nah, let her sleep on. Less fuckin' hassle anyway. He gathers his cigarettes and lighter and pulls a chair to the balcony and blows a smoke.

He's into his third cigarette, and she's still flat out. Jesus! This broad's gonna be here all day long if he don't make a move. He flicks the stub over the balcony rail and makes for the phone.

'Room service? Send up coffee, will ya. Room 1625 . . . yeah, make it for two . . . breakfast? I'll let you know, OK.'

She hears his voice, stirs some, then makes herself cosy again. Frankie pulls on the trousers of a dark blue two-piece, stands back and looks on in disbelief.

'Hey, baby, I know you're awake. You gotta get up an' get the fuck outta here. It's eleven o'clock, already.'

'Eleven o'clock don't mean a darn thing to me. Shake me when the coffee arrives,' croaks a voice below the covers.

Frankie can't believe his ears, but before he has a chance to throw the covers back there's rapping on the door. The service has been quick, but then it should be. Frankie tips no less than a five-spot on a bad night, and if he's at the tables winning some, you bet it's bigger. The kid walks in and places the tray on the coffee table, and Frankie finds it funny how the staff always take great interest in what's in the sack; like all three are now sharing some big secret. Perhaps the waiter gets lucky once in a while and spots a known face, the wife or girlfriend of someone important? Then there'd be a knowing look every time he held out for a tip. Everyone's on the fucking scam. Now get the hell outta here!

He doesn't have to say another word, she's stirring and shaking herself together. The duvet slips down revealing a face so bad that Frankie's glad he can't put a name to it. How in the world did I manage to bag that? She must have been the only fuckin' broad in the joint, he winces. Now Frankie ain't what you'd call handsome. He's built good. Five-ten and weighing in just under one-ninety. His face has seen some action, but his teeth are straight and white, and heh! Some gals like their men on the rough side. But this girl? He's sure glad the waiter *never* got a good look at her.

Sitting upright, the duvet pulled tight to shield her breasts, she pokes a finger at the coffee pot.

'Give it to me straight, Frankie.'

Frankie pulls back, surprised she knew his Christian name.

'What's all this Frankie business? You just get yourself dressed an' outta here. I got places to be,' he snorts, dumping the tray on her lap.

She sips slowly at the coffee, watching Frankie put his things together. His wallet and gold watch rest on a table in the far corner. He fiddles about in jacket pockets for scraps of paper. After scrutinising several pieces, he appears to have found the one he's after, then selects a tie, gives up and throws them into a pile. Once or twice he looks at her; that move your ass kind of look, but she keeps on sipping. Frankie's holding shirts against the outside light to choose a colour to match the suit.

'Try the cream, why don't yer? Naw – not that one. You colour blind?'

Frankie's holding shirts up for her inspection. Without warning, he slings the shirts across the room. Man! What are we playin' at here?

'Whatever your name. This is gettin' old. Get your ass into gear, and shift it.'

'The name's Julie. You owe me thirty, Frankie.'

He kicks out at the nearest shirt and turns so quickly she jumps, spilling coffee over the duvet.

Frankie opens his arms wide. 'Listen, Julie. Let's get this straight. When I pay for a hooker, which ain't too often, I always sober up so I can see what I'm gettin'. No disrespect now, you understand. But I wouldn't pay you in old pesetas.'

56

'Now you listen here, Frankie. When I need–'

'You listen, an' listen good. You've slept in my bed, I ain't gonna charge rent. You drank my coffee, still no charge. Just get the fuck outta here!'

Julie climbs out of the king-size, clutching the duvet tight to her body, careful not to let Frankie see anything she's not going to be paid for.

Her undue modesty is wasted on Frankie. He glances around now and then to make sure she's climbing into her clothes. His mind is on other matters, his fingers leafing through scraps of paper again for a Boston telephone number. Julie's into her high heels. Frankie grunts approval, fixes the strap on his gold watch and tosses a crumpled ten-dollar note on the bed.

'Now get the hell outta here!'

Julie snatches up her top coat and shoulder bag.

'Fuck you too, asshole!'

She left the door wide open. Frankie peered out into the corridor to make sure she'd caught the elevator, then slammed the door shut. Women!

'Hey, that you, Sal? It's Frankie. Is the old man around?'

There's a pause, as if Sal's looking around the walls of the social club.

'He ain't, Frankie. You still in Vegas? . . . the Flamingo . . . OK, gimme your room number, I'll find him.'

Frankie knows Carlo Grasano will be sat at a table near the phone. He never takes a call, he employs people to do that. And never is that telephone used to discuss business of any nature. Sometimes the guys fuck about on it to throw the cops a line of bullshine should they be listening in. There are men who do nothing else but run two or three blocks to use public call boxes. All day long they're in and out of the club, making calls, relaying messages to Carlo's number two, Vincent Riboco. Carlo doesn't talk business face to face with anyone unless they're in the mob's inner circle. But Frankie believes

57

he's one of Carlo's favourites, and Carlo will surely make the effort to get back to him.

'He'll call you. Sit tight, Frankie.'

Frankie cradles the receiver then paces the room. It could be hours before Carlo gets back to him, he's a busy man. Frankie has no choice, out of respect he'll have to hang in. He knows if he's not there when Carlo calls, the old man will hit the roof, and all those years of friendship will be shot to pieces. He wished now he'd let that ugly broad stay, fooled around with her some, got change for his ten. Perhaps she wasn't that dog-rough after all?

He leans against the balcony rail. Below him the sun beats relentlessly on to paint-work and chrome like tiny twinkling stars. Frankie glances down at his watch. 11.46 Christ! Step on it, Carlo. The day's gonna be over.

The refrigerator door slams shut with a bang. Where the fuck has Joey got too? Abilene would go next door and borrow a filter, but she had a bust up with the faggot's boyfriend over a bin liner of trash she left lying outside his doorway.

'A fuckin' bin liner! I ask you?' she'd screamed at Julian.

He'd flicked a dish towel at Ronnie's arm, threw his head in the air and minced off into the apartment. He never said a word to Abilene, and that bugged her. Julian was always good for the odd thing when she ran short. In fact, most days he'd knock her door and ask if there was anything she was short of. Not anymore, and now this cross-dresser, Ronnie, is top of her shit list. Right now she hates queers.

The channel dial is turned for the umpteenth time. Anything to break the wait for Joey. She should have asked him to bring back cigarettes, the soft pack lying on the dresser showing three. The bedroom floor is still littered with her clothing. She steps over it, opens the wardrobe door and searches about in Joey's jacket pockets. There's nothing in there, Joey wouldn't be so stupid. But she knows he must be skimming the picture

58

house. He'll have sticky fingers, just like the rest in this town, where everyone skims for common survival. He's got to be holding out on her. But where?

Tom and Jerry flick across the TV screen. She screws her face at it, turns off the set and decides to tidy the bedroom. Anything to pass the time. Stepping amongst the debris lying about the floor, her smalls are scooped, more or less folded and stuffed without forethought into the nearest drawer. Thinking this all too much trouble, she kneels on the carpet and begins to sling clothing on the bed. Close to the skirting, a stretch of floor creaks beneath her weight. Somewhat surprised, she moves back and topples against the bed, feeling kind of stupid.

Man! Two years and I never knew the board was loose. What board? Places these days have four by eight boarding, even she knows that. Her second husband George was a carpenter. He still might be for all she knows but, like everything else, he was fucking useless at that. She twiddles a pair of nylons between her fingers, looking at the carpet where the floor creaked. She wonders if this is a hiding place? Abilene scrambles over to the door and turns the key.

The carpet peels back easily. Her pulse is rocketing. The gap between the cut board and joist is big enough for her to place her little finger and hook it up. Bingo! Got you, Joey. In wood chipping's and sawdust lies a plastic wrap, she sees the green of folded bills. Whoopee! What a sucker! She gently lifts the package and spreads the money over the carpet. One hundred and eight bucks – cheers, Joey! You bastard!

Now she's debating what to do with her new-found wealth. Her first impulse is to collect it together and hide it somewhere different. But the more she looks at the money, the more unsure her thoughts become. Joey *is* taking from the picture house, that's for sure, there's every chance that tonight he'll be bringing more money home, Saturday night being their best day of the week.

Although they've lived together the past six months, she doesn't know a lot about him. If ever talk of the past crops up in conversation, Joey's lips are sealed. She knows he's had a plug-ugly past and can be a mean mother if provoked. There's something about Joey. The way all men treat him with respect, even the niggers around the complex who normally don't give a fuck for anyone, walk around him, 'Hi, Joey' is what they call.

What's the point in takin' it now, she asks herself. Let Joey build the kitty, and if he should act strangely she can always get there before him. Abilene folded the money the way she found it, and tucked it in the plastic wrap. The wrap was placed between the boards and dusted with sawdust. She replaces the board with her first smile of the day.

Abilene stands and wags a finger at the relaid carpet.

'I got you this time, Joey boy,' she smirks.

She's happy now. The television stays off. She scoots about the apartment, tidying this, stacking that, feeling pleased with herself.

The negroes fixing their wrecks below pull a smile as she hangs over the rail. Enjoying her last cigarette, she watches with amusement as they tackle an oily auto manual, scratching their heads and nudging each other in laughter. There's no music blaring today, she heard the apartment manager tell them, 'Shut the goddamned thing off,' but they're having a ball all the same.

Leon looks up and shouts, 'Hey, what's shakin', sister? Weah's the ol' man this mornin'?'

'Taken off,' she calls down, jokingly.

Skit throws the manual along the ground and they all look up.

'Well, baby. If yo're ever in need of heavy duty exercise. I'm yor man.'

They all laugh like crazy, slapping thighs and thinking their banter some big joke.

'Yeah, sure. I'll keep you in mind. Say? Any of you guys gotta spare smoke?'

'On tha dash, baby. C'mon down when yo're ready.'

'I'll be down.'

'Bet ya will, baby,' says Skit, thrusting his pelvis.

Joey turns on to Main. Underneath his arm in a brown paper bag are coffee filters, razor blades, two three-quarter pound steaks and a bottle of dago red. He gathers pace, smiling to himself, thinking on how those two creeps in the California had to suck around him to lay the low-down on Abilene. It's going to make life tough, could be a long while before she's re-employed; hasn't she just about worked every casino in the city? A car rides by and beats its horn. The sun impedes his view, he didn't see the driver, but waved all the same.

Cutting through a side gate into the complex, the first thing he spots are the Saturday morning mechanics. Jesus! Those guys strip that same old engine one week, and rebuild it the next. He's only heard them fire that old Ford Galaxie once. She blew so much shit that a blue cloud hung over the complex for a full half hour.

He's about to climb the steel staircase when he sees Abilene resting on the auto's benchseat. What the fuck! He stands for a moment, his hand gripping the rail, listening to the laughter. Joey can't believe what he's seeing and hearing. The paper bag is laid on the bottom rung.

Nobody sees him, they're in a world of their own. He's at them before they know it. He points to Abilene. 'What the fuck is goin' on! Get your ass up those stairs this second.'

She props on one arm, stunned. 'C'mon, Joey. Nothin's goin' on.'

She doesn't get the chance to upright herself. Joey's inside the cab like lightning, pulling at her T-shirt, throwing her to the ground. She knows better than to talk back when he gets this far down the road, but the negroes don't. OK, they're cautious, but what's he gonna do with so many of them against

61

him? Before Abilene has time to clamber to her feet, the negroes are circling Joey.

'Hey, man! Chill out! Abby only came down for a smoke. No need for trouble.'

'Come here!' Joey calls to the talker.

The black shrugs his shoulders, looking from side to side at his friends. No problem, Leon, they seem to say. Go on, brother, we're right behind you.

Leon moves forward, his friends stay put. He gets within an arm's length of Joey, and Joey lets go. The blows come in so hard and furious, Leon's still standing after a score of punches, his body jerks and buckles, his brain didn't have time to register the onslaught. Leon finally crumples to the floor. Joey steps back, adjusts his feet, regains his balance. He's ready for the rush. Nothing matters now. When Joey's ready to battle, a crowd don't frighten him.

By now there's a rumpus building outside Leon's doorway. His woman is dancing on the spot, screaming blue murder. Abilene watched the action from half-way up the staircase. Then she bolted along the veranda and took station outside their apartment door. Leon's friends stand helpless. They've seen street fighters aplenty, but none moved with such hand speed. That combination of head and body punches was something to see. Leon grunts and groans, clutching his stomach. His face is distorted, a swelling takes shape high on his cheekbone. One of his friends raises his arm in surrender to Joey. It's over, not a word is said.

From the balcony, Abilene watches Joey walk back to the staircase. He stops momentarily, jabbing thin air, shadow boxing an imaginary opponent, then casually retrieves the paper bag as if nothing had happened. He rolls his head, shaking off demon pain. Abilene shakes hers in disgust. You're some sick motherfucker, Joey. She was right to place the money back under the floor after all.

*

'That you, Frankie?'

'Hey, Carlo. Good of you to call.'

Frankie turns his wrist to check his watch: 12.45. It's all pleasantries now, but fifteen minutes ago he was cursing Carlo Grasano to hell. In the time he'd been waiting on the call, he'd drank a quarter bottle of malt, chain-smoked a pack of cigarettes and chewed a knuckle raw.

'So what you calling me for, Frankie? You ain't got enough goin' on down there?'

'Naw, just thinkin' on comin' back in a couple of days. Is everything OK?'

'Everything's fine, Frankie. Don't you worry none,' Carlo croaked. 'Just one thing? You'll be stopping at the Flamingo, yeah?'

'Yeah.'

'OK, Frankie. Buongiorno.'

'Thanks, Carlo. Catch you.'

Within seconds of the call, Frankie's whistling a tune and playfully juggling his room keys from hand to hand. He secures the room and shuffles his frame into a crowded elevator. A twelve-year-old kid looks up at him and smiles a mouthful of brace. Frankie looks down at her, his lips curling into a checked smile. As people jostle for extra space, he notices lipstick trace on the large mirror behind the girl's mother. She moves her head slightly to fix the ribbon in the little girl's hair – he sees the word CUNT so plain, he's wondering if he's the only one to notice.

As they come to rest, and people muddle off in different directions, Frankie holds back out of curiosity and reads the mirror – FRANKIE FRANCIONE IS A CUNT. He slams his fist against the wall of the cage and bawls an obscenity back at himself through the mirror. His body shaking with rage, he rubs the lipstick with the sleeve of his two-hundred-dollar suit jacket. He isn't too bothered by the CUNT, he's been called that

63

a thousand times. It's *his* name, scrawled in cherry red, that's killing him.

He manages to rub the wording to an incoherent smudge. Where's the fuckin' elevator operator? He'll have to reprimand the desk – they'll call the janitor – get that shit polished off the mirror. He knows who's done this: that ugly bitch that weaselled the ten from him. What's her fuckin' name again? He's so fired up he can't remember. Another thing, she left the room two hours ago, if she'd have written it then, surely someone would have reported it. No, the bitch must have known when he was leaving his room. Perhaps she was in the elevator, disguised as a witch. How would she know his surname? Frankie storms off to reception.

She was quick in seeing Joey ascend the staircase; her heart beating like thunder, she'd grabbed a razor sharp boning knife from the kitchen drawer. The apartment door bangs open. Abilene's grip tightens on the knife.

'Abilene!'

She turns, the knife gripped tight behind her back. She'll stick him without hesitation if he cuts up rough on her. Joey sits the wine on the breakfast bar and stands in the lounge doorway, leaning the jam, the bag swinging low in his hand. He knows what's behind Abilene's back.

'What you playin' at, Abilene? Ain't I told you about mixin' it with those niggers? Here, I got your things.'

He tosses the bag, it tumbles through the air. Out of natural instinct she reaches out to catch the bag, and drops the knife. She realises her mistake, stoops to make for the knife, but it's too late, Joey's at her, tying up her wrists with one strong hand. She's forced back against the wall, her head crashing plaster. Their faces brush, she smells coffee on his breath, but there's no fear in her eyes now, just anger that she'd been wrong-footed.

'What'd I tell you? he hissed into her face, kicking the knife along the floor.

'Go – go fuck yourself, Joey!'

Joey releases his grip, steps back and raises his arms, showing her the white of his palms.

'Enough is enough. You remember what I told yer. Go an' sort yourself out, you look a fuckin' mess.'

Joey walks on the veranda to see what's happening below. The negroes have moved inside their apartments. He knows right now they'll be popping beer cans, working up courage. Six cans later and they'll be voicing what they're going to do with Joey. Nine cans and they might dare a move. But it's unlikely. Those guys like the night drama, when it's dark and they can sneak about like thieves in the night. He's safe for the time being, they haven't the stomach for daytime one-on-one.

He's had trouble with this crowd before. The time he caught one of their teenage kids mooching around his lounge. He'd left the door open on account he was only tipping trash in the dumpster on the corner of the block. The kid was plenty old enough to know he shouldn't be in there. Anyway, Joey cuffed him some, then held him over the balcony and shouted down, did anyone want to claim him. Man! Those black mammas stampeded out like nobody's business, screaming the place down. The kid was so frightened he shit himself. Joey finally hauled him back in when a compromise was reached. That kid never climbed the staircase again.

Since that day, the negroes below have figured him plain crazy. Which suits Joey fine. He just wished Abilene would follow suit, then perhaps things around here would ride a little smoother. He locks the door behind him and tips out the paper bag. The filters and steaks are placed next to the stove, the blades tossed into a kitchen drawer. Listening to confirm Abilene's whereabouts, he hears her splashing about in the bathroom, the rush of water through waste pipe, the chrome ring clinking against wall tiles as she lifts a towel.

His arms rest on the work-top, eyes watchful, ears tuned for movement outside the apartment door. Abilene slides into the kitchen, quiet, like she doesn't want Joey to hear her. Joey takes scant interest, and after a while she becomes a little pissed off. After all, hasn't she made an effort, slipped on a high tight skirt and left off her panties so Joey can sneak a peep at her bush. She leans against the wall opposite, her left foot tucked high, pubic hair curling thick beneath the hem of her cream skirt.

She looks across, catching him take a peek between her legs. With most guys this manoeuvre would promote some kind of positive response. Though his eyes roll between her legs, his facial expression shows no immediate interest. It must be three weeks since they made it between the sheets. If he had another woman tucked away, she could understand it. She's sure he hasn't, it's not Joey's thing. She's introduced him to stacks of girls since they've shacked together, and he's not shown the slightest interest. This ain't gonna work. Her foot slides slowly to the floor, she tugs at the hem of her skirt, her eyes travel along the work-top.

'You bought steaks. You want I should fix 'em?' she said softly, looking back at him.

'Tell me it ain't gonna happen again. No more mixin' with that kind. You hear me?'

'I hear you, Joey. I ran clear out of cigarettes. Jesus! You'd been gone an age. Thought perhaps you'd met some friends and stopped off for a beer.'

He looks at her quizzically.

'What're yer talkin' about? I never drink daytime, you know that? And what's the story with the cigarettes? There's a machine across the way. You gettin' so lazy to walk that far?'

'Didn't have the change.'

'That's crock, Abilene. Why didn't you knock an' ask Julian? You normally do.'

'Me and that dick-licker don't see eye-to-eye no more.'

'Oh, yeh? Since when?'

'Ah, forget it. I'll go myself after I've fixed the steaks. You want it rare?'

'I always have 'em rare. What're thinkin'?'

Abilene gets busy preparing the steaks. To Joey's amazement, from deep inside a cupboard he finds salt and pepper, ketchup sachets and a tube of out-of-date mustard. On closer inspection, he sees the salt and pepper shakers bear the Mint hallmark. He should have known. The ketchup probably came from there too. The mustard must have been left by the last tenants.

'What're you tryin' to do to me, Abilene? Poison me with this fuckin' shit?' he said, squeezing yellow mustard crust into the sink bowl.

Her eyes dance mockingly.

'There ain't no need, Joey, those niggers 'ull stick it to you – you see. Look at the last time you had a beef? Fuck me, all week they're watchin' you – you're watchin' them. Jesus, Joey. It was like somethin' out the movies. This time though–'

'This time nothin',' he cuts in. 'I got change, I'll go down to the machine and buy those cigarettes myself.'

'I wouldn't.'

Joey stops by the doorway and turns.

'You realise you got fired over that Masie business last night?'

'Oh, yeah? Howd'ya know?'

'I seen Jake an' Eddie this mornin'. You know 'em, they deal craps.'

'I know 'em, sure.'

'They told me you're out, finished, on your way. No need showin' tonight.'

She looks at him a little surprised, tosses her shoulders and buries a corkscrew into the bottle.

'They've got it all wrong. I'll go see Charlie, the union rep. Who the fuck seen what was goin' on, anyway? Perhaps that bitch Masie tripped in her rush to make the startin' gate. Go get the cigarettes, I'll fix the steaks.'

Joey went for the cigarettes, and there was no one around to trouble him. Pinching at their curtains, they'd have seen him walking the veranda, tripping down the staircase, heard him dropping the change, banging the machine as the coins stuck. They'd have seen and heard it all, but no one came out. Joey knows these people; how they work. They know what time the picture house closes. What time Abilene's shift ends.

Tonight the .38 will be coming home with Joey.

7

Susie Jenkins pours milk into a saucer and looks about the room. He was here a moment ago, sprawled on the arm of the sofa. Where's he gone?

'C'mon, Henry, come to momma.'

Henry isn't having any of it, not this morning. Is it nine o'clock? Ten o'clock? What time do you call this to be coming home, Susie?

Henry has lived with Susie on and off for five years. Some of the time it's cream and biscuits, but most of the time it's lonely nights with the lights out. How did he, the best-looking cat on the block, get stuck with her? If she ain't swinging her tail evenings, she's stuck to the phone like glue, like now for instance.

'That you, Helen? Gee, Sheree, you still there? You must be whacked. You got anything for me? . . . That guy last night? Tommy what's-his-name. He's called in? What did he have to say? . . . Really!'

She reaches down, moving the saucer closer to Henry's sofa.

'Come to momma,' she calls again.

Henry cocks his head. The milk looks tempting, but he'll leave it a while, let her know who's the boss around here.

'No, just talkin' to the damned cat is all – he said *that*? I'll be darned! Well, if he's happy enough an' willin' to pay extra, he'll do. I'll leave the answering machine on just in case. I'm bushed, Sheree, gonna hit the goose hair. Take care now.'

Tommy, eh? Yesterday he was William what's-his-name. Who's it going to be tomorrow? Watching her hook the phone and light a cigarette, Henry slips down gracefully from the arm of the sofa, side-steps a discarded high heel, and laps at the cold milk.

'So, what have you been up to, Henry?' she calls down, glancing at the partly opened window. 'Some life you've got, mister.'

How old he is? She wouldn't know. Henry found her. Came in that very window one rainy day and claimed the place his own. They hit it off straight away. She lets him out come sundown to do his thing, wandering the Fremont neighbourhood, sat most nights on the ledge of that crummy porno movie house one block away. Perched on the ledge overlooking the main drag, Henry watches the action, sees every form of low-life come and go.

Take last night for instance. That fat guy in the check sports coat, rushing in late for the second half of that trashy movie. He'd like to have words, wise him up some. And what's he doing talking with that bozo who runs the joint? The fat guy's got to be loco. He'd have taken in the conversation, but a pigeon swooped down fifteen feet away and stole his concentration. By the time he'd chased off the bird the fat guy had gone. That guy really looked out of place, but sometimes you can't tell. Should the town and country coat walk by again, Henry's made a note to point him in the right direction.

Forget the streets, now he's tucked cosily in the warmth of bedroom carpet, watching Susie, taking in details. She stands naked in front of a full length mirror, brushing through thick auburn hair. Henry makes out the reflection, her ample breasts beating a tune with the hair-brush. The white of her flat stomach clashing with a rich dash of pubic hair. All in all, she ain't in bad shape, I'll bet that Tommy would like to be where I'm lying this second. She peeps back at Henry. Giving him a buddy look, then the wink of an eye. Life ain't all that bad, he reckons, clawing on to the quilt and snuggling down beside her.

Spinning the cigar stub along the sidewalk, Angelo Persaci climbs the three steps into the A.OK Social Club on 12th. Before entering the club, he looks up and down the street. Sure enough, tucked up the block some, sits a black sedan. He can't identify its make, but two guys sit in the front seat reading newspapers. Fuckin' Feds. Angelo would have liked to have met with Carlo Grasano some place different. But what can he do? Carlo snapped his fingers and he had to be here. Twenty minutes ago he was banging the ass off his mistress in a basement flat he rents on 4th. The phone rang just when he was about to blow his tanks. He had to pick it up, only a select few know the number, it had to be important.

He recognised the thick smoky Italian voice straight off. It belonged to Albert Greppi, an ageing mob member who acts as the telephone runner for the old man. Albert's calling from an outside box, he's about to run out of change, Angelo tells him he's kinda busy right now.

'You listenin'? Get your ass over here, Carlo needs to speak with yer.'

All the same, he rolled on top of Rosie some more and scored a home run.

On the ride over, he's speculating who the old man wants putting down. It's been months since he'd talked or done any business with Carlo. Angelo doesn't come here often, it's full of past-their-sell-by-date Mafioso hoods, narrating hour-long stories on how it used to be. Old guys like Albert, too old to be any use on the streets, are now sat on their fannies all day, drinking coffee, devouring large plates of meat-balls and peppers, yelling at the kid who runs the kitchen. The younger guys: talking deals, shooting bullshit and sucking up to the old man. In his forty years he's never had as much as a parking violation. OK, he's had his fair share of luck, but keeping your distance from places like this helps plenty. All that Italian bullshit, Angelo doesn't need to be around their company.

Angelo Persaci is different from the guys he's going to shake hands and hug with on the way to Carlo's tiny office. Angelo doesn't work mob rackets anymore, but he knows how it works. From container hijacking to ripping off cargo at Logan Airport. The numbers racket to extortion, and never had a dime from such activities passed through his fingers. He smiles. He must be the only one.

As he shakes hands with the dozen or so young bloods and old Mustache Petes, a chill will run down their backs. The younger ones who have never met him before will move back out of respect, but mainly fear, for the man who has taken more scalps than any living hitman. A thousand-dollar-a-week retainer secures Angelo's undying service to Grasano. The money is delivered in cash every week to his undertaking business on Stewart. So the name Angelo 'the undertaker' Persaci has stuck with him.

'Go call the undertaker,' Carlo would have said. And it's one big joke amongst the guys that Angelo buried two guys he had shot the previous week. The best part of the joke being he made a real good job, made them up so their mothers wouldn't know they'd taken one behind the ear. He even stood by the graveside, consoling the dead men's next of kin. That was a few years back after the Irish war business.

Angelo makes his way slowly through the smoke-filled room, every now and then stopping to shake someone's hand. Some of the old faces that were here on his last visit are missing.

'Where's Salvatore?'

'He's gone, Angelo,' came the reply.

No one lasts forever; he knows that better than anyone. Why the fuck didn't he get the business to bury him? What's the score around here? He should be getting all mob business.

Carlo's office is stuck at the far end of the games room, next to the john. The office itself used to be the ladies powder-room, but there's no need for it since they took the place over. They don't let women in no more. Angelo raps the door, and waits for Carlo to summon him. Word will have got to the old man that he's arrived, Carlo will make out he's busy and let him wait to show Angelo he still ranks as an employee.

It's only a matter of minutes before he's bellowed in and sitting opposite the old man. Carlo seems to look much older these days, and Angelo's sort of measuring his coffin length as he's handed a large cuban cigar. After several attempts to console his huge frame in the chair, he appears snug enough for Carlo to open up.

'How's business, Angelo?'

'It could be better.'

'You know, Angelo, there's only two places you'll find Cuban cigars – in this room and the White House. Here, let me light it for you.'

Oh, yeah! Angelo could take him to a store one block east where, if you slipped the owner a ten-spot, he'd slip you a full box, candy wrapped.

Angelo accepts the light and wriggles uneasily.

'No kiddin'? Thanks, Carlo, I ain't smoked one of these in years.'

The old man waves his hand, like it's no big deal.

'That's OK, don't think about it. I didn't drag you away from anythin' important?'

Carlo pauses. Angelo shakes his head.

'No, then that's OK. I got a small problem, Angelo. An' it needs fixin' – how's the cigar?'

'Good. So, Carlo, what's the problem?'

Carlo leans forward, elbows resting on the imitation leather desk. His face stern and serious.

'Remember Don Peppino's funeral last Fall? I had a kid stood alongside me.'

Angelo remembers well, it was the last one he did for Carlo.

'Yeah, I remember.'

'Frankie Francione's the problem.'

'No shit! He was glued to you like shit to a blanket at the funeral.'

Carlo wrings his knuckles white, his face racked with artificial pain. Angelo knows this is a load of bull. There's only one reason he's here; to earn his one-thousand-weekly retainer.

'I've treated Frankie like a son, ask anyone, they'll tell ya. But recently he's gettin' outta control.'

'Where's he at? Set him up, say a day. You want he should be found?'

Angelo said it so fast, Carlo didn't have time to tell him the guy's two thousand miles away.

'Frankie's in Vegas, booked in the Flamingo. While you're down there, there's another one – you're gonna love this.'

Carlo waits for a response from Angelo, but sees a blank face blowing smoke rings.

'That Irish scumbag, Joey O'Sullivan.'

Angelo straightens up, choking on his cigar.

'With Francione?'

'Nah. Talk has it O'Sullivan's been livin' there some time.'

'Where'd you get this, Carlo? I thought that son-of-a-bitch was long gone. Who the fuck told you?'

Joey O'Sullivan is an old score that needs to be settled. He was in the john, taking a leak the day Hughes and O'Sullivan hit the barber shop. They got Hughes afterwards, but that punch-drunk O'Sullivan vanished into thin air.

'Take my word.'

Angelo stubs the half-smoked Havana into the ashtray.

'I'll catch the next flight. You wanna see Frankie again?'

'Do what you gotta do, Angelo. I'm visiting my daughter next week, I don't want to see anyone.'

The talking's over. Carlo reaches below the desk and hands Angelo a box of Cubans. Angelo smells the rich aroma of box-wood and tobacco leaf, and accepts gratefully. The old man settles back in antique leather, watching Angelo stand and bow in old school respect, tucking the box under his arm and closing the door quietly behind him. You're some dumb bastard, thought Carlo. I bought those cigars at the corner store, one block down.

As Angelo leaves the building, darting right to avoid the Feds, Carlo rocks back in stolen leather and reflects on Angelo. How could he fault the guy? Eleven years he's been on the payroll, and never once has he let him down.

Carlo walks around the office desk, opens the door and shouts over heads for Albert to get his ass into the office.

'Make sure there's a ticket at Logan for Angelo, he's on his way to the airport now. Another thing. Call Vegas, talk with Pete an' tell him everything's going as planned.'

Albert will make the call. Sony will book the flight, and nobody will ever know the booking was down to Carlo Grasano.

All it took was a five-dollar fare and a cab driver's knowledge to find the Pink Flesh porno theatre on Industrial. No out-of-towner would ever dream of looking for this place, never mind find it. But Tommy's found it, and now he's sneaking through corridors of dark titillation, peering below ranch-style louvered doors, every now and then stooping to see if the booths are occupied by tell-tale feet. He passes several that appear unoccupied; they have company in the adjacent cubicle. Tommy searches on until he's free from intrusion so he can savour flickering images to come.

Cramped into the tiny booth, the doors swung back tight behind him, he shakily presses a dime into the meter-slot. He has a choice of three titles, and plugs for *The Mexican Maid*. By magic, the screen lights up in front of Tommy as he hastily unbuttons his fly and rubs a warm hand into his boxer-shorts. His cock is roughly pulled through, fingers stroking his small cock to a quick erection. His hand stroke is slow and calculated, he doesn't want to ejaculate just yet; he'll save that precious moment for the grand finale.

After a minute or two, the screen images fade away, his free hand frantically dips into his pocket for change, his eyes greedily search the menu. What shall he watch next? He settles on *Beach Babes*, although he's sure he's seen it before. The dime drops. Nothing happens. He slips in another coin. 'Fuck it!' he cries inwardly. He'd like to bang at the coin-meter, but knows he'll be slung out on his ass. He'd like to complain to the manager, but that would be a complete waste of time; there's no consumer protection act in a dump like this.

He scours the dark labyrinth one more time. Once or twice, a ghostlike face stares back at him. Their eyes veer from contact, like it's a bad omen to intercept each other's inner thoughts.

In the centre of the building, ten booths form an arc. By instinct, Tommy finds the booth that will provide him with his moment of masturbatory gratification. These doors are full length with switch locks for customer privacy. He pushes the door open, clicks the lock and by the light of a small fluorescent tube, feeds four quarters into the meter. Timing is of the essence now. The four-by-four window in front of him suddenly burns with brilliance, throwing him for a second. But the old stager is soon composed, fumbling with his trouser zip, ogling the dancers, masturbating slowly with thumb and forefinger.

Tommy closes his eyes – inhales the familiar fragrance of spent semen, his foot slithering on previous spillage. Then ever so slowly his eyes open wide and peer into the brightly lit arena. Two middle-aged women dance with amateurish enthusiasm, their naked bodies labouring under excess fat. An expressionless face draws up to Tommy's window. She's so close, cupping her breast, pressing it tight against the glass. He's sure she can see him. Shit! This has got to be better than the real thing. He leans forward, his mouth caressing the glazed nipple, his hand goes into overdrive, and soon he's spilling his load on to the greasy floor.

Tommy folds his limp cock back into his trousers and feels stickiness on his thigh. She blows a raspberry at Tommy and he rewards her entertainment with a one-dollar bill in a box beside the meter. The shutter comes down. In the light of the single fluorescent, Tommy straightens himself out.

Darkness wrapped its blanket around downtown neon two hours ago. Polished stars danced between threatening clouds rolling in from far away north. From her window, Ruby watches Mary drop Moe off at the Porno Palace below her. Moe leans forward and kisses Mary. Ruby thought it a nice touch. Her neighbour, Susie, had told her many a story about the old couple, nice ones, a change from all the bad she hears on the streets all the time.

Hey! Here comes that bruiser who works the cinema. The one with the broken face. He looks a tough guy, that one. I'll bet it would have been a different story if he'd have been around the night they shot the cab driver. She'd already reported her suspicions to a big detective who works the district. What're the cops doing? Diddly. Ruby sees who she thinks are the perpetrators almost every night when coming home from work. She'd seen them an hour ago on the corner of 3rd, they were huddled with another black, talking in whispers.

Joey left the apartment complex earlier than normal to side-step the negroes. This morning was different, he had surprise and venom on his side. But now, with them organised against him, he knows he wouldn't stand a chance. They'd come from all angles, and overpower him so fast he wouldn't have time to retaliate.

As he crossed the street he'd seen Mary's station wagon disappear down Fremont. He noticed a bunch of negroes hanging close. He strolled on, called in on Moe, they drank coffee together and shot the breeze. Moe was good company, just what he needed after the day he'd had.

'How's Abilene?' Moe had asked.

'She's fine,' Joey had replied hastily, remembering what happened after their steak meal. Abilene had run down to the call box and called the union guy, Charlie Powell. She came back all cock-a-hoop, saying, 'Charlie 'ull fix it,' and Joey's thinking; he'll fix it all right, Charlie's been screwing Abilene on and off for years. How else would she have kept herself in work all those years?

Joey relieves the day-shift and sits in the glass-fronted cubicle reading the Micky Spillane he'd shoved in his back pocket on the way out of the apartment door. There's a good crowd in already tonight, so between pages he's running the figures through his head, counting a thirty-dollar rake-off when last night's shadow casts himself along the corridor. Joey looks up at Tommy Mace, and shakes his head.

'You made it on time tonight,' said Joey, reaching for the five-spot.

The guy doesn't put his hand in his pocket, just leans on the counter, looking down at him.

'So, how you goin'? You remember me from last night?'

Joey looks up impatiently, his hand still hanging to take the bill.

'Yeah, I remember. You're the man from all our yesterdays. You comin' in? Or you gonna stand there flappin' your gums?'

Tommy shifts nervously from foot to foot, looking around the corridor, trying to find words that will coax Joey into dialogue. He's temporarily saved when a customer walks through the entrance. Tommy steps back from the counter, resting his back against cracked plaster. The customer is soon eagerly on his way through the turnstile.

'You comin' in?'

Tommy reaches into his breast pocket for his wallet.

'I'm comin' in. What other reason would a guy be doin' in a neighbourhood like this?'

'You tell me. I come here to work.'

Tommy rocks his weight off the wall, draws a crisp five-dollar note, and slowly steps across to the security glass.

'Listen, pal. We need to talk.'

'*We*! Pal! What're you talkin' here? I thought I told you already, go take a fuckin' walk!'

Tommy slides the note through the opening, Joey grips it, Tommy pulls it back some. Joey stares up in anger.

'Listen to me—' said Tommy, slowly.

Joey snatches the note from him, cutting him short with a look that could kill.

'Now you listen to me, fatso. Go back to Boston – write your newspaper stories, or whatever you do up there, and leave me alone.'

Moe sticks his head through the door.

'Hey, Joey. There's a great cabaret at the Roxy tonight. Do ya fancy it?'

Joey scowls at Moe, and the old guy dithers in the doorway, unsure why Joey's angry with him. What's he said wrong?

Tommy gives Moe an appreciative glance; this has got to be Joey O'Sullivan. He folds the five and sticks it in his pocket. He has no need for the movie now, just the need to telephone Jack.

'Think I'll take a rain check – Joey,' said Tommy, smugly.

For a time afterwards, Joey sat figuring out future moves. He realises he's been sussed, and what if this guy should make a long-distance call? At times like this, thoughts can twist irrationally; right now, this is how he sees it: the niggers? His eyes fix on the S&W revolver. No problem. If they come after him, he'll let them have it in good style. But this guy from Boston, that's another ball game. If those guys from up north should have a fix on him, his days in this town are numbered.

Where should he head? East into the boondocks of Arizona or New Mexico? Nah, slim pickings, they work for peanuts in those states. Back to southern California? At least there, he'd be able to fall back into regular construction work and familiar faces. His thoughts are interrupted now and then as movie goers trip the turnstile.

Then there's Abilene? Not exactly a kindred spirit. No great loss there. But to make his run, he's got to get at the cash squirrelled away under the floor boarding. Either that, or rob the night's takings from this place.

More than usual, Joey's glancing down at his watch, glancing to the open doorway, the .38 always within easy reach when he has to move any distance. Jesus! This would be the ideal spot for a guy to be whacked. If *he* was setting up the hit, this place would be ideal. Except for old Moe next door, there's no one around to hear the bullet. The crowd in the auditorium would hear the thud, but they'd be too preoccupied to take any notice. The more he thinks about it, the more he realises he shouldn't be here at all.

As Joey reads 9.45 on the watch face, Moe pokes his head around the entrance.

'Sorry, Joey. Did I say somethin' wrong earlier?'

'Yeah, sort of, but don't you worry none.'

'You want to talk about it?' said Moe, trying to reach out.

'No!'

'OK. I'm just about to fix coffee. You want some?'

Joey indicates a yes, and follows Moe to the doorway. Through a fine mist of rain, he looks up and down the deserted street, then steps smartly back into doorway shelter.

'Sorry, Joey. We only got instant,' grumbles Moe, passing over a mug.

'That's fine.'

They lean each side of the doorway, drinking their coffee, watching the mist turn to rain, out of their reach on the sidewalk.

'You walkin' up to the Roxy afterwards, Joey?'

'I'll be walkin' that way.'

A truck speeds past, spraying the contents of a puddle in their direction. They both jump back spilling coffee.

'Darn!' screeches Moe, looking down at the stains on his trouser legs. 'I only bought these goddamn cords yesterday.'

'What're you fussin' about? Mary will have 'em in the wash an' lookin' like new in no time.'

'Talkin' about Mary. She's picking me up around eleven-forty-five at the Roxy. She don't like coming this far down Fremont late at night – it's OK her dropping me off, but if there's a last-minute customer, a problem locking up, she gets nervous waiting for me. You understand what I'm sayin'?'

Joey's listened to him rattle on, and he can't make Moe out. They've always got on well and now he's having to explain himself to Joey. He should say no. He doesn't want Moe getting caught up in anything on the way to the Roxy. But he doesn't want to hurt the old man's feelings either.

'Sure, Moe, we'll walk together. You don't have to explain a thing to me, you know that.'

'I know that, Joey. Thanks.'

Sadness creeps into the nooks and crannies that form old Moe's weathered face. He'd always wanted to get close to Joey. How many times have Moe and Mary invited him around their trailer for a meal? A dozen or more, and Joey's never made it. Always some excuse. There's been reasons in Moe's head; silly, but could it be that Joey hasn't a change of decent clothing? He doesn't see it, Joey's always clean shaven and cleanly turned out. Could it be something to do with Abilene? Moe's met her just the once. She was OK – as far as it went. She stood with her back to him most of the night, eyeing guys and bitching other women.

Joey hands back the empty mug, watches old Moe scuttle back through the book store door. Tucked in the narrow leather belt in the small of his back, he fingers the .38. He takes one last look along the street.

Moe shuffles between magazine racks and shelving. A bulb has blown at the far end of the room, so he winds his way to the broom closet for a spare and step-stool. They might as well close this darn store, he mutters to himself, as he struggles with the steps. Climbing to the top rung, he balances precariously, easing the dud from its socket. New wattage throws magazine cover gloss back at him, he steps down a rung to steady his balance, then freezes.

Staring back at him from a cover, there's a girl who looks a ringer for Susie. He wants to lean closer, take a better look, he sees these magazines all day long, but this one is telling him to look away. The cover girl is bent forward, her large fleshy breasts hanging loose. She's smiling seductively at him, throwing him the glad-eye, asking Moe all kinds of questions he's finding it hard to answer. Susie's hair is different. That smile? Those teeth? It can't be Susie. Just can't be.

He steps to the ground and carries the stool to the corner of the room. Several times he looks back over his shoulder at the cover. He's still unsure. It's been years since he's seen Susie. Mary sees her regularly, but she is never discussed. Moe shakes his head to clear the memories, but they won't go away. He closes his eyes, images of Susie are in front of him: she's seven years of age, wearing that printed frock she loved so much, kicking her legs to make the swing fly higher. 'Look at me, daddy,' she's saying with a big smile and sparkling eyes. He never forgot that long hot summer day on the naval base.

His eyes focus back on the magazine. Strangely curious at first, then trying to blot out the face. It's useless, in and out Susie comes. So where did it all go wrong? Maybe it was all the moving around, or the years away at sea. He was never there when the important things happened. Susie learning to ride her first bicycle, intake day at school, and a million other things come to mind. In retrospect, the move to Nevada wasn't the smartest, but here was a town growing fast and the climate eased Mary's bronchitis. Susie was a teenager when they moved to Las Vegas, like all teenagers, she was easily impressed and influenced, and dropped out of high school. She took to the bright lights faster than a duck to water, and Moe saw the beginning of the end.

His old eyes travel swiftly to the store window. There's a face stuck to the glass. Is someone sounding out the merchandise? The face moves on. Moe drifts to the far end of the room. Those memories, he's held them back the best he could. His eyes begin to fill with pain and tears.

He looks back at the magazine one more time, then folds his aching body on the stool. His head bowed, elbows resting on scrawny thighs, fingers clasp and pinch slack flesh on his ageing face, his eyes begin to fill. On the meanest block, in one tough city. Moe Jenkins breaks down and sobs his heart out.

It's around ten o'clock when Angelo Persaci's flight touches down at McCarran. His face is set like granite as he treads tarmac and tugs at the back of his jacket collar. The width of the collar isn't wide enough to shield the rain lashing across the expansive airfield, it was just a futile gesture as he ran with his hand baggage for cover. It wasn't a particularly good flight. Two teams of high school basketball players were on board, and boy! Everyone of them must have been seven foot tall and climbing. Their legs stretched out into the aisle, it was like scaling a nest of giant spiders every time he needed to walk the aisle for the bathroom.

Angelo had arrived unannounced to the Las Vegas Mafia. Typically, any intrusion into another mob's territory without forewarning would be a no-no. One simple telephone call from Grasano to the 'office' in Vegas would have manufactured the hit on Francione. The Vegas mob would have taken care of everything, and Angelo would still be in Boston. Any goodwill between the two factions ended on a star-filled night last July.

Depending on whose narrative your ears and loyalties are tuned to, both sides have their own interpretation of events; but take Grasano's version. This is how it happened: three of Grasano's boys flew in for a one-week vacation after a 50,000-dollar US Mail blag at Logan Airport. Shortly after the heist, the heat came down from the cops, so Grasano thought it best they leave town for a while. The one week was provisional, if the heat stayed on, they stayed down. Anyway, they settled into a prime mob run casino-hotel, everything gratis on account of their New England connections.

Of the three, only one was a made man. His name was Tony Zinna, thirty-six years of age and long-time side-kick to Grasano's number two, Vincent Riboco. Zinna was an earner, he had turned over millions of bucks for Grasano; he was important to the New England mob. They were three days into gambling, boozing and broads, when an argument broke out between Benny, one of Zinna's pals, and some half wit wearing a loud Hawaiian shirt. Benny had drunkenly stumbled into him in the Sands crowded lobby. Benny made an apologetic gesture, but the guy cried out for blood and things rapidly got out of hand. Before they know it, casino heavies are escorting them out of the building. Tony thought, fuck this, there's been some mistake, I'll make a call in the morning and get things straightened out.

There were twenty or thirty people milling about outside and, in the confusion, Tony lost sight of the guy who caused all the trouble with Benny. They figured the guy must have barrelled back into the casino, and went after him. As they neared the casino entrance, through the opened doorway they saw the guy talking with security, 'What's goin' down? Who the fuck does he think he is? C'mon, Tony, let's have it out with these shmucks,' hollered Nick. Tony was pretty sober, he read the picture, the guy must be mob connected to the home team. Tony settled them down. Let it go; he'd make that call.

It took a lot of persuasive talking, but Tony finally got

through, and they collared a cab to the dunes. Now and again one of them would slide off to play the tables, but mainly they stuck together, swapping jokes and ribbing one another. They were fooling around with a bunch of Oklahoma housewives, when out of the corner of his eye Benny spots the Hawaiian shirt.

All of a sudden the laughter stopped. Benny was on his feet, and made for the guy. Before Tony had a chance to intervene, Benny caught the guy with a slugging cross and decked him. Benny was quickly under house arrest and frog-marched out of the building. Tony scoured the tables for Nick, but couldn't find him, so he gave Benny a couple of minutes to cool down, and followed him outside.

Tony stepped out and braced himself against the early morning chill. He buttoned his jacket and walked the wide drive looking for Benny. There was no sign of him. After a while he sat on a low wall and fished a cigarette. Benny can't be too far away. Maybe he's gone someplace to cool down? Take a leak? What the hell! He'll be back any second.

As Tony lit his cigarette and stared for a fleeting moment into the warmth of the lighter's flame, he wouldn't have noticed the black Coupe de Ville turning off the Boulevard. He wouldn't have noticed its speed increase as its headlights focused and temporally blinded him. By the time he'd got to his feet, the car was on top of him. The rattle of automatic fire was the last thing Tony ever heard. Benny was around the corner, heard the rat-tat-tat, and fell against the tree, wetting the front of his pants.

That's the real story how they got Tony Zinna. Carlo Grasano was as mad as hell. He whipped up the families and they held a meet. This was serious business. Tony was a made man with the New England mob, and without Grasano's authorisation no one, but no one, should have touched him, let alone killed him. Someone's got to pay, and those bastards down there better come up with a body pretty soon. The Las

Vegas crowd admitted nothing, and to this day never showed remorse or produced a body.

Angelo heads for a bank of telephones hanging in the baggage-handling area. There are twelve, each one linked direct to the hotel of his choice. Angelo scans the glossy photos plugging hotel advertising. He's stayed in most of the classier joints on past visits. They came gratis on account of his mob connection. But for the next few days he needs someplace quiet, a regular place like the drive-by tourists use. He lifts the receiver for the All-Star Inn.

8

She looks back at herself in the mirror, pinching tight the slackness on her cheeks and jaw line. The unlit cigarette inches angrily between her fingers, spilling dry tobacco amongst cotton wool and dime-store cosmetics. Abilene frowns and leaves her stool to hook the long-player arm. She watches as the needle finds its track, waiting impatiently for David Newman's sax to blow her favourite, 'Hard Times', sweetly into the room. Apart from the daily chore of temporary disguise, this is a time of day she likes best, just her and that old jazz record she picked up in a junk shop someplace on her travels. For a moment she ponders where, but there has been so much junk in her life, she can't figure where.

The needle reaches out for the next track. Abilene glances up at her half-made face and pulls her top lip. A pack of Marlboros prop the mirror, reflecting back on this afternoon's rumble in the courtyard below. And how, after Joey'd hit the sack after their steak meal and bottle of red, she'd crept out of the room, cat-like, and made that call to her union rep, Charlie Powell.

The call went as she knew it would: a trade-off. Tonight she'll spend in Charlie's arms, tomorrow she'll be back at work. The make-up scattered in front of her, she's wondering why all the effort. With Charlie, it'll be all between the legs, his breath reeking from chewing tobacco, and a reel of feeble excuses why he's tucked in beside her, and not his wife in

Henderson. She'll take it between the legs, like she's done so many times before. She wished she was out on the town with the girls. They'd made their arrangements mid-week, before all that shit with the late bitch, Masie. Never mind, she'll do the rounds next week; working their way through Strip casinos on the look out for pinkie rings and men who know their way around.

She peers into the mirror. It seems the make-up takes a little longer at each sitting. Long gone are the days when simple strokes of blusher and a dab of lipstick did the trick. Now, rich foundation has to paper the lines that etch the corners of her eyes and crease of her mouth.

George had crept in and out of her thoughts since she found the loose board this afternoon. He always said she'd turn to shit; if only George could see her now!

They'd met in '63. Times were good in those carefree adolescent years in Litchfield, Illinois. She'd flunked her high school grades, so what? By this time she was dating George who, it appeared, had things running smoothly. Too naïve to realise the Dodge Phoenix was daddy's money, and George's only interest was to get inside her pants, she gave in to George one hot and lazy summer's afternoon. Three months later she found herself carrying extra baggage.

George did the decent thing and married her. He was four years older and tried his best, she'll grant him that. But the writing was on the wall, or in George's case, his unskilled hands. Every night he'd return home with bandaged fingers and glowing thumb from misplaced hammer blows. An indentured carpenter, his mastery of the wood saw was that of a one-armed fiddler. Before too long George had almost demolished their home town, and was travelling forty miles daily to demolish another.

She needn't have married him in the first place. The baby was still-born. They struggled on, Abilene working down at Connie's ice cream parlour, George working miracles to stay employed. At eighteen she embarked upon her stripping career, and was soon knocking 'em for dead down at the Parisian Nights. George's father disowned him on account of townsfolk gossip, and before too long repayments on the two-storey clapboard slid into arrears.

Six months later they were in deep water. She moved up and along in the show business world. The last she'd heard of George, he had remarried and was general manager of a fast food deal north of Dixie. She moved slowly west, town by town. Except for a fling with a slick used-car salesman in Lubbock, Texas, this six months with Joey is as long as it's got since her divorce.

Why Joey? The man's rough trade, but he has his points. He don't lean too hard, and goes about his day, which can't be too rosy, and shakes it off once he's back home. But she's figured his move. That roll under the floor? It's take off dough, you betcha. The thing is, for all her bitching, she needs him around. At least she knows where she's at with Joey. If he goes, before too long some creep will mosey in. That's the way it is, and she guesses that's the way it'll always be.

Joey places an old ticket stub between the pages and folds the book. He's lost count how many times he's tried to read the book and given up. There are too many ifs and buts taxing the brain tonight. The shift has dragged. In the last forty minutes he hasn't seen Moe or a customer, just some creep mooching about outside. He'd gripped the .38, swung out off his chair, and moved guardedly to the doorway. The mooch had disappeared. He'd secured the main door before his routine walk-about; didn't want any shock surprises as he exited the auditorium. Tonight was different in many other ways. He didn't see the jerk-off beating his meat on the rear row. The stale air didn't throw him; in fact he didn't see or feel anything at all.

Twenty minutes to go before he hits the lights and locks the building. In the chair, unsteady hands flip pencil stubs, loose change, and objects he never realised took up space until now. He's nervous, he'd thought it through and the odds didn't total in his favour, not by a long chalk. This shit is much different than the bad old days in Boston. There at least he had territory, a neighbourhood safe enough to walk once the dust had settled. Here he's isolated and vulnerable, feeling the negroes might strike tonight. A cold shiver runs his back.

In a basement tenement, two blocks north of Joey, four negroes crouch round a buckled coffee table. Serious business has brought them together; a brother has been whipped in a one-sided fight on Main. Ruff, Cracker and Blade are old school, badasses sporting a mean reputation. The fourth, James Stockton, is the eldest brother of the courtyard victim. He's here to put heads together, his kid brother's been hurt and he wants their help.

James looks about the room as Cracker reaches into a dented cooler for iced beer. They eye the dude from Main with distaste and suspicion, as cheap Milwaukee Lite is passed around the table. James knows people live like this, he's seen it on the TV, seen it in magazines, he never believed it happened. This place is a shit hole: a shadeless lampstand struggles petty light along bare cinder block walls, buckled and blistered ceiling plaster hangs below second-rate plumbing housed in the joists above. There are no windows and the total furniture comprises of four torn bus seats. The place doesn't smell too healthy either. James looks at their main honcho, Blade, and realises he's out of his depth.

He'd made the approach through a friend in the apartments right after the knock-down. 'No problem, bro,' is what his friend had said. Though now he feels he's made one big problem, 'cause these guys are the real McCoy, real-live scumbags. He can't back away, and lose face. He's hemmed in by dizzy laughter as the three to-and-fro a reefer smoke. He refuses a draw on the hemp; got to keep his wits about him here on in.

'Weah you at, man? You ain't gonna take with yo'er brothers?' said Blade, with heavy suspicion.

James shakes his head. All this brother nonsense is getting to him. Blade draws on the weed and blows it in James's face.

'Ah, fuck you. Why should you want some honkey squared away for what he done to your kid brother? I seen you before. We all fuckin' seen you before, hangin' round the white trash on Main, and such. We know this guy you're lookin' at, he lives in the same palace, don't he?' barks Blade, his eyes hardening as he passes the smoke and sucks on the beer. Ruff and Cracker nod their heads in silent agreement. They wait on a reply from James.

James feels their eyes biting into him.

'I live there 'cause I gotta family. You know that, man. Weah the fuck am I supposed to be? Out on the streets? You came recommended. Jazzin said, you were the guys to see.'

'It's gonna cost yer, ma'man,' Cracker cuts in, 'You gotta be comin' along with the Doe-ray-me, bro. This ain't no two-bit outfit you're talkin' with. We's The Three Musketeers–'

Ruff chokes on his beer, as Cracker slaps him on the thigh with great laughter. Blade slams his beer on the table with fury.

'Shut the fuck up!' Blade screams, slapping Cracker hard on the side of the head. 'You gotta excuse these niggers, James. Too much smoke, an' slack black pussy has turned their brains to shit.'

James isn't seeing the funny side of anything.

'So, what'd ya want we should do with this Joey guy? You want we should blow him away? Stick him real good. Break bones? You're in the drivin' seat, James – you're payin' the dough.'

James shifts uncomfortably in the ripped bus seating. Don't everyone get along with Abilene? Sure they do. And this Joey fella? Well, he ain't so bad; remembering the time Joey tipped-up a deck of Lucky's when the boys ran short, or the time Joey watched his back as they walked for a can of gas late one night. OK, this business with Leon was bang out of order, but perhaps?

'C'mon, James! We ain't got all fuckin' night. He'll be walkin' his way home shortly. What you say?' snaps Blade.

'Can't yer knock him around some? Make like we got somethin' back, at least. Un'erstand what I mean?'

They look at each other in disbelief. Where's this guy coming from? Knock him about some! Yeah, right!

'We know what you mean, James. Slap him around?'

James nods. Blade smiles reassurances.

'You better be runnin' along, James. Time's gettin' short an' we got things to resolve.'

They rise from their seats as one. James keen to break away and beat a path back home. The others rattling their limbs for the opening bell. They're still goofing around as James makes the top step and tugs the ill-fitting door. He looks back and shakes his head. Oh, brother!

Once James had slammed the door, they huddle back around the coffee table. What Blade said to James was just crazy talk. They haven't any guns to blow Joey away anymore. They've been shaken down by cops on the street so many times over the past months, it would be plain stupid to carry them. The cops have smashed through the door twice this month looking for drugs and weapons, they didn't find a thing. All they carry now are knives, and they are stashed behind a loose wall brick in the alley out back.

'Did you hear that motherfucker? Some dumb nigger! What the fuck? His kid brother takes a beatin' an' he sits there askin' if we should go a little easy, just slap him around some? We'll stick him real good, hey, Blade?' snorts Cracker.

'Sure – but don't he walk with that old man?' said Ruff, tightening his jean belt.

'Yeah, so fuck the old man, they both work for that fat bum, Turner. We're gonna have Turner on our backs over this Joey any case, so we may as well do two for the price of one. What'd say, guys?'

'Fuck him, too,' said Ruff and Cracker simultaneously.

They smile. They're a team.

'Gimme skin, bro.'

They stumble together, slapping palms.

Freddy leans the far wall, making hand signals to Joey.

'Not a fuckin' thing, Joey! The movie goers musta had their dicks tucked away tonight. Saturday night! I ask yer? Ain't Saturdays always good for loose change?'

'Win some – lose some – what's the matter with you, Freddy? Always on the fuckin' take.'

Freddy straightens up, popping a cigarette between his lips.

'Yeah, yeah. Talkin' about take. What's the rake tonight?'

'Two-fifteen an' I'm handin' it to Maurice myself. Make sure he gets what's due,' Joey replies.

Joey knows Freddy's not going to like this sudden change of drill. It would need Maurice's consent, and he'd have briefed them both in person first. But Joey needs the dough more than Turner, and what can Freddy do about it? Sweet FA. To try and manhandle it away from Joey would be madness. Fuck it! He bets Freddy'll run around Turner's office tomorrow morning and straighten things out. This ain't right, he'll be sayin', don't my years with Babe Enterprises count for nothing?

'You can't fuckin' do this, Joey!'

Joey banks up the last few seats, making it easier for the cleaner. He stops, rests both hands on the arm of a seat and glares across at Freddy.

'Tonight, Freddy, this is what's happenin'. If you got

93

anything else to say, say it. Otherwise, shut the fuck up, an' let's get the fuck outta here. I got someplace to be.'

Freddy's stunned. Jeeps! Joey's never been like this with him before.

Moe's waiting on the sidewalk and hears the rear door clank as Joey slams it tight. All is quiet on the street now, but a moment ago he thought he saw a bunch of negroes hitting in and out of doorway shadows further up the block. He'd focused a while, he's sure it was the same kids they'd seen last night. He couldn't hear no music. Don't those kids always carry a coon-box?

First to appear from alleyway darkness is Joey. Close behind struts Freddy, his face screwed tight, like he's sustained a bad experience.

'What's with the face, Freddy? You backed into one of those creepos in the can? Caught you bendin' over for the loose change and slipped you one from behind?' Moe cracks, impatiently treading air.

'Shut the fuck up, Moe,' snorts Freddy.

Joey pats Moe on the shoulder.

'Take no notice, Moe. He's only bitchin' 'cause he didn't feel a thing,' said Joey, winking an eye at the old man.

Joey turns sharply on Freddy. 'Let's get goin'. You gonna walk with us tonight, or take your chances?'

Freddy looks up and down the street, shuffles his feet, then digs his hands into his pockets in child-like fashion. He feels foolish, knowing he's no option but to walk the street in numbers.

'I'll walk with you guys. Three's a crowd, eh?' he bleats.

'Three's a crowd,' said Moe.

Joey reaches into his coat pocket, making sure the .38 is tipped nose down for an easy draw. He feels gingerly around the stainless rim butt, got to be careful on a misfire, this gun comes double action – no safety. Tooled up on the street like

94

this takes him back to his Boston days, and he's hoping against all odds he won't have to draw the piece.

Moe cocks his head, then cups his hands to fend a light breeze as he lights a cigar. He watches Joey caress the lining of his coat pocket, knowing darn well what's inside: he watched from the doorway earlier, saw Joey fish it from beneath the counter. He'd watched Joey's movements with increased concern tonight, but couldn't quite pinpoint the reasons for his uneasiness. Moe reckons the fat guy who suddenly appeared out of the blue has something to do with it, but couldn't muster the words to ask.

They step off down Fremont. Moe swings cautiously on the opposite side to Joey's gunhand. Freddy tucks in behind the two lead men. Apart from the wail of distant police sirens and the occasional police helicopter clipping overhead, the street is as quiet as a graveyard.

9

Joey's eyes fasten on an alley half a block ahead. He's sure he'd seen a head bob back inside alley brickwork as an auto splashed its beam as it cut a left off 5th. The car slacks its speed, like it's going to stop, the driver maybe ask directions. Joey squints into the windshield, an overhead street lamp checks out the driver is female, Joey sighs with relief, the car lifts a gear and passes by. They walk on, the street lamp casting long shadows before them. Joey's seen movement, there, where the tip of his shadow is about to fall. He stops suddenly, lightly grabbing Moe's arm. Freddy stumbles into the back of Moe, senses the muted tension, and curses beneath his breath.

'What's up, Joey?' whispered Moe.

'There's some bastard in that alley up ahead. Look – see. Just beyond the old liquor store.'

Moe strains against Joey's grip. 'What'd you think?' said Moe, looking anxiously up at Joey. 'Best we cross over?'

'Let's do it!' wheezed Freddy.

Joey's eyes stay with the alleyway as they angle for the kerbside in silence. Stepping on to pavement, they hear the blast of an auto's horn. Instinctively, Moe and Freddy jump back, Joey feels someone tugging at his coat. Whoosh! It sweeps by, brushing Joey's loafers.

'Hey! Ass'ole! Why the fuckin' hurry?' shouts Freddy, at the speeding car. They look at each other in surprise – Joey never heard the horn. Fuck! Joey's on the move, his left hand pushing

Moe back against Jimmy, his gun hand drawing the .38. Moe and Jimmy waver, confused to what's happening.

Joey had quickly made distance between him and the old man. Twenty feet in front of Joey, three negroes emerge out of the darkness. Moe's eyes dart from the negroes to Joey's stationary silhouette, the revolver resting peacefully in the small of his back. For a split second there's a feeling of security, knowing the man in front will level the weapon if the negroes make a play. But the negroes are standing much the same, their hands hidden from view as if they too are concealing something. Shit! could they too have guns? Old Moe's heart beats like a steam hammer. Jimmy slides back a stride.

Moe senses movement behind him, then feet pounding sidewalk. He side-glances, sees a whirl-wind of arms and legs as Freddy makes his getaway. Fuck you, Freddy! he wants to bellow after him, knows the words won't come, his throat so dry, his tongue stuck to the roof of his mouth.

The negroes begin their move, taking slow, deliberate steps. Joey's seen these guys before. The same negroes that walked over to them last night? Yeah, that kid on the end, where's the blaster? No need for music tonight, Joey knows this time is for real.

Joey begins to build a picture: if these guys were carrying shooters, they'd have produced them by now. It'll be knives and the need to get in close. Any second now, they'll open up with some kind of spiel, try and ease the tension, catch him off balance.

As if by some pre-arranged signal, Cracker and Ruff move away from Blade. Joey got it wrong, there isn't going to be a parley. They begin to circle their prey – in for the kill. He heard Freddy cut and run. Freddy wouldn't count in a situation like this, he'd get in the way; fuck things up. Moe's somewhere close, he can hear his breathing. Stay back old man. There's rapid movement – knives are drawn and glint their menace –

the .38 swings from behind Joey's back, levels up, sweeps an arc to cover all before it.

Blade realises they have fronted a guy who will take them out, but it's gone too far, they are revved with dope and raring to go. They've been here before. The streets belong to *them*, not some whitey thinking he can dump on a brother. C'mon guys! This 'ere mother's pullin' our chain. He ain't gonna shoot the fuckin' thing, he's tryin' it on, is all.

Pakooosh! Joey lets go at Ruff circling to his right, hits him high in the thigh, hears the clatter of steel as the six-inch bladed Schrade rattles paving stone. Blade rushes in, Cracker hesitates. Joey squares up. *Pakooosh*. Misses – Blade's at him, his knife slashing downward at Joey's gunhand. Razor steel slices the knuckle – Joey lets go another shot in Blade's direction, the bullet clips his shoulder bone, spinning him to the ground. Moe moves in to protect Joey. Where's the third? Fuck! Cracker's at Moe's side, thrusting the knife forward – Moe stumbles, crashing to his knees.

For a split second, Cracker rocks off balance, recovers and lunges forward to stab Moe a second time. In his eagerness, he doesn't see the .38 locking on him. Cracker feels barrel heat against his forehead, freezes, and stares up into the crazed eyes of the gunman. The bowie falls away, his arms spread wide, staring dog-eyed, pleading a breathless mercy. The thumb lifting back the hammer appears cartoon size. *Booom!* The side of Cracker's head skims claret along the liquor store door.

Blade and Ruff scramble about in blind panic. As soon as Joey had drilled Cracker's head, they knew the four remaining bullets had their names on them, and accelerated down Fremont.

The weight of Cracker's body lay slumped across Moe's legs, pinning them down as Moe tries to draw his knees to his belly. Joey looks about him to make sure the other two have scarpered. Shit! There's been enough noise to wake the fuckin' city. He heard window sashes chinking the odd window, people shouting in high pitched voices. The blooded handgun is stashed in his coat pocket. He hauls Cracker aside, and sees blood oozing between Moe's scrawny fingers.

Joey turns Moe on his back and drags him into the murk and trash of the liquor store doorway. His intention is to leave Moe for the ambulance that will have been called on a 911. Joey looks down at Cracker, has second thoughts, he ain't gonna leave his friend lying next to that piece of dead shit. Moe feels featherweight in his blood drenched arms, shop fronts and doorways flash by as he makes for Leepers Deli.

From his strategically positioned seat behind the glass display case, Lenny Lewis can see plain the entrance doorway. Not that he should be worrying about who comes in and out of the place, that's down to a security guard hired from Gold Star Nightwatch. The guard took off ten minutes ago for a pack of smokes, and now Lenny's having to keep watch on the place himself. Some fuckin' outfit! He'll hit the blower first thing in the mornin' and tell 'em the contract's over.

He glances at the wall clock, twelve minutes the guy's been gone. That's it! I'll give him another three, an' if he ain't back I'm callin' the company right now for a replacement.

Fuckin' hell! What was that! He springs from his seat as Joey bursts awkwardly through the door. Where's the fuckin' guard! Jesus! He's carryin' someone. These guys are in trouble – this can't be a stick-up – they're swimming in blood. Joey rests Moe to the floor and props him against a Coke machine. He pinches the old man's cheeks and removes his dentures, and lets his head fall back on his chest. Hearing police sirens, Joey knows he's got to get the hell out of there.

'Dial 911, now!' Joey yells, placing the dentures in Moe's top pocket, then he bolts out the door.

Lenny slumps into his seat, white knuckles gripping the arm of the chair.

*

Standing in The Roxy's foyer, nursing a tall Tom Collins, Tommy believes they've Jewed him with the gin, and suckered him with ice. He'd showed up half an hour ago on the off-chance of bumping into Joey. It's getting late now, Joey would shut bang on the button, and by now he could have walked the length of Fremont, and back again. He'd had plenty of time to settle his bulk and rehearse his lines, but it looks like a futile exercise. It was a long shot, he'd tried, sorry, Jack. He traipses over to a billboard next to the reception, leafing through promotional handouts, thumbing shows and tours he's never going to make; he's booked on a scheduled flight to Boston tomorrow night.

He's got one hour to kill before his date with Susie, so he turns and walks to the cabaret room to take in the show. Mid-way along a crowded bar he impacts onto a stool between a stiff ginger-haired guy and a dumpy blonde. For a moment, she doesn't observe Tommy's head lifting in the waft of her expensive perfume. Leaning closer, almost caressing her intricate silver and turquoise earrings, the scent is driving him wild. It's familiar, not hooker familiar. But where from?

Mesmerised, he doesn't see the blonde's shaky stare at the bartender standing in front of him.

'What'll it be, Mac?' the bartender snaps impatiently. Tommy takes one last sniff, then zeroes on the red and black checked waistcoat.

'Tom Collins. An' easy on the ice, *Mac*,' Tommy bats back, with an icy glare. 'The name's Tommy, by the way.'

The bartender begins to shake the mix, unscrambling the fat guy's thoughts with his twenty-year fix. Twenty goddamn years! Dreamers and drop-outs. Wiseguys and washouts, he's seen 'em all. Then, there are degenerates like the fat man. He can spot his kind a mile off. So can the lady, she slides her glass across the bar-top and swings off her stool. Tommy shrugs and slips a beer mat. What the fuck, everyone's on his case, he'll be sure glad to get back to Boston.

The bartender places the drink.

'Fifty cents – sir.'

'Stick it on the tab,' Tommy replies, keeping his hands on the bar, like he can't be bothered scratching around for change.

'She's gone, mister, there ain't no tab,' said the bartender, placing his heavy hands on the bar in front of Tommy. 'Fifty cents, or you're in for the fastest walk of your life. You get my drift?' he snarls, nodding towards a floorman. Tommy turns his head and sees the gorilla, dips into his pocket and tosses down two quarters on the bar.

'Fuck – you.'

The bartender leans over, wags a thick finger in Tommy's face then balls his fist.

'Drink it, cueball, an' take that walk. I got a break comin' up in fifteen minutes an' if you're still around, I'm gonna ask that guy to walk you outside. Guess what?'

'What?'

'I'll be waitin'.'

Tommy brushes the threat aside, lights a cigar and thinks he's got better things to be doin' than sat in this pisshole looking at some sorry bastard who's about to chin him for nosing up some fat blonde's hairpiece. Hey! She probably got a kick out of it anyway. With this town! Who knows? Further down the bar, a guy's yelling at the checked waistcoat.

'Hey, Paulie. Joey's on the line, askin' for a Tommy Mace. Ring a bell?'

'Joey who?'

'Joey! Works the skin-flick.'

'Gotcha. Nah, ain't heard the name Tommy Mace – what do'ya think I'm runnin' here, an answering service? Gimmie a break, Sol. I'm busy.'

Tommy's feet grip the stool-rail, throwing himself forward.

'Hey! That's me, I'm Tommy Mace. Tell him to hold.'

He wobbles off the stool, throwing a dollar bill in front of Paulie.

'There you go, *Mac*.'

Paulie shakes his head. 'Get outta here,' he hisses as Tommy takes off for the phone at the end of the bar. Tommy's out of breath, pressing the earpiece tight to the side of his face to drown out a female vocalist, warbling 'Killing Me Softly with His Song'. She's killing it, all right.

'It's me, Tommy. You changed your mind, eh?'

Tommy hears laboured breathing.

'Nothin's changed. There's been some trouble. I'm one block up from the Starburst.'

'How'd you know I'd be here?'

'I knew, that's all. Catch a cab, an' *I'll* find you.'

'Sure, sure. One–' Tommy talks back at himself. The line is dead.

10

Incandescent red and blue spins and bounces off grilled store fronts and patrol car windshields. Camera bulbs flash and pop, illuminating the scene like a movie-shoot. Detective Sergeant Danny Driscol sits the hood of his Dodge Charger, torches a Pall Mall and looks over the location. What a mess, somebody sure done a number on this guy. He scratches his head, turns and checks his watch in a cruiser's side-light: 11.42 precisely. When they had hit through the red stop-and-go on Fremont, there wasn't a soul to be seen on the street. Now a crowd of more than thirty people are bunched around the ambulances and patrol cars. A Mrs Ruby Goldstein had made the initial 911 but, like everyone else on the block, she said she hadn't seen or heard a thing till the shooting was over.

Driscol slides off the hood, opens the Charger's glove compartment and palms a fresh pack of gum. Planting his rump on the rear seat, rooting his size twelves against kerbstone, he watches a news crew arrive. This one has a touch of mystery. He'd pulled back the tarp, had an officer shine his flashlight on what was left of the dead man's face. Some number!

There was no way they were going to ID this person without dental records. Officer Gleason tracked the flashlight's beam, as Driscol searched through the dead man's clothing. There was no plastic ID, but around his neck, the mock gold medallion placed a name in Driscol's memory bank.

Theo Thomas, street name, Cracker. Driscol pulls the tarp roughly over the victim. This is one mother he's glad to see out of the system, Cracker and his two cronies have given him the run around for long enough; one down, two to go. A dozen times he's had them in the slammer on suspicions, ranging from rape to robbery, hauled in over the cab murders, and every time they've weaselled out with the help of a bent attorney.

At first sight, this could have been a drug deal turned sour, or a gang fight over territory. It don't add up – the other victim, who is as old as a Redwood, is on his way to Community Hospital. Where does the old guy fit in? As Driscol sped down Fremont, the manager of a deli had flagged him down. Some guy inside, shot, stabbed, couldn't say which, but the guy's in bad shape. The old man got star treatment, Cracker got the tarp. Cracker had to be the assailant on the old guy, but how could this frail old man defend himself? An officer had turned out his coat pockets. No ID, just a twenty-dollar note, a half-empty pack of cigars and flip-top matches registered, The Roxy. It's a start.

Driscol hunches his shoulders and lifts his six-foot frame out of the rear door. His 220 pounds shave bystanders aside as he makes his way back to the crime scene. He's been on these streets long enough for people to respect his no-fuck-about style, and those who don't, fear his presence.

He knows the torn up face belongs to Cracker, and good fuckin' riddance. Two knives were found at the scene, blood is splattered all over the sidewalk, and Driscol bets Cracker's two partners in crime were involved. If the old man did it, he deserves a medal, but he couldn't have, he's half dead and Blade and Ruff wouldn't have left him that way. So, who's the shooter? Pressing his bulk through frenzied pressmen, he asks for the first officer on the scene, rookie patrol man, Esequiel Cordova.

'Got here maybe a minute before you guys,' said Cordova,

looking down at street-worn sneakers protruding the tarp. 'You know this guy, sergeant?'

'Yeah, I knew the shitbag. Who's lookin' after the deli end?' said Driscol, discreetly kicking the dead man's sneaker.

'Abe Lincoln. He's over with the captain.'

Driscol turns, waving bystanders back from the cordon tape.

Abe's standing alongside Captain Drome, their heads locked together. The captain taking final details before he heads back to Central.

'Some eyesore, hey, Danny?" said the captain, out of the side of his mouth. 'Do ya recognise what's left of the face? Any ideas?'

Driscol screws a cigarette butt under the heel of his shoe.

'Early days, Captain, but I know the face. Theo Thomas, street-name, Cracker. One big shit, so he won't be missed, an' I tell you this. Bring me the guy that done it, an' I'll shake his hand. That motherfucker bought what's due.'

The captain sighs pensively.

'That so, Driscol? Keep your thoughts to yourself, these press-guys will pick you up faster than that.'

'You got anywhere with the deli guy, Abe?'

A camera flash pops off to the side, blinding them for an instant.

'Yeah, the deli manager says the old guy was carried in by his friend—'

'What shape was his friend in? Was he injured? Did he recognise him? Why did he take off?' interrupted Driscol.

'The manager said he recognised the guy that carried the old man in, he works the porno joint along the block, goes by the name Joey. He wasn't sure if he had a flesh wound to his right hand, or it was comin' off the old guy. We ain't got a surname yet, but Maurice Turner will clear that one. But get this. The old man is apparently the manager of the mag store. Do ya fuckin' believe that? The guy's as old as the hills!

Anyway, this Joey props the old guy against a Coke machine, then took off.'

There's a break in conversation as they watch Cracker being loaded into the meat wagon.

'Sounds simple, don't it?' said Driscol, dryly.

'About as simple as it's gonna get tonight, Danny,' said the captain, squaring on the detective, 'Go and find Turner, he'll be on 5th. Get the full name of the shooter, find out where he lives, what kind of car he drives. He could have been injured, so check the hospitals,' said Drome, pointing a finger at Driscol.

'If he's on his toes, there ain't a dog's chance he'll be visitin' casualty,' said Driscol.

'Check the hospitals anyway. Get the street cleared. You check the deli manager, Danny. See if you can get anything else out of him.'

Patrolman Cordova appears from the crowd, bursting with enthusiasm.

'I think I got somethin'. A Mrs Ruby Goldstein seen three negroes hangin' around earlier in the night. She also seen the old man lock the store, an' walk off with two guys that work the picture house. She thought there was somethin' wrong – about two minutes after they set off, one guy ran back past her window.'

For a moment, the cops look at each other in silent appraisement.

'We got the shooter, Danny. Get a name, an' get after him.'

The captain talked briefly with the press, then pulled out. A television news crew appeared at the last moment, finding Driscol the most senior officer left at the scene. Driscol was about to follow the meat wagon's tail-lights up to the deli, but got caught in the whirlwind of reporters and camera men. He wasn't comfortable with the media, never had been. He talked tersely into the camera, elbowed the crew aside then made strides for the deli.

*

Five blocks north at the Fremont and Las Vegas Boulevard intersection, the scenery changes dramatically. Huge stage curtains have suddenly been raised, from darkness into neon madness. There is no warning; no rehearsals for what's about to hit the naked eye: the glitz and glare of Glitter Gulch. Here the downtown casino-hotels pack together in a blaze of dazzling triumph. This is where starry-eyed visitors to Vegas will feed their first dollars, crave its addiction, then starve in its futility.

Thousands of people will criss-cross the street tonight, trying their luck somewhere new. For them it's fantasia – for the night-shift working the Mint, it's the start of another long shift.

'How ya doin', Masie?' asked Karen, dumping her empty glasses on the bar-top. 'You still hurtin' from last night?'

'Just a little,' Masie replied, wiping down her tray.

Karen leans in. 'Some fuckin' animal, that Abilene. An' you know what I heard?'

'Yeah. She's been promoted up to management. Let me guess; public relations. Tell me I'm right, Karen,' quips Masie.

Karen sees her coming the smart ass. 'You're close – Abilene's keepin' her job. Charlie Powell fixed it.'

Masie looks about for confirmation. There's no one close except Mike, and she wouldn't ask him in a million years.

'You're shittin' me? This your idea of a joke?'

'Heard it as I came on shift.'

'Where the fuck is she then? I don't seen her tonight,' said Masie, looking around the walls.

Mike looks on, polishing a shot glass.

'You ladies gonna make tips tonight? Or stand there jawing?'

They make like they don't hear him. Karen steps back, sizing Masie. Some dumb bitch!

'She ain't here 'cause it's her night off, an' just about now, Charlie's gonna be pokin' the ass off her. Get the picture?'

Masie slams the cloth on to the tray in frustration.

'This ain't fuckin' right, an' you know it, Karen.'

'It's all down to Charlie, Masie.'

'Fuck him, I hope his dick drops off, an' there's every chance of that happenin'–'

She stops short, catching Jimmy Jinks in the corner of her eye.

Jimmy sees Masie looking over and veers to avoid her. He saw that *who's-side-are-you-on look* as he hurried by, but what can he do? His shift crew comprises croupiers, stickmen, boxmen, shills. They don't have union rights, but cocktail waitresses and kitchen staff come under Charlie Powell's domain; he calls the shots when it comes to hiring and firing. Anyway, he's too busy for all that bullshit with Masie right now. The floor manager, Jake Marrante, has tumbled a crooked rookie dealer, Hicky Watson, who's been thrown out on his ear, and now he's heading upstairs to shake down the dealer's partner in crime, Kenny Muff.

Thirty minutes ago, Kenny was on a roll. The floor manager had switched dealers to throw Kenny's play, and the casino began to claw back some of its losses. Jimmy had been called across for a head-to-head with his superior, Jake Marrante. They suspected Watson and Muff of collaborating to scam the house. The dealer is new, so what's his history? How long has the guy been employed by the casino? Where was his last place of employment? The office upstairs ran a check, while the rookie dealer took his break in the coffee lounge.

They scrutinised the player. He looked a green-horn, wet behind the ears, and about the same age as Hicky Watson. Jimmy Jinks has seen all manner of scams during his ten years with the casino, and ninety-nine per cent have involved the dealer. While Watson blew cool the scalding coffee, Jimmy placed a peroxide shill two seats along from Kenny. She will be the casino's ears and eyes for the next session of play. Jake whistled Watson from his break.

Ten minutes later, the blonde reported back to Marrante that the two men were definitely acting in collaboration against the casino's interest. She explained: as she'd joined the table, Kenny had three different chip values in front of him: one green twenty-five-dollar chip, four red five-dollar chips, and a stack of silver-dollar tokens. Playing against the unfamiliar dealer, Kenny limited his take to one token bets, maybe two if the dealer turned a poor *hole* card. Kenny won some, lost some, he was playing it straight up the middle, no problems.

The dealer was switched. Hicky stepped in and took up his station at the table. Kenny's pattern of play began to change. He started to bet five-dollar chips with the tokens, making out he was stepping up a gear. The cards were dealt – Kenny holds with a Jack, nine – Hicky pretended to concentrate on another player. With lightning-fast fingers, Kenny adds the green twenty-five-dollar chip to his bet. It's simple, it's laughable, but it's one of the casino's biggest problems in its war on cheats. A straight dealer would have spotted Kenny's move before he'd fanned the cards. He'd have told Kenny to place the largest value chip on the bottom of the stack, then the lowest value token on the top. Hicky didn't tell him, and bust with an eight, a six, and a ten. Thirty-six dollars' worth of chips were pushed into Kenny's betting area.

'The shift is over, son,' Marrante whispered into the dealer's ear.

Kenny read Hicky's ashen face, the presence of Jimmy at his shoulder, looked pensively at the pile of chips in front of him, and felt his stomach sinking.

'Come with me, sir,' Jimmy said, politely.

Kenny looked up in shock, he didn't notice the pretty cocktail waitress feeding the table with drinks, or hear the steady rattle of slot machines behind him. His stomach hit rock bottom, he'd heard stories of what happened to scam artists who rip off Vegas casinos. Busted heads, broken bones, a late-night swim in the Hoover Dam. He'd held his breath and forced the cheeks of his arse together, wishing he'd never listened to Hicky Watson. He knew this was one crazy idea, he shouldn't have listened when Hicky convinced him Vegas would be easy pickin's.

'What's your name?'

'Kenny.'

'C'mon, Kenny. These people are waitin' to play.'

There was false softness in Jimmy's speech. Kenny must have realised this passive diplomacy is to remove him from the table with the least possible commotion, and once he's locked in isolation with the razor-sharp eyes of Jimmy Jinks, things would be so much different.

A new dealer was quickly installed, the table back into service. As Kenny trudged plush carpet, all he saw was security, with every step the guards seemed to have grown taller. He'd been allowed to carry his winnings, the stack of chips clutched tight in his small hands made the situation look worse, like he'd *really* robbed them. It was all Hicky's idea, he'd wanted to blurt out, but knew it wouldn't hold water with the guy gripping his upper arm.

Although Hicky Watson pleaded his innocence, he was about to be convicted without a jury. Morrante's pugilistic face didn't change Hicky's mind, he'd give it sweet innocence. Who! Me? What the fuck's goin' on here? But gave up the game when Morrante's stubby finger poked a hole in his chest. He was warned with gangland vernacular which way the Greyhound terminal lay, and if he showed his face at the casino again, he'd be clipped. 'Clipped!' the word stuck in his head as he was accompanied by two burly guards to the main doors. With his tail between his legs, he traipsed up Fremont to the Greyhound terminal. He guessed his friend wouldn't be too long. Surely they'll give Kenny the same message.

Watson's reluctant admission of guilt is signifcant. Until that moment, all they have him on is suspicion to defraud, and technically this wouldn't hold up in a court of law. If there was such justice, Watson would say he took his eye off the game for a second or two, and he'd walk. The thing that's bugging Jimmy as he walks back amongst tables is the incompetence of personnel in the first place. He'll look into it first thing in the morning.

The chips clutched tight in his sweaty palm, Kenny slinks back against the wall of the tiny office. Jimmy enters and dismisses the guard. Panic stricken, Kenny finds he's alone with a guy who takes ripping-off company money like it was his own, he's scared shitless. This pit box can't stand much over five-ten, but he's got something about him, everything on the outside relaxed and calm. Inside? Who knows what's in Jimmy's eyes? Kenny sees the calculated coldness of a man who wouldn't hesitate to kill him.

'Where you from?'

'Racine, Wisconsin – hey, mister. I think you got the wrong idea,' Kenny blurts.

Pointing to the chips in Kenny's hand, Jimmy fixes him an ugly glare, 'You came a long way to shaft me, pal. How much?'

'Dunno. Maybe one-twenty, one-thirty. Honest. I dunno.'

'Spread 'em on the table, let's have a look.'

Jimmy's eyes flash over the chips as they hit the table, and counts out 140 bucks' worth.

'Empty your pockets. C'mon! empty 'em I said.'

Kenny fumbles in his pockets and peels out a wad of notes.

'Count 'em.'

Kenny gets to fiddling the notes and making count. He would have stuffed them in his socks, but everything happened that fast, he didn't get the chance. He counts 250 and lays it down beside the chips.

Jimmy walks forward and scoops up the cash, 'Listen to me, kid. If I see your pimply face in this casino, on the streets, any fuckin' place, I'm gonna nail you to a fuckin' cross – you got that?'

Kenny's mouth falls open, he'd saved all last year to come down here and be with Hicky. Okay they done wrong, he'll hold his hands up to that, but the casino got their chips back, surely this guy wouldn't rob their fare home?

'Security is waitin' outside the door. Now beat it.'

Kenny looks at him with pleading eyes. 'You got my dough, mister.'

'What!'

'How are we supposed to–'

'Now!' orders Jimmy, opening the door.

Nobody's going to know what went on in here tonight. The chips will be returned to the cashier's cage, the neatly folded notes slide into Jimmy's side pocket. This is his to keep. Is the kid gonna run to the police? No chance. Nobody would give a fuck anyway. Casinos and City Hall run hand-in-hand, it's all down to revenue and taxes to keep the city's machinery oiled and running. Who's gonna care about a couple of young grifters?

Tommy had cradled the handset, his heart beating ten to the dozen. Strangely, it takes him back to the old days when a call such as this held out a possible front page headline. For a second he stood motionless, relishing the fact he was right all along about Joey.

There wasn't a cab to be seen outside the Roxy, so he cut through Third and Fourth, and shuffled about nervously till a cab swung by. The driver tried light conversation, Tommy stayed quiet, thinking why the call? Out on the sidewalk, five blocks from the Starbust, two hookers swing their tails for passing trade. Tommy instructs the driver to slow some, the driver looks over his shoulder, and raises his eyebrows. This guy don't have to look for street-walkers, in his head he's a list as long as his arm.

'Slow, some? Sure, fella. You lookin' to party?' said the driver, adjusting the cab's rear-view mirror on Tommy.

The passenger isn't showing interest, just gaping out the side-window, the cabby flips the rear-view back into headlight dazzle and shifts a gear. Two blocks short of his motel, Tommy pays the fare and weaves his way through a crowd of bewildered sightseers. They envisage the neon must stretch forever, and stop Tommy for insider knowledge. He brushes past them and looks hard along the sidewalk. There's no sign of Joey.

Tommy drifts along, his excitement and sense of urgency depleted. This is some fuckin' wind-up, Joey's got him on a wild goose chase. Passing the telephone kiosk that Joey said he called from, he hears movement from behind a billboard. Frightened and unsure, he hurries to the delusory safety of kerbside. He hears the rustle of parting foliage. Christ! The shadowy figure of Joey begins to emerge from behind Holiday Inn advertising.

There's something strange about his appearance. Why is his coat inside-out, and where's his shirt? Tommy steps forward, Joey stands, feet apart, not attempting to step back into shadow cast by the billboard. Tommy doesn't need to be a brain surgeon to know the shirt is an improvised bandage, and Joey's in trouble.

'Holy mother! You all right?'

'I'm OK, let's get the fuck outta here,' said Joey, turning in the direction of the Starburst.

'Jeez! You look a fuckin' mess–'

'One more time, mister! I'm OK. Let's go.'

'C'mon, I know a back way into the motel,' Tommy said, brushing past Joey, signalling Joey to follow him.

Tommy angles across a dirt lot for the side entrance to the motel. Joey follows, unsure about this guy from Boston, but left with no other option. The instant he took off from Leepers Deli, he'd turned into an alleyway to catch his breath and gather his thoughts. Where could he go? Who could he turn to? The apartment was out of the question, and the only person he knows really well, he'd left propped against a Coke machine. He needed somewhere to clean up and move along. Tommy sprang to mind. Hadn't Tommy heard Moe mention the Roxy? He'd wrapped the shirt around his hand. Felt his blood soaked trousers, their sticky warmth clinging at his legs. Realising it wouldn't take too long before the cops picked him off the streets, and there was no one to turn to he could trust, there seemed no alternative, but the limited security of the Starburst motel, whether he trusted Tommy Mace, or not.

Joey hangs by the gate as Tommy checks the coast is clear. The torn hand throbs with pain, his good hand slams the gatepost in frustration. He'd been wrong-footed, it wouldn't have happened years ago, he'd have given it to 'em right off the bat. If only Moe had stayed back, things could have been different. He leans against the post, looking across at the riot of colour from nearby Strip casinos, at aircrafts' lights as they blink in an inky sky. It's Abilene's night off. She'll be out there somewhere with her friends, making whoopee. Joey hears a low whistle. The coast is clear.

II

Hicky Watson squats in the litter-strewn corner of the downtown bus terminal. For the past ten minutes he's occupied his time toeing empty milk cartons and screwed cigarette packs out of arm's length. Hicky squats sad-eyed and long-faced, pondering his lot. Kenny's carrying their bankroll, and he's hoping to hell Kenny had the smarts to hide it before the pit boss got him to the office. Things haven't worked out as he'd planned. But who said it was going to be easy? It had worked up in Reno, hadn't it? They'd bussed into Vegas, feeling good, and ready to take on the town.

This city isn't a first for Hicky. He'd drifted into Vegas six years ago carrying ten bucks and a battered suitcase. He'd slept rough in a patchwork camper shell at the rear of a used car lot. The owner figured Hicky some kind of security, and that suited Hicky fine, daytime working a fast food deal on Paradise. About a month later, he enrolled evenings as a trainee croupier in a dealers' school. The school didn't charge a dime, the tab was paid by the State of Nevada, and once he was in full-time employment, he'd repay the loan back in monthly instalments. This, too, was fine by Hicky. He could see himself covering the repayments on tips alone. After all, aren't these streets paved with gold?

Three nights a week, Hicky climbed the concrete stairs and learned his three disciplines: craps, baccarat and blackjack. He stuck it out and, before he knew it, the twelve-week course came to an end. They could shove the fried chicken right up their sorry arses now, 'cause that thin-paper diploma clutched tight in his expectant hand meant he was ready to make the big time.

Hicky had saved his money pretty good while in his rent free accommodation. A motel room was needed now, just somewhere cheap to shower down and crash between casino shifts. He found a place on 5th, a real flop house, but figured it was a start; got to be better than that old camper shell. At the conclusion of each course, the school find employment for eager students, and Hicky hears the popular words spoken by all prospective employers, 'You got to pay your dues, son.' Words he's going to hear time and time again during his next eighteen months in Vegas. Dues means starting rock bottom, at casinos so far removed from mainstream action, that they're not even listed in *Yellow Pages*.

He starts in a nickel-and-dime, two blocks north of downtown. The place is something straight from the old west, but there were no silver-dollars wheeling in this establishment; just social security checks. On rock-bottom minimum wage, plus tips that wouldn't feed a household cat, Hicky's pavements of gold quickly turned to deep shit. He began to struggle finding the rent payments, his social life bottomed to twenty-cents-a-pop hot-dogs and the occasional beer. If he met a girl he fancied, he couldn't afford to take her anyplace. If he found a pal, he couldn't afford to drink with him. Life sucked, for Hicky Watson.

After twelve months he got his break; he'd paid his dues. It was to a small casino on Fremont, a short step, but in the right direction. Trouble was, he was now two months adrift on school repayments, one month in back rent and had exactly three dollars sixty-five in the bank. He'd accumulated bar tabs a mile long, and every week he'd have to walk further afield to skirt bars to take a drink. After wearing down his last pair of decent shoes, he gave up the walking and nursed six-packs on the end of his bed. Hicky finally caved in. Las Vegas had the beating of him. But one day he'd be back, he'd promised himself. And so he had, three times with different IDs, and he'd skinned them good.

This is the first time he's brought this kid, Kenny, along. His other partner, Flames O'Tool, is about to receive sentence for arson, and he's looking at a long stretch. He'd looked around and found this kid with an angel face and thought he'd fit the bill. Why not? Who's gonna suspect a dork like Kenny Muff? They'd bussed it to Reno with Kenny's savings, had holed up in a low-cost motel, and waited a couple of days for Hicky's casino clearance. They'd been a little edgy, but security isn't as tight as it used to be. The Nevada gaming industry is having babies on account that Atlantic City is constructing casinos at a furious pace and will soon be poaching valuable labour. Hicky had no problems with his clearance. They hit for 400 in three days of play. They hit too hard, too fast. Quick-silver eyes began to follow their every move. It was time to blow.

Bleary eyes peer at the flotsam floating in and out the terminal. The place bleeds human tragedy. Derelicts and dipsos slumber in rigid plastic seating, their meagre belongings tied about their feet with string. Just when these lost souls are about to drift off into a kinder world, a fifteen-stone guard wakes them roughly with a night-stick. The drifters are the wiseguys amongst this lot, younger, most with cranky features and keen eyes that ward off wanabees who look to steal their patch. Latter-day hippies sit on the floor, passing joints, their psychedelic talk foreign to Hicky. Service personnel with razor sharp uniforms thread their way through. These are serious looking men returning from liberty, heading for Nellis Air Force Base, north of the city.

The longer Hicky squats, the more desperate he becomes. It's like these strange people are rubbing off on him in some weird kind of way. He shouldn't be here. Just this morning they were walking on water. What went wrong? Where the fuck is Kenny?

For what seemed an age, but it could have only been ten minutes or so, Kenny squeezed through the terminal doorway. His sloping shoulders and hangdog appearance clue Hicky that things are not as they should be. Their bankroll comes straight to mind. Hicky jumps to his feet to meet him, signalling Kenny over to a quiet corner.

'What happened, man? What kept yer?' Hicky cries, excitedly.

Kenny slumps against the wall.

'They fuckin' nailed us, Hicky. All along I seen it coming.'

'Fuck 'em. We'll try Sam's Town, I heard–'

'We ain't got a red cent. They took the fuckin' lot.'

'What d'ya mean! Took the lot? Who took fuckin' what, Kenny? They just can't take it, it don't belong to *them*!' Hicky screams, the veins standing out on his neck.

'They took it, it's gone, so much for hittin' the big time, Hicky.'

'Big time! You stupid bastard.'

Hicky's lost for words, shaking his head in disbelief. Kenny looks sheepishly about him. People are pricking up their ears, Hicky's getting loud.

'It ain't no problem, Hicky. Let's get back to the motel and get our bags. I'll call my ol' man, he'll wire us the fare through Western Union. C'mon, at least we'll have a ride home.'

'Home! Racine might be home to you, but it sure ain't home to me, buster, I got plans. This was goin' to be the one that set me free for the Golden Gate. I was goin' to be in California this time next month, an' here I am, stuck on this crummy fuckin' bus terminal with a pocket full of change, and some dick-head who can't tell the time of day. Fuck you, an' fuck your ol' man. Call him if you like, I'm stayin.'

'I dunno, Hicky. What we gonna do for food?'

'Food! Christ Almighty!' Hicky scowls, turning sharply, striding for the exit.

'You comin'?'

Kenny takes a quick look at the deadwood propped in seating and resting the floor, their glazed eyes unburdened by reality. The guard slaps his night-stick, his nose twitching at smoke-filled air. This is a world he's never travelled before, far removed from home-town comforts, and suddenly he's at the mercy of Hicky Watson. He's got no choice, his ol' man ain't got no cold cash, it's pissed against tavern walls seven nights a week.

'Wait for me, Hicky,' he calls out.

The blood-stained loafers were discarded on the doormat. Joey had walked in and shook them off like he was returning from a regular night out. He'd tightened the improvised bandage and held his hand high to stop blood dripping on the carpet. Tommy fussed about, said he'd find a drug store, pick up bandage and antiseptic. Joey told him not to bother, it was no big deal, it's just a scratch.

Tommy scurried about the room like a headless chicken, securing windows, closing drapes, and rechecking the door lock. He'd told Joey to shower down, use his robe, then he'd take a look at that hand. As Joey took a shower, Tommy was in need of a stiff drink. He lifted a fresh bottle of Vodka from the bedside cabinet, unscrewed the cap and poured a generous measure. Listening to the shower beat the curtain, his eyes zeroed in on the doormat. What the hell am I doin'? I gotta get rid of this guy. Fuck you, Jack, I ain't gonna sit here an' take the rap for something Joey's done.

The suspense was killing Tommy, as Joey undressed, he'd asked him what the hell had happened. Joey said he'd tell him later. Tommy got the feeling this whole thing had backfired on him.

Joey appears in the shower-closet doorway, the over-size

robe tied at his waist, pulling flannel tight against his bull-like frame. For a split second, Tommy travels back in time, seeing a youthful fighter climbing into the ring, his robe brushing the top rope, his trainer pivoting the stool.

'Bring over the bottle an' some ice,' said Joey, turning back to the handbasin.

Tommy shunts off the bed, grabs the bottle and a tray of ice-cubes out of the small refrigerator. As he enters the bathroom he sees cold water running freely over the torn hand, washing away a trickle of blood. At first sight it doesn't appear to be too bad. He gets in closer, and winces at the four-inch gash running across its back and down to the small knuckle. Joey opens the wound to flush it some, pinches it tight and looks over to Tommy.

Tommy screws his lip, it's not the wound that's gaining his attention; his eyes focus on the butt of a .38 protruding slightly from the robe pocket.

'You're gonna need the hospital. I'll make a call–'

'Oh, yeah? Like fuck you will!' said Joey, whipping out the revolver with his good hand.

'Fuck!' said Tommy, cowering down, 'OK, OK, I'm only tryin' to help.'

'Like fuck. I know what you're up to. You'd be straight on the blower to Boston, if you haven't already.'

'I ain't, Joey. I'm not, I swear on my life,' grovels Tommy.

'You ain't in no position to swear on anythin'. Get your fat ass in the lounge, an' take a seat.'

Tommy half-crawls over to an easy chair, all the time looking over his shoulder, petrified of what Joey will do. Joey slips the .38 into the robe pocket and walks over to the bedside cabinet. Tommy mindful that they could be in for a long night, the Vodka was dispensed sparingly on Joey's wound. The wound was bandaged with the tail of Tommy's sports shirt, its back and arms ripped into wide strips in case of further bleeding.

Joey rocks the pint bottle, it's three-quarters full, just enough to knock Tommy out for the rest of the night. Joey pours a tall glass, and passes it over to Tommy's shaking hand. He pours a small one for himself and glances down at his wrist watch: 12.55. He'll watch the one o'clock news on the local station, there's bound to be a report on the shooting, and hopefully, news about Moe. If he watches the news, Tommy's going to know what's happened, but fuck him, he'll be out of here before Tommy wakes. Joey hits the TV button.

'You made the news? I think you owe me, Joey.'

'I owe you nothin'.'

Tommy slugs the remains of his glass in one take.

Good evening. This is Jenny Williams with all your top stories, this hour. News has just come in of a shooting on Fremont Street, downtown Las Vegas. One black male was killed and one Caucasian wounded. The wounded male is said by a Community Hospital spokesman to be in a critical condition. Asked if this incident was connected to the recent spate of cab killings, Detective Sergeant Driscol, who is heading the enquiry, said it was too early to tell for certain, but it looks unlikely at this stage of the investigation.

There was good news today for the residents of Maryland Parkway, with the signing . . .

Across the screen, a fleeting shot of Fremont, the detective looking uncomfortable in front of the camera. The camera pans to where Cracker had fallen – Tommy's head spins towards the patio window, he's sure he heard movement outside. His head snaps to Joey – the chair is empty, Joey's already on his toes, moving at speed towards the drapes, the .38 held high; cop fashion. Tommy panics, he can't figure which way to turn, what to do next. There's light rapping on the door. Fuck! Tommy tumbles off the chair, falls to his knees. For a second or two he's blind with fright, looks up at Joey parting the drapes slightly with the revolver.

'You expectin' company?' whispers Joey.

Just like Hicky's first casino wasn't listed in *Yellow Pages*. The Welcome motel on 6th has yet to feature in the *Good Hotel Guide*. Hicky said the two single cots squeezed side-by-side in the ten-by-ten would do them for a couple of days. Kenny looks round the room. No TV, no radio, no nothing, just the stench of old piss and stale tobacco. They'd turned their suitcases inside out when they returned from the terminal. Kenny hit zero, Hicky hit a crumpled ten-spot. Kenny was bilked he hadn't found it. Hicky is stingy, he can go days without food, so it looked like Kenny would have to beg every time his stomach got to growling.

What happened to all the promises? They were gonna be high rollers by now, with a block-long stretch limousine, and peach pussy swinging off their arms. He watches Hicky smooth out creases and stretch the ten, like it's going to make it go further. Kenny's hungry, his patience with Hicky about to snap.

'Say, Hicky? Do ya think we could pop out an' get us a burger and fries? What'd think?'

'*Pop* out, eh, junior? I think you've been watchin' too much television. Are you fuckin' crazy? *Pop* out to fuckin' what? It's four blocks to the nearest casino, do'ya think I'm gonna risk my balls at this hour, for burger and fries?'

Kenny somehow knew that would be the answer, but he bets Hicky will spend wisely on a pack of smokes first thing in the morning. How he wished *he'd* found a ten-spot.

'So, how far is this ten gonna get us? You gonna stretch it till it makes a twenty?'

'I'll stretch this baby all the way to the Golden Gate. You'll see.'

'And yet it won't stretch to a plate of fries? You're full of shit, Hicky.'

Hicky throws a mean stare. Kenny's treading dangerous ground here, Hicky Watson can turn ugly, real quick. The words were just a cry from an empty gut. He craves food, a decent bed, a normal father who'd wire the money to set him free from Hicky and this goddamn city.

'What're we gonna do in the morning, Hicky?'

'We're gonna get us up 'n' runnin', that's what.'

'How?'

Hicky slices his hand across his throat.

'Listen, Kenny, an' listen good. I'm up to here with your pissin' an' moanin'. If we have to steal it, we'll fuckin' steal it. Got it!'

'Guess so,' muttered Kenny.

Susie raps at the door one more time, it's obvious there's someone in there, sound was heard from the television as she'd walked past the window. What's with this guy? Is he deaf? The drapes had folded back a touch, a chink of light had caught her eye. She's thirty minutes late, but thinks Tommy won't mind; he seemed pleased with last night's performance. Her last trick, a tall, raw-boned wildcatter from Oklahoma, had kept her back with the promise of a thirty-dollar bonus. The headlights from a pickup swinging onto the parking lot mark her out with its headlights. She turns to shield her eyes. The lights fade as the driver cuts the engine. A cowboy steps out and gives her the once over, then strolls to a room along the veranda. She's about to walk away from Tommy's door, her mind set for downtown, closer to home.

The door slowly opens, the faint rattle of safety-chain, Tommy's head glowing in a wedge of fluorescent light. He looks scared shitless, his face oozing sweat, his jowls shaking with laboured breathing. Beady eyes squint, then run up and down the veranda, skimming the parking-lot, taking special interest with the pickup. He asks her to hang on, and shuts the door.

Susie's poised on the balls of her feet. He'd made her edgy, she was ready to run. Usually a guy would come to the door somewhat relaxed, showered and in casual dress. He wasn't ready. Is it because she wasn't on time? Along the veranda, the cowboy opens his door and gives Susie the glad-eye, indicating: 'If he don't want ya, baby. You just step right up.' She turns and makes out she's about to step inside Tommy's room. The cowboy salutes her with a can of beer and closes his door.

She didn't like the look of that creep. Her mind flashes back to the time she took a beating in a motel room on High 40, west of Albuquerque, New Mexico. She was twenty at the time, an oval-faced starry-eyed apprentice, turning the odd trick to support her hippie travel along desert highways. That beating cost her plenty, apart from two shiners and a bust lip, the bastard cornholed her and stole what little cash she had. Since then she'd stuck with the agency and the city.

This Mace's used the agency before, so they'll have some idea if he's into bad habits. The motel room will have been paid for with a check, the mob own the agency, and they'll have cross-checked his bank and credit credentials for future reference. This isn't for Susie's benefit, but in case the name comes good in politics, Internal Revenue, or any other government agency. Then one day, when the guy forgot he even visited the city, the mob will put the squeeze on. 'Remember that time in Vegas?' That's how it happens. How do you think they bag so many judges and politicians? Patience, that's how. Tonight's twenty-dollar ejaculation will be tomorrow's million-dollar meal ticket.

Tommy put Joey in the picture, told Joey there was a hooker outside. Joey said to fuck her off, didn't want Tommy messing about outside. Tommy protested, he needed to give her money. Joey bunched his shoulders, who else but a hooker would be knocking doors at this time of the morning? Let her in. She isn't a cop, those bastards would have had the door down by now. The door cracks open. Tommy's going to pay up the

124

twenty and stay good with the agency. Susie steps warily into the room, looks at the guy sat in a bath robe, the sweat pouring off Tommy. Her heart begins to pound. Shit! She should have known something was amiss, but Tommy isn't rushing to bolt the door, he's heading for his sports coat draped over the bed. She looks closely at the guy's roughly bandaged hand. He hasn't moved, never once looked at her, just sat there staring at the dead TV.

Tommy reaches inside the jacket and pulls his wallet. She relaxes some. These guys aren't about to fuck with her; they're going to pay her off. Her hand remains on the door handle.

'Sorry about this, Tommy. Got my timin' wrong, is all.'

'That's OK, Susie. I met up with an old friend, an' we're havin' a drink an' talkin' old times. I'll call you back. Leave me your card.'

'I'll be runnin' along then, Tommy. Call me when you're ready.'

'That'll be great,' said Tommy, holding out a twenty bill. 'Let me call you to a cab at least.'

As far as Susie's concerned, Tommy's made good with the twenty.

'That's OK. I can call a cab from the pay phone out front.'

'I insist. It's the least I can do,' said Tommy, picking up the handset.

Two guys in one room is always a shaky deal, but so long as she's got command of the door, she feels relatively safe and isn't going to argue and upset them. Their minds seem to be on other things anyway. While Tommy's on the blower, she takes a long look at the guy in the chair. She's certain she's seen that face before, but can't figure where. He still hasn't moved a muscle, or said a word. She's sure she's seen him walking Fremont. She drifts to Tommy, his chest smothering the mouthpiece.

'Where to, honey?'

'The Frontier. What's the company?' said Susie, softly.

'Chilli Pepper Cabs. Why? You got a preference?' quips Tommy.

'They'll be fine. Tell 'em it's Susie Jenkins.'

Joey stirs, and picks up his ears, her name jolting his memory. His left hand begins to knead the muscles at the base of his neck. She watches him for several seconds, then, as his head rolls up, he stops and looks inquisitively into her eyes. He stays on her for a moment, then back to Tommy.

'The cab's on its way,' said Tommy, cradling the phone, tilting his glass towards her. 'You wanna shot while you're waitin'?'

Susie shakes her head, declining the offer. So far, so good.

'This your friend?' said Susie, nodding in Joey's direction, making light conversation.

Tommy walks over to the bedside cabinet and pours a drink.

'Sure is. Just called in to say hello.'

Susie noted the caution in Tommy's voice. Just called in to say hello? Look at the state of him! Two old buddies getting together for the first time in many years? Wake up! The air would surely be filled with talk and laughter. This has the feel of a wake. Her eyes roam around the room, looking at nothing in particular, just whiling time until the cab arrives. The room's tidy, nothing's really out of place, not like you'd expect when two ol' boys get together. Her stomach turns as her eyes sweep the carpet – not five feet away she spots the blood-stained loafers hobbled against skirting.

She glances to Tommy for reaction to her sighting. His back is to her, combing through the bedside drawer.

'You sure you won't take a drink with us, honey?'

Her heart begins to pound again. The bandaged hand? The blood-soaked loafers? Christ! What's happened here? Like a thunderbolt, it hits her where she's seen that face before – walking Fremont with her father. Four months back, Mom had told her about daddy's new job. Susie was alarmed, told her mother the place was a dump, the streets weren't safe, how's he going to cope, locking up that time of night? Mother said she'd argued black and blue, but he hadn't changed none, still as stubborn as a darn mule, and challenged her anxiety by saying he walked so far with some tough guy, called Joey, and that everything would be fine.

On the rare occasion when she happened to be at home that time of night, she had watched her father and Joey make their way along Fremont from her apartment window. Her father looking old and frail, bowlegged and ill-shaped against the swashbuckling roll of the younger man. She'd wanted to shout to her father and attract his attention, say things could be different between them. She hadn't shouted, and as they disappeared from view, she stood in silence.

If they walk together; where the hell is daddy?

'I need to use the phone – please – it's an emergency,' she blurts.

Side-glancing Tommy, Joey's eyes narrow with uncertainty.

'Who do ya need to call, honey?' said Tommy, quietly.

'My mom. I think something may have happened to my father.'

'Your father's Moe Jenkins? Works Turner's place on Fremont?' said Joey.

The mention of her father's name sends a shudder through her body. Her hands shoot up and clasp the sides of her face; she senses something serious has happened. Wouldn't this guy be at the hospital right now, if he'd been involved in a minor traffic accident?

Susie looks pleadingly at Joey, her hands pressed in prayer.

'You're his friend, right? Please tell me what's happened.'

Joey wished he could say there's nothing to worry about.

'I'm sorry. There's been some trouble. Moe's in hospital.'

'Which hospital? What happened?'

'He's in Community. There was a fight.'

Susie clasps her hand to her face and reels against the door jamb.

Tommy's ears are burning. Some fuckin' coincidence these two should know each other, even from a distance. What the fuck is Joey thinking? Telling her all this shit. She's gonna call the hospital, that's obvious. But what's she gonna tell 'em? The other guy involved in the shoot-out is resting up in the Starburst Motel? Get real, Joey. The place will be swarming with cops the minute the line goes dead.

Tommy covers the phone with his hand.

'Hold on! We need to do some serious talkin'. If the hospital start askin' questions, what are you gonna tell 'em?'

'I swear I won't say a thing about what I seen in here tonight. Please let me use the phone.'

Tommy shakes his head.

'No way, baby. You gonna make a call, go some place else – we don't want a trace. One more time, Joey was only lookin' out for him. Don't you be droppin' this guy in the shit. OK?'

'I won't let you down, Joey. I believe you were tryin' to help Moe–' said Susie, cutting short, distracted by the sound of a vehicle squealing to a halt.

Joey spins out of the chair, makes for the window. Susie opens the door and bolts outside. Tommy hesitates a second, then makes a beeline for the bathroom. Joey watches Susie jump the cab, and take off. Tommy's head appears around the bathroom door.

'What the fuck you doin' Joey? If she shoots her mouth, we'll both be in a fuckin' line-up, come sunup.'

'Shut the fuck up,' said Joey, locking the door.

12

Driscol lights a Winston and rolls down the Charger's side-window. He was sat these same goddamn lights one hour ago. With twenty minutes of his shift remaining, a call came over the radio, said there'd been a shooting on Fremont, 'The captain's on his way, Danny. Better get your sad ass into gear.' The controller had done the right thing by Driscol. The captain's on his back these days, and in another five minutes, Driscol would have been off police duty, and inside the Flamingo Hotel; talking turkey with racketeers.

Captain Drome was drafted in twelve months ago to make changes, sweep away officers like Driscol who had become fat cats under the rule of fifties' gangland Vegas. But their perks turned to shit during the sixties, when legit corporations bought out the hotels, and one particular individual moved east from California. Howard Hughes had just sold TWA for 546 million dollars. Hughes set about buying up Las Vegas with a vengeance. Within a decade, 65 million dollars had secured one-fifth of the city. Not satisfied with controlling the Desert Inn, the Sands, the Frontier Hotel, two local radio stations and McCarren airport, he also bought most of Tonopah, Nevada, and 14,200 acres in Nye County.

Hughes changed the city almost overnight. He stopped the traditional use of cocktail waitresses and showgirls as prostitutes. Any girls or management who disregarded the rules were fired. Shows were cleaned to laughable caution.

Casino security was tightened, hidden monitors installed. There was no more skimming of undeclared revenue, the casinos became as tight as any banking institution. Driscol was on duty the night Hughes had Frank Sinatra thrown physically out of the Sands. That night, Frank was the maddest man in town!

Before the call came over the air, Driscol was on his way to a meet with Mitch Griffin, when some crazy bastard with no regard for his outside business interests dragged him back downtown. He'd made some notes, listened to the captain's talk on crime scene procedure, and heard nothing he didn't know already. He had made out to walk to the deli, but when the captain had turned the corner, he didn't go inside. Go talk with Maurice Turner, the captain had said. Fuck! He'd no need to chase up Turner there and then, he'll be seeing Maurice in the morning for his weekly fifty-buck kickback, anyway. The old guy's face rings a bell, was introduced one time when he checked out store security with Turner. Driscol knows the punchy face of the guy who probably fired the shots, he'd seen him a couple of times leaning out front of the picture house as he'd cruised by.

Driscol gets a green, tosses the lighter on the bench seat and nudges the gear stick. Riding light traffic, he checks the time, thinking how the incident has thrown his schedule twenty minutes adrift. He tucks in behind a Chrysler New Yorker making a left on to the Flamingo's parking lot. The limo heads straight for the lobby entrance, Driscol peels off for a delivery bay at the rear of the huge building.

The '70 Dodge Charger 500 looks a poor relation against the four sleek sedans parked in the long shadow of a delivery truck. He turns his head as he locks the driver's door and surveys the chrome and polished paint-work of Mitch Griffin's handsome Lincoln Continental, looks the line of top-dollar vehicles belonging to owners who wish to shield their registration plates from the prying eyes of the FBI, their bodyguards drinking coffee in the hotel kitchens.

Driscol lightly kicks the Continental's white-walls. Eighteen years on the force and only once did he get close to making payments on a car such as this. In some ways he wished he had. Something flash for all the years of graft and public service. He could have done it easily with the thousands of dollars he's skimmed off casino management and Mafioso hoods. Every Saturday night he makes his rounds, collecting upwards of 200 bucks. He's slowed down now, but in the early days, come Monday morning, every penny would find its way behind some lousy bar, or back inside a casino counting room.

Just the once he'd got it right. That time the local boys plugged a wiseguy from Boston outside the Dunes. Driscol led the enquiry team into the death of Tony Zimmer and within twenty-four hours had three suspects in for questioning. One of them was Griffin's twenty-two-year-old son, Jerry. Driscol had a witness that saw Jerry's Coupe De Ville riding off the Dunes forecourt straight after the shooting. It shouldn't have got as far as bringing Griffin's son downtown for questioning, Driscol would have shuffled paper-work and that would have been the end of it. But a witness had walked off the street and reported in person to the desk sergeant. Driscol had no option but to follow up on information received.

Even if there had been no witness, to bundle the enquiry would have cost Mitch Griffin at least a grand. Now it's going to cost Mitch an even two, because the witness had to be paid off, or silenced by the mob with Driscol's full knowledge. The case against Jerry Griffen was dropped when the twenty-seven-year-old plumber never made it into work one morning. Driscol came home that afternoon to find a case of Chivas Regal on his doorstep, and a chunky brown envelope in his mailbox.

Later that evening, Driscol sat out on the patio and counted out three big ones. For what seemed an age afterwards he stared vacantly into the distance, conscious of the fact he'd overstepped his mark, played big into Mitch Griffin's hand.

The sun dipped behind steel-blue mountains. The moon surfaced big and bold. Driscol tore into the ten-year malt, got smashed for the first time in many years and fell asleep by the poolside. The following week he paid off his ex-wife and settled up his outstanding mortgage.

Considering the hullabaloo inside the building, there's an eerie silence out back as Driscol's brogues echo along the thirty-foot concrete loading bay. He pulls hard at a fire-door. Silence is broken by the sound of cooking utensils clattering against stainless steel worktops. Amongst great confusion, chefs and waiters bellow their instructions with great excitement. Burning oil and spicy aromas replace the crisp night air as he shuts the door behind him. Heads had turned to welcome the change of air from the opened door, then got busy again when they saw it was Driscol. They'd have tipped their heads in respect to a mob guy, but not a cop, sneaking through the back door like a thief in the night.

A short walk from the kitchens, three men sit around a red Formica table in the hotel's linen storage room. Mitch Griffin reaches into the ice-bucket, steers ice and bourbon into a tumbler. Jerry pinches a tooth-pick between his teeth, looks over to his old man.

'Where the fuck is that son-of-a-bitch?'

'We'll give him another five, an' if he don't show, fuck him. What'd yer say, Mitch?' said Arnie, following Jerry's lead.

The three men are growing impatient. Normally Mitch wouldn't give jack-shit, he'd have given the cop fifteen minutes tops and called it a day, but this meet is important for all concerned.

'He'll show,' said Mitch, tapping the brown envelope inside his jacket pocket.

Jerry looks round the storeroom. Of all the places to hold these weekly meets, his father has to choose a fuckin' storeroom. Last week it was chock-full of glassware, this week, linen. At least amongst the salt and pepper shakers they could take a smoke, now there's no chance. If anyone was to light up, the whole fucking hotel would go up in smoke. He glances at boxes of paper doilies, napkins and assorted paper goods, shakes his head, and makes to leave the room.

'Hey, Mitch. I'm gonna join Barney, see what's goin' on,' said Jerry, reaching for the door handle.

'Sit your tailbone, Jerry. You wait another ten minutes, *then* choke your fuckin' self to death on a cigarette.'

Jerry hunches his shoulders, sits back down and begins counting sugar caddy boxes. Arnie folds his arms, gets to thinking on changing his Pontiac convertible for a British racing green Jaguar.

'How long's Driscol got left on the force, Arnie?' said Mitch, drumming his fingers impatiently.

Arnie tosses a glance between father and son.

'Two years.'

Arnie knows Mitch has a hard on for Driscol, ever since he bailed his kid out of hot water over the Dunes thing. The rest of the crew couldn't give a fuck who takes the pay-off, one cop's no different to another. Jerry took off soon after his release, so never fully understood the significance of Driscol's efforts on his behalf.

'Get Pacheno on board, why don't yer? What's the matter with you guys?' Jerry snaps.

The two older men look at Jerry with scorn. At thirty-two, Jerry is regarded young and foolish amongst his peers. After the Dunes shooting, Mitch made a long distance to Lou Shots in Florida. Mitch and Shots go back forever, so Lou said he'd do him the favour; send him down. It didn't take long for the Miami crew to figure Jerry bad news; they shipped him back six months later.

Mitch looks at Jerry sternly.

'That so?'

Arnie takes a deep breath. He wants out of the room. He's

heard this kind of bitching between the two men that many times, it's getting old on his ears.

'What you say I take a look for Barney? Make sure that guy's still in the hotel?' said Arnie.

'We're gonna fuckin' wait. What's up with you guys? I say when it's time to go,' hollers Mitch, clasping his hands behind his head.

Jerry pops ice into a tumbler and tops up. Mitch gives him a stare that says to take it easy; we're here on business. Arnie was about to refill his glass but thought better of it. Where's it all going to end up? Arnie thinks to himself. Mitch is sixty-five and losing touch. He's no chicken himself, and Jerry's next in line.

Mitch signals to Arnie.

'OK, that's it, let's wrap it up. Go find Barney, tell him we're goin'.'

Driscol peers through steam to a tiny office in the top corner. Behind hazy glass, chauffeurs elbowroom a small table, shoot the breeze and play stud poker. Driscol begins to outrun unfamiliar cooking odours and noise, dodging tray-laden waiters, knowing these guys can turn meaner than cat piss if stepped upon. A swing-door leads into a wide corridor, within seconds, he's rapping a door marked PRIVATE.

Jerry opens wide and waves Driscol in, takes a step back as the cop fixes him with the hot eye. The stare didn't need rehearsal, the cop hates this man more than any other. As Driscol entered, Mitch and Arnie were standing, finishing their drinks, rubbing creases out of their expensively tailored suits.

'You're late, Driscol,' said Mitch, sternly.

'Too fuckin' bad . . . What's this bum doin' here, Mitch? How many times do I have to tell ya? This punk ain't sittin' at no table with me. We clear?'

Mitch points Driscol to a chair.

'Take a walk, Jerry. Go keep Barney company.'

The cop doesn't move, waiting on Jerry to leave the room.

'Fuck you, Driscol. One day I'll–'

'Name it,' cuts Driscol.

Jerry grunts, and slams the door.

They sit. Driscol's offered a drink and refuses. Mitch glances down and taps his time piece.

'Had to turn back for a downtown shooting,' blows Driscol, leaning back in his seat.

Arnie looks over at Mitch. The old man nods like he understands.

'Another cab driver?' asked Arnie.

'Naw. Some guy blasted a nigger up against Murphy's Liquor on Fremont.'

'Old Ryan's place? Didn't he shut the joint down last year?' enquires Arnie.

'Same one,' answers Driscol.

'Nigger, eh? That's OK then,' wisecracks Arnie, laughing out loud.

Mitch doesn't see the joke, and looks seriously at Arnie.

'What's wrong with you, Arnie? This cab shootin' business is startin' to hurt Turner's trade, an' if it hurts Turner, it hurts me. You know I got three big ones on the street for the guy who bangs these motherfuckers causin' all this shit. Let's get down to business.'

'I was only–'

'Fuck it, Arnie! If I want to know what's been happenin' on Fremont, I'll ask Driscol, or buy a fuckin' newspaper.'

'Sorry, Mitch,' Arnie said, mutedly.

Mitch slaps the brown envelope on the table, 'Got you a little extra tonight, Danny. There's a guy I want you to look at. He's staying here at the Flamingo. We think he's outta Boston.'

Mitch tips his head, like the undertone is obvious.

Driscol fingers the envelope. He knows the implication and this guy must be a top act for Mitch to be packing an envelope this thick with twenties.

135

'He's got ID? What name did he book the room under?' said Driscol, tucking away the package into his jacket breast pocket.

'Frankie Francione.'

'You think the name's genuine?' Driscol enquired.

'Yep.'

'How'd he pay for the room? Cash or credit card?'

Arnie chips in, 'Cash. He ain't used a credit card since he's been here. An' he's been throwin' dough about like there's no tomorrow.'

Driscol looks Mitch in the eye.

'You think this might have something to do with the Dunes shooting?'

'Do I think! Where you comin' from, Driscol? Who's the fuckin' cop around here?' said Mitch, rolling his eyes to the ceiling.

'Yeah, but–'

'But, shit, Danny. We both got a fuckin' interest here. Right!'

Driscol sighs. He always knew covering up for Mitch's loony son would come back to haunt him.

'Has he been seen with anyone that might look suspect?'

'Yeah, that tramp you used to knock around with – what's her name – Julie Tomkins. Suspect! Where the fuck have you been, Driscol? This fuckin' town is all suspect,' screams Mitch.

Driscol reddens and makes to leave his seat. Mitch waves him down.

'Francione's playin' the tables right this minute, check him out later, I got something else. Another guy checked through McCarren late last night.'

Mitch's eyes flit uneasily around the table and settle back on Driscol.

'Angelo Persaci. The name mean anything?'

'No. But he's from Boston?' Driscol wisecracked.

'Yeah. But this Persaci, we do know. He's in town on a hit. There's no fuckin' doubt about it.'

'You sure?'

'Sure! Of course I'm fuckin' sure! He's been on Carlo Grasano's payroll for years. Just when I thought we were gonna smooth things over with those New England grease-balls, Grasano ships this whacko down.'

Driscol knows plenty about the Boston crime boss, Carlo Grasano.

'So where's Persaci? Which hotel is he stayin'?'

'We only got word on Persaci an hour ago. He didn't use an airport cab an' he ain't booked into a regular hotel, that's for sure,' said Arnie.

'Someone's picked him up, maybe he called a courtesy car? You checked out the airport hotel listings?' said Driscol.

'You gone fuckin' deaf! I just told yer we only found out an hour ago. Earn your money, Driscol. You fuckin' check,' Mitch explodes.

It took Jerry ten minutes to find Barney. He'd meandered around the casino floor, first the blackjack tables, then the poker room, finally nailed him at a craps table. Jerry had weaved in and out of the crowded rooms looking out for Barney's distinctive mohair jacket. When he eventually caught up with him, Barney had the darn thing slung over his arm.

'Where the fuck you been, Jerry? Hangin' on to this guy has been a nightmare, he musta played every goddamn table in the house,' said Barney, rolling the mohair over his shoulders.

Jerry darts a glance at Francione. The mark has a crowd around him. He's loud, calling the shots, big time, a wad of greenbacks in one hand, blowing luck on dice in the other. He shoots – hits a seven. The stickman yells – bystanders roar in delight. Frankie leaps in the air. Jerry counts the chips piled high in front of the Boston high roller.

'This guy's havin' some fuckin' luck, I tell ya,' said Barney, lighting two Camels, handing one to Jerry, 'What's with Mitch? Has that cop arrived?'

Jerry steps to the side and tips ash into a tray, swings to face Barney with a fired look and nods his head.

'Fuck the cop! Mitch wants yer. I'll keep tabs on this guy.'

Mitch walks around the table and pours Driscol a drink. It's been pretty quiet the last five minutes, just the odd mumble from Arnie and every time Mitch cut him off. Arnie's got a problem that needs airing, he could have called Driscol in the week but thought he'd leave it till tonight, make it person-to-person. Now that Mitch is on the move with the bottle, Arnie feels the moment is right.

'I need a favour, Danny.'

Driscol glances over. He's done Arnie a favour or two in the past. Arnie seems to have been around as long as him.

'Sure. Fire away.'

'It's the wife, Danny–'

'Holy shit! Not again, Arnie?' squeals Mitch, jumping back, almost dropping the bottle.

'Yeah. Last Sunday on the Expressway – I'm gonna throw the fuckin' keys away this time, I swear it.'

'Fuck me, Arnie. You said that the last time. You gotta throw 'em in the Lake like I told ya. Hidin' the keys is like hidin' the Scotch, it don't fuckin' work,' ribs Driscol.

'What's with Millie? She tryin' for the record books? Give us the count, Arnie. Six, seven?' said Mitch, taking his seat.

Driscol looks at Arnie seriously.

'It's the seventh time – you gotta listen good, Arnie. This is it, then no more. You ain't doin' her any favours, sure as fuck she'll kill some poor bastard one day – I'll do it, but you got to give me your word.'

Mitch listens in with a half-smile. All the time, Millie's gonna ditch the drink – take the pledge. Millie's a lush, she'll never change.

'She ain't had a drink all week, I swear–'

Mitch leans across, 'That's twice you've swore tonight, Arnie. Give me break, why don't yer. Millie an' booze are an item, just like Jerry and his big fuckin' mouth. Go live by Lake Mead, buy her a boat, make her a sailor instead of a driver, she'll only kill herself that way.'

'You gonna do it for me, Danny? Or you gonna listen to this fuckin' shmuck designin' my life?'

'It ain't a case of designin', Arnie. Take the fuckin' car off her an' I'll shred the paper. A deal's a deal, OK?' said Driscol.

'Sure thing, Danny. What's it gonna cost?'

'Not a bean. *Gratis* to you, Arnie.'

Mitch chokes on his bourbon. He can't believe what he's just heard.

'*Gratis*! You gone soft in the head, Driscol? Charge him two, like the last time,' Mitch bawls.

'Naw, this one's for old times. Me an' Arnie go back before Bugsy Siegel.'

'Before the fuckin' Ark,' said Mitch.

There's a rap on the door, Barney strolls in and tips the remains of the bottle into a glass.

'Where the fuck you been, Barney? We were about to call mountain rescue!'

'Sorry, Mitch. Jerry had problems findin' me–'

Mitch snatches the bottle from Barney.

'Findin' you! Where the fuck are we? Long Island?'

'Jerry's covering Francione. Francione's in for the long haul, I tell ya. He's hittin' the tables real good. He ain't goin' anywhere.'

Mitch spreads his arms and looks around the room.

'What fuckin' table is he playin'?'

'Craps.'

'Right, Danny. You go find your old pal, Jerry. Take a good look at this Francione an' see what you think. Call me at Dilly's on Apricot in one hour's time and we'll bang our heads together on him, and this guy, Persaci. While you're up there, send Jerry back, I need him to drive me tonight. Tell him to meet me by the kitchens. Let's go.'

Mitch dropped his regular driver a week or two back. Jerry might have the biggest mouth in the Union, but he can wheel a car better than most, and has balls as big as a bull when the chips are down.

13

Sat across from Charlie Powell in a Tex-Mex restaurant isn't Abilene's idea of a swell night out. Charlie's stuffing his face with enchiladas and fried beans, while Abilene picks at roast beef and mashed potatoes. If Charlie's bloated face doesn't unsettle her, the shit he's eating does. Abilene was brought up on three-square and who, in their right mind, would want to eat beans anyway? She's sure if those old Mexicans below the border had a choice, they'd plump for roast every time. Pretty soon he's going to harp on again how lucky she is to know such a hot-shot as Charlie Powell; without his help she'd be out of work. She pushes the half-finished meal to one side. Charlie scoops his last fork of beans.

'That was great, Abilene. Try the pumpkin pie, I hear it's the best in town.'

'You try it. I ain't hungry.'

A pretty Hispanic waitress hovers over the table, Charlie tries his Spanish and makes a complete asshole of himself, but waves her away like it's no big deal. There's a moment's silence as Charlie opens a soft pack, and directs smoke at people sat at the next table. They glare across in disgust, but Charlie doesn't seem to notice or care.

'You're a regular here, Charlie?'

'Sure am. How'd yer know?'

''Cause you ain't never tried the pie,' said Abilene sarcastically.

Her eyes wander round the half dozen occupied tables. A good-looking Latino glances away from his partner and gives Abilene the gladeye. She feels herself blushing and lowers her eyes, then feels the presence of the waitress placing a dish of pumpkin pie and fresh cream on their table. Charlie hurriedly screws his cigarette into the remains of the Taco salad basket. Abilene cringes as the foul smell hits her nostrils and reddens again as the waitress shaves the basket from under Charlie's nose.

She studies the top of his greying head as he buries it into the dish, and chuckles inwardly at the sight of his large cauliflower ears. She guesses Charlie must have been a punch bag at one time. For a second he lifts his head, smiling with thick creamy teeth. Abilene smiles back.

Mother Nature never had been kind to Charlie Powell. Even as a kid, he had features akin to a bull dog chewing a wasp. As time rolled on, Charlie's mug rolled in folds, pinched at the nose and slack at the jaw. The ears, it was said jokingly, came by way of the midwife, not in the ring. Charlie realised from an early age his grotesque infliction could frighten and bully. He tried about everything when he left high school. Frightened customers as a shoe salesman. Scared the living shit out of kids on the ice cream delivery. Finally he embarked on a careeer with the Longshoremen's Union in New York State, where terrorising port authority management brought promotion and travel.

Charlie was quick on the uptake, cunning and ruthless. By the time he was thirty-five he'd made his mark. No longer the kid with the shook down face, now a man with power and ambition. Other people were taking note of Charlie's progress and, in 1951, Jimmy Hoffa made him an offer he couldn't refuse. The Teamsters wooed him to Las Vegas with a fifty per cent hike in salary and promise of promotion. Las Vegas was different then. Mobsters tooled around the city like they owned it; which they did. Charlie mingled on the fringe, hovered close, but never made the top tables.

The mob had their own men positioned inside the union. Charlie had been brought in to administer paperwork and run errands for guys in pinstripe. He tossed it around in his head to move back east, but his wife couldn't understand what all the fuss was about. Wasn't their standard of living better? The climate dry and free from bugs? Isn't this city well policed, the very place to bring up children? These things were brought to his attention every time the move was mentioned. Charlie compromised with Rose: they stayed, but they never had children. Charlie and Rosemary dribbled along, Charlie half-heartedly toeing down to union business. Rose upping her handicap on the Country Club fairways.

Charlie finally surfaced and wiped clean with a napkin. The gladeyed stranger two tables along had paid his bill with ready change, and as he walked away from her towards the exit, Abilene noted low-cost rigging and down-at-heel shoes. Fuckin' typical, she'd thought. The one decent-looking guy in the joint, and even he's a fuckin' derelict.

Charlie waves over to the waitress and orders coffee. Abilene rolls her eyes everywhere but Charlie. He looks up, watching her tired, detached observations. For a second or two, he finds himself looking over the same trashy restaurant fixtures.

'We'll make it someplace else, next time. Drink your coffee, Abilene, or it'll go cold on ya.'

Abilene sips at black bitter coffee, apprehensive in the thought that soon they'll be piled into Charlie's Mercury, riding to some second-rate hotel room. It's never anywhere fancy, just some doss Charlie and his buddies share the key for union services rendered.

Charlie glances over her shoulder at the wall clock, 'Jesus! Look at the time, will ya?'

She knows what the clock reads, she's been glancing up at it most of the night, wishing the time away. Suddenly, Charlie's all business; paying the tab, throwing on his top coat, steering Abilene out of the door so fast she didn't have time to use the restroom to straighten her face.

Charlie swings on to the parking lot of Circus Circus, driving on until he near hits desert. He kills the lights, cracks the side-window, reaches across Abilene and flicks open the glove compartment. Abilene's tongue-strapped, what the fuck is going on? They're in the middle of nowhere, the tail-light of the nearest vehicle must be 400 yards away.

'What the hell is goin' down, Charlie?'

She stares in disbelief, as Charlie roots about in the compartment, its bulb flickering intermittent light as his hand combs amongst the objects inside. He doesn't answer her, but keeps searching. Abilene grabs for the door handle, Charlie curses, and seizes Abilene's arm.

Charlie pants with sexual expectancy, 'Fuck it, Abilene. I'm sure I had a rubber in there some place.'

Abilene's surprised. Charlie's not got the physique for back seat acrobatics. She sees a rush job, perhaps he's got to get home to Rosemary?

'You think you're gonna fuck me on a parkin' lot? You got to be dreamin', Charlie. Turn the key an' get me home.'

Charlie leans back, lifts his arse off the seat, unzips his trousers, 'Aw, c'mon, Abilene, I got a boner down here, blow me an' we'll call it quits.'

Charlie's too preoccupied masturbating a full erection to heed Abilene quietly opening the door, her heel gently touching asphalt.

'You want it sucked? Suck it your fuckin' self,' shouts Abilene, slamming the door.

'You owe me!' she hears him shout after her.

'I owe you fuck all.'

Outside the rear entrance of Circus Circus, she looks over her shoulder to see if the Mercury had moved. It hadn't. Inside the casino, she dials a cab and guesses the only thing that was sure to be moving out there in the desert was Charlie's wrist.

Driscol eases the gas pedal, swings a right and eases away from neon onto quiet urban roads. Polished autos rest wide driveways, here and there sprinklers spin mature neat lawns. Driscol rolls down the Charger's window and checks down his speedo to an even thirty. Glancing out, charging his lungs with the rich honey sweetness of moist grass, thinking how, in every sizeable city, neighbourhoods can switch from shit to shine in a two-minute ride.

He rides back in time to his early years as a young patrolman in Detroit City. Shrinking back into his seat, images flash across the windshield of desperate migrant car workers cooped in old brick cold-water tenement blocks. Entering the tenements, ground into its graffiti walls, the stench of boiled cabbage, decaying garbage and excrement. On the stairways, in the corridors, so bad he could taste it. Inching along at third floor level, keeping back behind seasoned officers, waiting for the heavy guys to bust a door open. Sheer terror on the black woman's face, her baby pressed tight to her tit – 'Fuck it! We got the wrong apartment number,' someone shouted. The woman so frightened she could barely speak, the door hanging at forty-five on one crippled hinge; who's gonna pay the damage? A cop beat the door with a night-stick and they withdrew down the stairways, exploding chock-a-block bin-liners with the toe of their boots, scattering putrid garbage every place. It was a game; the place stunk twice as bad now. The smell of boiled cabbage stays with Driscol forever.

Driscol worked Motor City until February '52. He remembers a cold damp Friday. It's early evening, a light drizzle of rain shimmering in the headlights of bumper-to-bumper early evening traffic. The sidewalks crowded with people making their way across town, heading home after a long day. Driscol ducks under a store front awning to shield the rain, pulls his hip flask, takes a slug of Kentucky's finest to drive out the cold. He shouldn't be drinking on the job. Every cop does it, what's the beef? A kid wearing a white T-shirt and apron weaves through slow-moving traffic at break-neck speed. The kid reaches Patrolman Driscol and blurts broken English. Driscol barely understands a word but flags down traffic and follows the kid across Winston and into a bakery.

Inside the bakery, two old polacks are beating their arms and dancing on the spot. The kid sits on a stool to gather composure, slows his speech. Driscol gets his drift: there's been a stickup. The kid tries his best to describe the perpetrators, but it's no use. Driscol finally catches the kid's arm and they barrel out into the street. The kid's light on his feet, weaving a pattern along the crowded sidewalk. Driscol's struggling to keep pace, the alcohol taking effect. The kid stops dead on the corner of Winston and 6th, jabs a finger at two desperado Hispanics up ahead. It all happened so fast. Driscol drawing his service revolver – rain trickling off his thick eyebrows, impairing his glazed vision – shouting the men to stop. The two men make for the kerbside and leave themselves open. Wait! There's a bystander closing with the suspects. Driscol shouts one more time. The bystander stumbles into the back of one of the Hispanics. Jesus! It's all confused, they're just a blur as he squeezes the trigger – two rounds echo out, people dash for cover or belly wet pavement. Driscol missed his target, two Hispanics leg it across Winston, Driscol had drilled the bystander.

Fifteen minutes later Driscol was relieved of his .38 special by a delirious lieutenant. The next twenty-four hours saw his badge, uniform and pension in the gutter; six years of service down the drain. For the next two years he stumbled through factory gates and powered an air gun on the Chevrolet assembly line until the smell of cutting-oil and mindless worker politics drove him west, into the small town of Beaver, Utah.

He settled into a single-wide in a trailer park on the outskirts of town and took low-pay wages at a gas station over on High 21. He lived frugally, kept away from booze and, come the morning, sucked in the desert's clean thin air. He was quiet, kept himself to himself, stood apart from most men in that tight outland community. John Doe pulling over for gas caught steady steel in those dark brown eyes as they checked over oil and radiator levels. Bar talk had it the guy out the filling station was from some place east, a quiet sort, and not to be fucked with. It suited Driscol fine. He became something of a mystery, and word on this new guy on the edge of town spread like a prairie fire amongst Beaver's womenfolk.

It wasn't too long before Sissy Grant heard the news and rolled in for gas. Sissy stepped down from a dusty stepside pickup, straightened her hair and braved bright blue eyes at the talked about man as he wiped the dip-stick clean. Driscol caught the spark in her small pretty face, her corn coloured hair hanging free over check shirt and denim bib and brace. Sissy's stepside got the whole nine yards that Friday morning. Sissy owned a five-acre smallholding ten miles north that had turned to seed in recent years. There was no one around to help fix fences and service the swamp-cooler, her old man being a MIA statistic from the Korea War. She'd given Harry two years to make it home. She'd heard nothing from the Marine Corps and reckoned if Harry was still alive, he could have walked back in that amount of time.

Sissy made her play and he readily surrendered. Six weeks later Driscol gave up the trailer park and moved in with Sissy. He curved a claw hammer at broken fences, fed hungry chickens scratching powder-dust about his feet and fooled around with Sissy in between. She moved him into her circle of friends, he became less of a mystery to the folk of Beaver. The fences now a glossy white, the chickens fat and oven ready, Driscol was home and dry with a woman he loved. He proposed marriage one Sunday afternoon, Sissy accepted and they planned a ride into town the following day to see the preacher. Later that evening there was a knock on the flyscreen. Harry had made it home.

The Chinese liberated hero Harry into Beaver's one and only ticker-tape procession. Dupe Davis, the sole attorney-at-law in town had a field day sorting out legalities. Harry was national news and in all the excitement, Sissie wasn't too sure which way the wind was blowing. Driscol sat around a couple of days, sloped Harry's cast-off Stetson to the back of his head, walked out the door, and said good-bye to Utah.

Driscol landed in Vegas the next day and found work on a construction site. At the end of a shift one day, he decided to call an old police buddy in Detroit City. Ernie Snarl was still working his old precinct, he had some interesting news for Driscol: there had been a fire at City Hall, all record of Driscol ever serving with the DCPD had been destroyed. Driscol asked Ernie to make double sure, he'd call him back the next day. Ernie substantiated his claim, 'The whole fuckin' wing went up in flames.' Three months later Driscol was back in uniform with the LVPD.

Eighteen years he's drove these city streets and, for the past seven, he's been on the take. So what, other cops were getting moneyed. If his past ever crept up on him, he'd be out on his ass anyway, so why not hedge his bet? Once the kick-backs started, there was no turning back, with promotion to sergeant, came bigger favours, bigger bucks.

Neat colonial-style housing rolls by to his left, to his right, a neat park where kids play minor league. He meets a 4-way, slows, then barrels through. As he'd pulled off the Flamingo parking lot earlier, he'd gunned for Pete's All-Night Diner on Rancho, made four blocks before deciding to cut across town and drop by the hospital. Pete's an old cop friend who took the dough and opened up the diner on retirement. Messages from the likes of Mitch Griffin go to Pete instead of Driscol's answering machine, that way it keeps everything clean. Driscol makes a mental note to call on Pete before his next business meet in the Silver Slipper.

For a while he listens idly to crackled police affirmatives coming over the radio, then shuts down the power. Lighting a cigarette, he thinks on his meet with Mitch and that scumbag son of his, and how he'd love to ring his fuckin' neck. This thing with Francione has him puzzled. Why doesn't Griffin sort him out? Send in the troops? Perhaps Mitch's wary on upsetting the Boston outfit again? Mindful, it'll be cleaner for the LVPD to move Francione on.

Driscol hasn't seen Julie in over nine months, so why the fuck did Mitch have to bring in Julie's name? That was below the belt, and it rattled him. Mitch knows she's history now, so was it just a cheap throw-away remark, or was it intentional? Whatever, Driscol sucks heavy on the Winston and credits Julie with bigger balls than Jerry and his old man put together. OK, she never would make the Miss World, but they'd got it on together in a crazy kinda way. She'd moved in, cleaned his place and cooked breakfast. About a year went by, things were looking good till she got stir-crazy and moved back with her pimp on the north-side. Driscol tracked her down, it was easy, and beat the living daylights out of the pimp. She found another pimp; Driscol never ate breakfast again.

The nurse on the hospital emergency intake desk eye-balls Driscol and banks her head in the direction of the south wing. There's no need for ID, Driscol's part of the furniture, either handcuffed to some poor bastard that took his beating, or interviewing suspects barely breathing. He clips along white tiled corridors, through several reception areas looking for a uniformed officer. Batting through a swing door he sees half a dozen worried-looking visitors, off to one side Patrolman Dave Smith. Smith looks up at Driscol with surprise and folds a glossy.

'What'ya doin' here, Danny? Thought you'd be home by now?'

149

Driscol signals the officer away from earshot, 'Naw, thought I'd drop by, see if there's any news on the old guy they scooped off Fremont a while back. You got a name?'

'Yeah. Moe Jenkins, an' it's fifty-fifty if he makes it – but I heard the doc say he's a tough old bastard.'

'Who'd he say it to?'

Smith peeps around Driscol's shoulder, indicating to the row of hopefuls sat on a black leatherette bench.

'Those two on the end. Mother and daughter, I guess. They came in about half an hour ago,' said Smith, expecting the obvious.

Driscol can hardly contain his surprise, 'You guess? Ain't you talked to 'em yet?'

Patrolman Smith veers from eye contact, 'No, sir. That wasn't my brief. Nick Martinez is handlin' the case, he said he'd be here presently and–'

'That's OK, Dave. Forget it – I'm goin' over to have a word with 'em. Say fuck all to Martinez, I ain't been near, OK?'

'OK, Danny. I ain't seen yer.'

The patrolman ambles back to his seat and lowers his eyes into the magazine. Driscol draws a light-weight tubular chair over to the two women.

'Excuse me, my name is Detective Sergeant Driscol. I wonder if I might have a word? Mrs–?'

'Mary Jenkins. This is my daughter, Susie,' said Mary, squeezing Susie's hand.

'I know how you must be feelin', Mary, so I'm not goin' to ask too many questions, just enough to get me back on the streets. Is that OK?' said Driscol softly.

Mary glances tentatively at Susie.

'How old's your husband, Mary?'

'Sixty-seven.'

Driscol looks at Mary sceptically.

'Sixty-seven is a fair age, Mary. You know that one man was killed and two seriously injured last night. If you don't mind me sayin', do you think Moe was capable of such an action?'

Mary eases her grip from Susie and reaches into her handbag for a tissue, 'No, sir.'

'It's all right, Mary. I know for sure your husband didn't pull the trigger,' he said slowly, switching his eyes between the women. 'We know there was another guy with him, do you know who it could be?'

'Joey always walks so far with Moe – he wouldn't hurt him, Moe thinks the world of him.'

'Tell me about this Joey?'

'He's all right, he always makes sure Moe's safe, I can't understand what happened last night.'

'It seems this Joey made sure your husband was looked after, but he took off, and I'd like to know the reason why,' said Driscol, observing a sudden alertness in Susie's eyes.

'Ain't Joey out of town, mamma?'

'You sure, honey? Daddy only said at breakfast to pick him up at the Roxy. Said he'd be in there with Joey.'

Susie looks at Mary for assistance.

'You know how daddy gets things mixed up these days, mom. Only last week you was tellin' me how absent minded he was getting these days.'

'You have an address where I could find this Joey?'

'No,' Susie said defensively.

Driscol's heard enough, the girl obviously knows more than she's letting on. He'll call Maurice Turner on a public pay phone on his way out of the hospital, and get the address. The detective leans forward, takes Mary's hand, and looks into her eyes with genuine concern.

'Your husband's gonna pull through, we believe if it was Joey with your husband, he's been injured. I'm gonna leave my card. If he should get in touch with either of you, call that number. This looks like a case of self-defence, the guy ain't got nothin' to worry about – make sure you call, OK?'

*

151

Driscol made the call to Maurice. Maurice came over all excited.

'Fuck, Danny, I'd just heard the news on television, one of my boys came crashin' in an' told me it was old Moe – you met him once, remember? I told him it can't be, then figured he'd have Joey along . . . Yeah, Joey Burke, fronts the picture house for me . . . Nah, Burke ain't his real name, but who gives a fuck, he does his job . . . You takin' the piss, Driscol? I don't give a flyin' fuck about social security numbers . . . An address? I ain't got an address. What do'ya think I'm fuckin' runnin' here, a welfare programme? . . . OK, OK, I'll ask around . . . Jesus! Driscol, get off my case will ya . . . Fuck you too. See you in the morning.'

Angelo Persaci looks dismally around the room, and dumps the black holdall onto thin carpet. He measures out the room with an undertaker's eye, then jabs at the mattress for signs of life. Don't the mob always travel first class? Not any more, he reflects, thinking on his flight out with all those string-bean kids and how he's holed up in a crummy All-Star Inn. To make matters worse he waited twenty minutes in the airport terminal for the courtesy car. If that wasn't bad enough, the driver turned out to be Guatemalan, and didn't seem to understand Angelo's verbal instructions.

First of all, Angelo asked José to ride by the Flamingo. He tells José it's on the Strip, he can't go wrong, everybody and his uncle knows where it's at. José makes a fuck up on Paradise, and ends up hopelessly lost on Maryland Parkway. Persaci's sat in the rear seat about ready to palm the .44 out of his holdall, and blow him clean away. José apologises, gets his bearings and beats the shit along St Louis, hits the Strip on amber, throws the car on two wheels and rockets in the opposite direction to the Flamingo. Persaci's going ballistic. He orders José to pull over, the car screeches to a halt, Persaci drags the Guatemalan over the bench-seat, swipes him with the .44, and takes the wheel himself.

Heading back down the Strip, José's mumbling 'Hail Mary's,' and polishing a brass crucifix around his neck. Persaci doesn't take any notice of the carry on from the back seat of the cab, he's too busy looking out for the Flamingo Hotel. Turning into Tropicana, the guy in the back seat plucks courage to shake Persaci's shoulder. What the fuck! Persaci slugs José in the side of the head, the car loses control, and swings erratically on the All-Star lot, fish-tailing to a grinding halt beside a palm tree. If José had a wife, seven kids and four sets of balls, Persaci menaced death or removal of all sixteen.

An offensive carload of tourists happened on the parking lot as Persaci shook the Latino up and down the courtesy car. Bill stopped and reassured his wife and kids, this sort of thing didn't happen on a public car park in the good old US of A.

'I'd leave it be, Bill,' said his wife.

Bill puffed his chest and slid out. The kids cheered, 'Go on, dad.'

He could have called out, but the thick Italian accent echoing loud and ugly over the lot made him cautious. He could have walked directly across, but he skirted round the palms, occasionally peeping back to his wife and kids, their expectant faces glued to the side-window.

Bill was twenty feet away, and realised he'd dropped a bollock. This Italian looks a real mean bastard. Why's he getting involved anyway? Hey! Perhaps the little guy had hassled the Italian for money? Maybe tried to pick his pocket? Bill had heard stories about this town. Yeah, bet your bottom dollar, that guy's gettin' all he deserves. He's about to turn, explain to his wife and kids that the guy is a wetback, and the big guy is Immigration. Yeah, Hilary, you know the kind, always on the mooch for an easy buck. They'll believe him, they believe everything he says. Bill turned, faced his family and spread his hands wide to tell them everything's OK. He heard the Guatemalan's tiny feet race into the night, didn't see the Italian bearing down on him. Hilary's anxious face in the side-window should have alerted Bill, it didn't, all of a sudden Persaci's breathing down his neck, like a fiery dragon.

Things turned suddenly unpleasant for Bill. An uncontrollable twitch appeared in his right eye, he needed a restroom like he'd never needed one before – too late – he shit himself. He looked down to collect the smell, move it someplace else. Looked up to see its reason, the hard, cold face of the undertaker. Angelo didn't need to say a word, he'd terrified hundreds of men with that evil stare. Bill took off at a gallop, dived in and flooded the engine. The last Angelo saw before he strode into the motel was Bill beating his fists on the steering-wheel. He didn't see any kids, they must have sunk low in the back seating.

Angelo turns the bedspread and checks the sheets, gives them the OK, thinks about turning on the TV, gives it a miss. It's late, there's plenty of heads to hunt tomorrow. First, he's got to hire a car with his false ID. He'll need to ride over to the Flamingo first thing, make on this Francione guy. Then find this Mace, break his balls and get to that piece of shit, O'Sullivan. It's all quick with Angelo now, he's thinking blood, the holdall tipped-out. Out of habit, the big barrel .44 stuffed under his pillow, he hits the lights, thoughts of Joey O'Sullivan and bygone Boston days drift him into an uneasy sleep.

A cheer goes up around him, Frankie Francione fills his lungs and reaches for the ceiling. Three times in succession he's hit the even money pass line. They can't take it away from Frankie, just when they thought he'd burnt his luck, Frankie blew those dice, came good, and knocked the house for six. Congratulatory hands slap at his back, a raven-haired beauty wraps her arms around his waist, a pit boss leans in on the stickman's ear.

'Touch me for luck, mister.'

Frankie turns and grips the woman's hand, pressing it on his pelvic bone. His free hand unblends his winning chips into separate stacks of colour value.

'Sure thing. What's your name, baby?'

'Cherry.'

'I'm Frankie, stick around. The party ain't even started.'

'You bet.'

If Frankie wasn't so carried away with his successes, he'd probably ask himself why this pretty unattached woman is making eyes. Would it bother him to know she's a shill working on behalf of the casino? Possibly not, he'd done nothing wrong, just got lucky. But casino management have to be cautious. Cherry would normally breeze amongst the blackjack, sit a slow table, display her cleavage, encourage jaywalkers to sit and play. Sometimes, like now, she'd be sent to check a guy out. Within five minutes Cherry would know all there is to know, and report her findings to the shift manager.

'You got Lady Luck on your side tonight, Frankie.'

'*You* betcha!'

Pete's All-Night Diner is a regular hit for the city's night owls. Cabbies and cops drift in and take checker cloth tables at one end. Teenagers and street bruisers take up the juke area. A couple of kids hang over the box, popping dimes, selecting their favourite disc. Over coffee-stained cloth, a dozen cops shoot the breeze, cabbies listen in, they're part of the night-time crime scene too; the cops might pick 'em up, but before they do the cabbies have had their head-to-head with prostitutes, pimps, enraged husbands, their free-fuck wives and every type of low-life.

At sixty-five, Ruby Jordon must be the oldest waitress in town. She's been with Pete five years now, keeps telling him this is it, c'mon Pete, I'm too old to be working these goddamn graveyard shifts. Six months ago Pete said he'd switch her to daytime and every time she brings it up, Pete says, 'Give it till the weekend, Ruby. See how you're feeling.' Ruby leans against the counter, and rubs the ache from her ankle. She looks along the counter for Maria. Where has that darn girl got to?

A cop leans sideways out of his chair into the middle of the aisle, 'C'mon, Ruby. We're about ready to order.'

Ruby slowly makes her way over to the tables. The cops are her favourites. They come over playful, sometimes saucy, but they never bad mouth, and if one of those freaks at the other end of the diner should get stroppy, they'd drum their nightsticks against table legs and that would be the end of that. Ruby would miss these old faces if she switched to days, that might be the reason she hasn't pushed Pete all the way.

'Times of your life' echoes from the juke.

'I'll have a pastrami on rye with mustard.'

'Give me roast beef on wheat with lettuce and tomato, no mayonnaise.'

'Club sandwich, Ruby. Toasted bagel with cream cheese.'

Ruby jots down the orders, out of the corner of her eye she looks for Maria.

Pete Morelli sits in his supply-room-cum-office. A glass partition gives him view to the kitchen. For the past ten minutes he's been chewing the arse out of a dead cigar, watching Peppy, the slippery dish-wash hand, flirt with his niece. This Maria is a real pain in the ass. He'd told his brother he'd look out for her. Jesus! She's hotter than a smoking pistol. He lowers his head, scratches lazily over January's IRS returns and tosses the biro; he can't concentrate, what if she should become pregnant? He finally attracts her attention through the glass and beckons her into the office.

'This ain't no good, Maria. What have I told yer about screwin' around with the help? One more time an' I'm on the blower to your father. Hear me?'

Maria looks at him confused.

'What have I done wrong?' she questions.

'Plenty,' replies Pete. 'Now fuck off back to the kitchen an' work your wage – any more, Maria, an I'm makin' that call to your father. You got that?'

Maria frowns, turns and stumbles into the cop standing the doorway. He moves aside and lets her through, looks at Pete with told-you-so eyes, and closes the door behind her.

'What did I tell ya, Pete?'

'Don't give me that shit, Driscol. The girl's no fuckin' good, I got my brother on my back, Peppy cleans plates cheaper than a dish wash machine, an' one of 'em's got to go. This ain't no nine-to-five. Who's it gonna be, Driscol?' said Pete, glancing down at the paper work.

'Don't I get coffee, at least?' said Driscol, taking a seat.

Pete opens the door and barks the order to Maria.

They small talk for five minutes over coffee. Driscol keeping check on the time, he's still got a lot of ground to cover in the next couple of hours.

'You got anything for me, Pete?'

'Yeah, that fat bastard, Tommosso called. Said he'd have to cancel the meet in the Frontier tomorrow night. Trigger Mike wants you to call him, he's in the shit over his gun permit.'

They both laugh out loud, Trigger's always in gun trouble.

'Maurice Turner just called, said he's got an address for you on Joey somebody, it's on the pad. You also had a long distance . . . it's also on the pad. That's it, Danny. Bingo!'

'Thanks, Pete. I got a few bucks here to cover the IRS shit.'

Pete motions no, but Driscol slaps the greenbacks on the desk.

'You take it, Pete. You know where it came from, it's bad dough anyways, let the fuckin' IRS have it back.'

Pete tears the messages from the pad and hands them to Driscol. The cop eye-balls the messages, folds three and tucks them into his top pocket, the fourth he takes time over, then places it in his wallet.

'Do ya need to use the phone for that long distance, Danny?'
'Naw. I'll dial it later,' said Driscol quietly.

It was just after one when the cab dropped Abilene off. By the activity inside the complex, it looked like there was one big party going on. She thought how much fun it would have been if she'd stayed home; lights were ablaze, people were moving in and out of each other's apartments; the place was buzzing. She climbed the stairway, noticed most of the activity was outside her door. In the half-light, faces that had joked with her only yesterday, now looked stern and threatening.

'You seen your ol' man, Abilene?' said a hidden voice.

'Yeah, just before he took off for the picture house – who the fuck has he upset now?'

'There's been bad shit, one of our brothers got killed on Fremont. Joey done it,' said James.

'What! Over that shit yesterday? You gotta be crazy – you see him do it?'

'He done it, alright. You bet the cops have him already.'

'So, what you boys doin' here?'

'In case they ain't.'

'Fuck it, let me through. He ain't here right now, but if he shows, I'll send him down. How's that?' said Abilene, thinking Joey could well be in the apartment.

They let her through. Joey wasn't in there. Abilene got to thinking on the positive side, lifted the loose board and checked her windfall was still intact. It was.

Driscol had a rewarding night. Along the way he took another 300 bucks in back-handers. Picked up on Francione's room number at the Flamingo. Made a run to McCarren airport and tracked down Persaci to the All-Star Inn on Tropicana. He made a call to Mitch Griffin, but told him little. The less Mitch knows, the better. Mitch needed Driscol more than he needed him. The only query Driscol had was confirmation on the 3000 for the cab killers. Had he heard it right? If so, was it three G's a head? Mitch said, yeah, and for that he wanted to see the heads on the table in front of him. It was four a.m. when he pulled into a gas station for cigarettes and soda pop. Tired and leg-weary, he headed home to catch some shut-eye. There was plenty of mileage left to be covered, and Driscol just knew he was going to be busy.

14

Las Vegas neon evaporates into the blush of morning light. Joey turns away from the motel window and reflects on the night's events.

After Susie left, Tommy hit the bottle in good style, and within an hour he'd picked up courage to talk on the old fight days. Joey had nursed him along, talked middleweight fighters of his day; Griffith, Benvenuti, Fulmer and the likes. He let Tommy ramble on about anything and everything, so long as it didn't get personal. The more Tommy talked, the faster he sunk the vodka, and that suited Joey. An hour or two later, Tommy was out of the picture, sprawled fully clothed on the king-size.

Now that Tommy was flat to the boards, Joey had to make his play. He needed clothing and, if he ate for the next fifty years, nothing that Tommy owned would fit the bill. He double checked Tommy's inebriation with a poke in the stomach. Having locked the room, and checked there was no one around, he headed to the side of the building in search of the boiler house. The door to the boiler house was easy, it was fastened with a simple catch. Pipework and conduit shimmered under the bulkhead light. On the far wall, draped over a gate-valve, was a pair of coveralls, all he needed now was footware. His luck was in, in a locker he found a pair of work boots. They were two sizes too big, he figured Tommy's socks would sort that out.

Tommy hadn't moved a muscle. Joey got busy with his wallet, tossing the credit cards aside and pocketing 150 in cash. Susie's business card has him thinking. Apart from a Greyhound bus, he had no other means of escape. Same old fuckin' story, on the run again, no ID, no fuck all, and where to this time? He takes a chair, looks at the card, Susie could be his only ticket out of here.

Kenny spent all night scratching and chasing bed bugs. Twice in the night he'd woken Hicky and took verbal abuse. Hicky said he didn't give a monkey's fuck about bed bugs, lice or anything else that crawled around in the dark, and rolled over. Kenny sat on the end of the bed, wondering if to relieve Hicky of his ten-dollar find and chance the streets for food. He came close a couple of times, but heard drunks fighting and stumbling about in the corridor every time he was ready to make a move.

Threadbare curtains filter morning light, Hicky's still crashed and Kenny feels now is the time. He lifts the ten from Hicky's jeans, wets his hair with saliva, tentatively opens the door, and sneaks a peek outside. He's going to do it, fuck Hicky and his Golden Gate, Kenny's stomach tells him he's in need of breakfast.

Inside the Gold Spike, Kenny looks on with envy at people playing tables and queuing in line for cooked breakfast. Kenny inches towards the line, backs off, thinking it ain't fair on Hicky, but if it wasn't for that dumb son-of-a-bitch, they wouldn't be in the hot spot they're in. Fuck Hicky, they're up shit creek without a paddle, he might as well go the whole hog and join the queue.

Kenny makes a modest start. Bacon, eggs over easy, toast and coffee. The young waitress smiles, refills his cup and asks if there was anything else. Whether it was the fresh morning air that had boosted his appetite, Kenny wasn't sure, and didn't care. He reorders the same with hashbrowns, English muffins, and tips the waitress a dollar bill. Kenny considers himself part of the casino's culture, what's a buck? She wouldn't know Kenny only had five and change as he ambles out of the dining area.

Hicky wakes, rubs sleep from his eyes and looks around the room for Kenny. Where is the bastard? He swings off the old piss-stained mattress and grasps his jeans. Holy fuckin' Moses! The ten-spot is missing – he's gonna wring that cocksucker's scrawny neck when he gets a hold of him. Hicky pulls on his jeans, throws on a T-shirt and begins a search for his socks. He hears footsteps, someone whistling; the tune familiar. It's gotta be Kenny! The cheeky bastard! He begins to shake with uncontrollable fury – the door opens with a flourish and in breezes Kenny. Hicky can't believe his eyes, through an enraged blur he sees Kenny holding out a cigarette packet, tell-tale egg stain on his shirt.

Kenny smiles, pleased with his peace offering. Christ! Hicky's flipped. He backs off to the false security of the open door. Hicky's mouth is going round in circles, desperately trying to voice his anger.

'Where's the fuckin' ten-spot, Kenny? Where you been, you slimy little bastard?' bawled Hicky, lunging at Kenny.

Kenny dodges to one side, wrong-footing Hicky. Hicky sails into the door-post, catching hold of Kenny's shirt as he trips. They stumble to the ground. Kenny's no brawler, Hicky's been this way dozens of times and overpowers the weaker man easily. Kenny stares up at fired eyes, feels Hicky weighing down on his full stomach.

'C'mon, where is it?' screamed Hicky.

Kenny's speechless, gasping for breath, 'I – I just bought – you cigarettes, is all.'

'We'll fuckin' see then.'

Hicky pats around Kenny's jeans pockets, pulling out the five and change.

'What's this, birdturd? You bought a fuckin' carton? I know

it – you fed your fat face when you was out, didn't ya?' said Hicky, screwing the five, pitching it across the room.

Kenny stays prudently glued to the floor like a defeated animal. Along the corridor, a head pops out of a door to see what all the commotion's about, sees no blood or fatality, and slams back the door. Hicky paces up and down the room, damning their lot in a high-pitched voice.

'I'll call my pa, he'll wire the—'

'You'd be callin' an empty bottle, an' you know it, Kenny. Get real, man! That sawbuck was all we had in the world. What we gonna do? I'll tell you what were gonna do. Some poor bastard's gonna pay for that breakfast you just devoured. You happy now?'

'What'd ya mean? Gonna pay?' mutters Kenny.

'What I said, peckerhead. You stay close here on in. Got that?'

Aching eyes slowly open and squint against the morning light. The room is deadly quiet. Tommy raises his head a little, feels the pain, and gently lowers it back on the pillow. Turning his head, he sees he's alone in the room, the empty bottle and his opened wallet sitting on the bedside cabinet. He rolls back and closes his eyes – what a night – his eyes pop open. Dammit! The wallet? Where's O'Sullivan? Scrambling off the bed, he stands on strewn credit cards, with automatic reaction, grabs for the telephone. The wire has been cut, the line is dead. Bastard!

Throwing his jacket on, Tommy makes for the pay phone at the front of the building. The dialling tone seems to ring forever. C'mon, Jack. Where the fuck are you?

'Hey, Tommy! Where the fuck you been? I've been waitin' on your call,' Jack shouts with anger.

'O'Sullivan! I had the bastard, an' he's got away.'

'Hold your horses, Tommy. What'd you mean, it's Francione that's got my ass on the line, never mind O'Sullivan,' said Jack.

'I ain't got nothin' on Francione, I'm gonna look this mornin'.'

'You're too fuckin' late. Tomorrow, I gotta hand the house deeds over to Grasano. Can you work a fuckin' miracle before midnight, Tommy?'

'It's askin' a lot, Jack.'

'Yeah, exactly. Give my love to the porno queens, why don't ya?'

'Oh, yeah? Give my love to your new trailer park,' Tommy said, slamming the receiver down.

Tommy's angry and disappointed, an old friendship down the tubes, and all over a smart ass wiseguy. He walks to the restaurant for coffee and aspirin. The young waitress looked at him suspiciously. Is this the same guy who came in yesterday morning? The one that ogled her tits and tipped the five. It's him, all right. What'd he do last night? Sleep in that doggone suit.

Abilene hit the sack fatigued and heavy-eyed. She was kept awake for hours by the constant banter outside her door. Twice she rolled out of the sheets and brewed herbal tea, sat and watched the local news station on television, and shook her head as pictures of Fremont flashed the screen. These dudes have it all wrong, she had said to herself, Joey might get punchy now and then, but he's not stupid enough to kill anyone – is he? It was around four when she yanked the quilt over her head.

Heavy knocking disturbed her sleep. Abilene's reaction is to wrap the quilt around her ears – if it's that motherfuckin' James – it went quiet for a second or two. She couldn't hear no mumbo-jumbo talk outside.

BANG!

Abilene dives out of the bed in her baby-doll and runs to the window. Below her and over the way she sees the negroes huddled together, staring up at her apartment. She presses her nose up to the glass, trying to see who's at her door. She can't get the angle, make out who it is. One thing's for certain, it can't be Joey. The negroes below would have hacked him down before he even reached the staircase.

'POLICE! OPEN UP.'

Abilene leaves the safety hooked and dubiously cracks open the door. CRASH! The door busts open, the chain snapping on impact. A gold badge flashes before her eyes, she's momentarily stunned as the cop moves systematically from room to room, his gun drawn high in the fire position. There's a pause, she hears him curse, a porcelain figurine splinters the lounge floor. He appears in front of her, the search is over. Abilene watches as he slips the special into his shoulder holster.

Abilene swipes out blindly at the broken safety chain.

'What the hell's goin' here!' she screams.

The cop kicks the door closed.

'Sergeant Driscol. LVPD. I got some questions. Get yourself decent.'

'You better have a fuckin' warrant, Driscol,' shrieked Abilene.

She storms into the bedroom and slips on a sweater, her eyes glued to him she walks back into the room. She's seen this bull in the downtown area many times. Only last week he'd strolled into the Mint like some big-shot. It made her stomach turn to watch the management suck his ass.

'Button your mouth an' take a seat, lady. I'm lookin' for your room-mate, Joey Burke. When did you see him last?'

Abilene looks up at Driscol, feels she'd like to tell him Joey doesn't live here, take a jump off the balcony. But realises Driscol's done his homework, and Joey must have done wrong.

'I ain't seen him since he took off for work yesterday.'

'Have you any idea where he might be? Has he any friends–'

'Friends! You gotta be jokin'. Joey ain't got a friend in the world,' said Abilene, smirking.

'What about *you*?' Driscol said, smartly.

Driscol's hit a sore point. Abilene explodes off her seat and rounds on him.

'You'd know all about that, wouldn't you? I seen the way it is, Driscol. Swankin' around like you own the fuckin' city. Go take a walk. You want him – you find him.'

Driscol felt like punching her to the ground. He knows her story. He was outside Binnion's the night she beat the shit out of that girl. He'd have stepped in, only he was on the wrong side of town, with somebody he shouldn't be seen with. Fuck you, bitch. One day I'm gonna set you straight.

'Listen to me, you low rent piece of ass. The interview is over, my belly can't take much more. I'm leavin' my card. You see Joey, tell him do himself a favour, and call that number. Right?'

Abilene slammed the door, it was a signal for the negroes to stay clear as the big man growled his way along the terrace.

Angelo Persaci hooks the handset; Sharky's Rent-A-Car will have a Chrysler outside the All-Star in twenty minutes. He booked it in the name of Ernest Hemingway, figures some dumb broad's going to be staring into the phone and scratching her head, wondering what Ernest's doing in an All-Star. He grins at himself in the dressing table mirror, then gets serious again. Thick fingers flick through the *Yellow Pages*.

'The Flamingo. Can I help you, sir?'

'Give me room 956, will ya?' said Persaci.

Persaci rocks his foot impatiently as a voice keeps telling him he's connected and to hold the line. At last he hears a scratchy voice.

'Yeah. Who is it? What'd ya want?'

'Hey, Frankie, it's me, Angelo Persaci.'

'Where you callin' from?' said Frankie, surprised.

'I'm in town . . . yeah, Vegas . . . I'll be round at eleven o'clock. Have everything ready to go. I got the tickets home.'

'Tickets home? What're talkin' about?'

'The old man sent me, Frankie. Just be ready. OK?'

'Like I need a fuckin' baby-sitter all of a sudden.'

'Something's come up. Carlo needs you for a job. That's all I know.'

'A job? Can't it wait? . . . Yeah! That I can understand. But why the chaperone, Angelo?'

'Hey! No more fuckin' questions. I'm down here on other business, you're just a fuckin' message. Pack your things an' be waitin'.'

Angelo cradled the phone and stretched out on the bed. It was never like this in the old days. These kids today are too smart for their own good. Why Carlo wants Frankie bumped off, he doesn't know and doesn't care, but he knows it must be serious shit. His thoughts go back to Carlo's daughter's wedding. Every chance he got, Frankie was hanging around Laura like a bad smell. But that was years ago, perhaps he's back making a play for her. If that's the case, he'd have to be a foolish man; nobody fucks around inside the family and gets away.

Mary dropped Susie off around eight a.m. Susie freshened up and poured sweet tea. Her eyes stinging from tears and lack of sleep, she sat back and lit a cigarette, remembering how she'd held her father's hand, and he didn't even know she was there. Why did it take something like this to bring a family back together? It had been a long night. Apart from Driscol, one other cop had spoke with her and Mary. A guy by the name of Martinez. The interview was brief, Martinez was in a rush to be someplace else, he'd picked up another homicide on the west side.

Her eyes begin to fill once more. She searches her bathrobe pocket for a Kleenex to wipe her tears. Struggling to sip her tea, she's too choked up. Images of her father and Joey on the street last night, fighting with those black guys. Picturing Moe's sluggish movements as his old body was trying to keep pace with his friend, feeling the pain as the knife enters, the desperation in both men's faces.

She closes her eyes to relieve the soreness. The phone rings, her heart misses a beat, terrified it could be the hospital calling with bad news. She falters – the bell keeps ringing – she squeezes her eyes tight, lifts the handset.

'That you, Susie?'

'Yeah, this is Susie. Who's that?'

'It's Joey. You on your own?'

There's a pause.

'Where'd you get my number?'

'Offa Tommy. It was in his wallet.'

'What'd you want?'

'Thought I'd call an' find out how Moe's doin'?'

'It's touch 'n' go, he lost a lot of blood, we're just hopin'.'

'I just wanted to say I'm sorry. They were lookin' for me, an' Moe got caught in the action.'

'The police are lookin' all over. Where are you? Who are you with?'

'I'm on my own, callin' from a pay phone, on Highland.'

'So where's your friend Tommy?'

'He ain't no friend, I ain't got no friends. I need some help, Susie. Howya fixed?'

Thinking back on her mother's words. How Moe was close to Joey. How they enjoyed a beer, and cracked jokes together after work.

'Make your way to Highland and Sahara. I'll loan Mary's wagon and pick you up in fifteen minutes. Is that OK?'

'I'll be waitin'.'

Since his call from Persaci one hour ago, a cigarette hasn't left his lips. During that time, Frankie's worn the shag off the carpet, rang room service half a dozen times for food and drink he hadn't touched. He's irritated and fazed, a far cry from the euphoria he felt at last night's tables. For what reason would Carlo detail him an escort back to Boston? Naw, it can't be Laura. She showed him the door right after the honeymoon. They'd stayed in touch on a friendly basis, enjoyed each other's company over dinner a few times since. Frankie knowing the risk if they should be seen, they'd always eaten somewhere quiet, out of the way.

To distract his thoughts he picks up the sports pages and reviews next month's title fight between Muhammad Ali and Jimmy Young. He's edging his bet in favour of Ali when the phone rings.

'Frankie, it's Angelo. You on your own?'

'Course I'm on my own. I already got enough with one baby-sitter.'

'You all set?'

'Yeah.'

'I'm comin' up.'

Frankie's adrenaline begins to surge. He's met with this Persaci a few times; the man's an animal. He remembers when he was in the office with Carlo, one time. Persaci was summoned to make a hit on a wiseguy who'd turned stool pigeon, and was now in the hands of the Federal Protection Agency. This guy was going to be hard to get at, the Feds had secreted him into another state. Persaci listened, never said a word. His eyes stayed cold and fixed. Persaci got the snitch on the courthouse steps in Washington DC. Persaci was a legend.

The two men greet each other with a feeble handshake.

'You been havin' a good time, Frankie?' said Angelo, glancing to baggage, a full ashtray and the newspaper opened up on the sports page.

'What time's the flight, Angelo? We got time for a drink in the bar?'

'We got plenty a time. Just relax. The flight ain't till six.

Angelo strolls to the balcony, making out he's interested in the view outside.

'Pretty nice up here, hey, Frankie? You should see the dump I've been stayin'.'

'Where's that?'

'The fuckin' All-Star,' Angelo grinned, stepping out on the balcony. 'Do ya fuckin' believe that?'

'Let's go down the bar, Angelo. There's a couple a broads I'd like you to—'

'Jeez! C'mon look at this, Frankie. I ain't seen a Caddy like this since Don Baiona's funeral.'

Frankie moves forward, dithers with uncertainty. Angelo waves him on excitedly, his head moving slowly with the flow of traffic.

'C'mon, Frankie! You can't miss this showpiece.'

Frankie's not too sure, couldn't Persaci have whacked him as he'd walked through the door? Hasn't Grasano been like a father to him?

'You're gonna miss it, Frankie.'

15

Lying stone-still on the single cot, Kenny bluffs he's asleep, when he feels it's safe, squints a cautious eye at Hicky. His stomach feels a little sore after their altercation, but at least he didn't throw his double helping of breakfast up. Hicky had marched up and down the room, screamed blue murder. An old inmate two doors down had come to his rescue by threatening them with management and certain eviction if they didn't simmer down. Hicky told him, go fuck himself, they were leaving at twelve o'clock anyway. Hicky did keep it down, needed someplace to think on what to do next.

'C'mon, Kenny, it's fifteen to twelve, we gotta be leavin' soon.'

Kenny wants to stay put. This flea-ridden room being his only salvation from the cruel world outside. It's not what's outside that's bothering Kenny, it's what schemes Hicky has dreamt up once they hit the street that's causing him a problem. Kenny's running through all the possibilities: from robbing the Wells Fargo Bank to kidnapping Howard Hughes. The bank's a possibility. Is Hughes still in town?

'Move it, Kenny! You're a lazy bastard, next time I'm gonna pick somebody with what it takes between the fuckin' ears.'

Kenny stirs and stretches out of his pretend sleep.

'Gee! Is that the time already? What's happenin', Hicky?'

Hicky scoops up Kenny's holdall and hurls it at him.

'Let's go, Kenny. You're startin' to piss me off again.'

Kenny caught the bag and propped it under his feet. He isn't going any place without a fight; he'll fake an illness.

'I've been gettin dizzy spells.'

'You're about the dizziest person I ever met, Kenny. You fuck up in the casino, steal my money and now you're belly-aching – fuck you, loser. You got your wish, I'm gonna leave you behind. *You* find your next meal ticket.'

Hicky slopes out the door. Kenny places his hands behind his head and adjusts his feet into a more comfortable position.

Kenny looks on with a cocky grin.

'See yer, Hicky. Give my regards to the Golden Gate, why don't yer?'

Kenny hears footsteps in the corridor. It's got to be Hicky, returning all apologetic. He can't wait to see his face, tell him, that's OK, at least we know where it's at.

A purple face emerges around the door frame. It isn't Hicky. It's the motel manager.

'What's it say on the ticket, son? It says twelve o'clock. Sling your hook.'

Kenny's up and on his feet, grabs his holdall and shoots out the door.

'Wait for me, Hicky,' he yells, sprinting hell for leather up 6th Street.

Kenny caught sight of Hicky on the corner of Carson. He followed Hicky at a sensible distance all the way to Ogden. When Hicky stopped, Kenny stopped. On it went until Hicky swung left into the Golden Spike Hotel and Casino. This must be part of Hicky's grand plan, thought Kenny. Suddenly Kenny was at his side.

'Hey! Shitface. What the fuck are you after? A free lunch? Thought you'd be outside the Western Union this minute, waitin' on your ol' man's cash?' said Hicky, sarcastically.

Kenny slung the holdall on to his other shoulder and fell in step.

'Don't be like that, Hicky. I'm with you all the way. Anything I can do–'

Hicky lengthens his stride.

'Go fuck yourself, that's what you can do. I ain't trustin' yer no more.'

The Golden Spike is a cheap joint. No sharp suits and pinkie rings, just nickel and dime and denim cloth. If Hicky thinks he'll score in a place like this, he's going to stay poor. Hicky's no stranger to this place, he'd worked it after his dealer course and hoped things had changed. After a quick scout around, he realised it hadn't, and made for the exit.

Hicky's stuck between a rock and a hard place. He can't afford to walk the downtown casinos, not after last night's fiasco in the Mint, and it's one hell of a walk to the Strip casinos. He's got no choice. He's got to take his chances on the Strip.

'You with me?' Hicky said.

'All the way, Hicky,' Kenny beams.

'Well, no more pissin' an' moanin', OK?' said Hicky sharply.

Tommy siphoned 400 bucks from his Savings and Loan account and sat in the opulence of Caesars Palace with coffee and pastries. Whenever it was discreetly possible, Tommy dabbed a napkin to his head. The initial pain had reduced to a plodding throb, the hangover had almost diminished, and the only person taking any notice is a nosy little brat sat with his parents at the next table. A slug of water helped down two more codeine tablets. He threw the kid a frosty look, and left a pastry.

He breezes the blackjack tables and blows a quick twenty as he devours a young croupier's flesh. The croupier triggers Tommy's need for his daily fix. His mind flashes back to yesterday: to the porno parlour where he'd lost his money in the flick booth with the two girls dancing naked in the tropical garden. Tommy's hit a high. Hey! Maybe they've changed the girls around. To save time, he trades in a sawbuck at the cashier's cage for a five-dollar quarter wrap. Striding out in blazing sunshine, Tommy flags a taxicab.

The cab halts half-a-block away from the parlour. The heat from the cab and coming expectations have risen his body temperature to boiling point. He removes his coat, loosens the top button on his shirt and drifts along the block.

'Hey, mister. You got a light?'

That's the oldest trick in the book. How many guys have been suckered with that one? he thinks, giving the kid the thumbs down and quickening his pace. The kid sprints alongside, darts in front of Tommy.

'C'mon, mister. I'm dyin' for a smoke,' pleaded the kid, waving the cigarette in Tommy's face.

Tommy looks expeditiously about him, there's a dozen or more people on the block, he doesn't think this kid will try anything. Taking no chances, he delivers the Zippo's flame at arm's length. The kid thanks Tommy and scurries off.

Around the corner, Hicky had placed a blank of wood across a pile of bricks and took a seat. He'd spotted the fat guy getting out of the taxi, guessed a visitation to the porno joint and detailed Kenny to make sure. Hicky brushes dust off his faded jeans and mops belly-sweat with his T-shirt. He's bollixed, it had been a long slog down the Strip. He rubs his shoulder where the holdall had bitten and takes a pull on a can of warm Pepsi.

Kenny scoots round the corner. Hicky rocks back on his plank, momentarily surprised at Kenny's enthusiasm.

'He walked right in the stroke joint. Just like you said he would,' blurts Kenny.

'You don't say,' replied Hicky, nonchalantly.

'What're we gonna do now?'

Hicky stands and pitches the empty can across waste ground then points to a clump of bushes.

174

'We'll hide the bags over there. After that – just do as I tell yer.'

Kenny picked up his holdall and fell in smartly behind his guardian angel, Hicky Watson.

Inside, Tommy's eyes slowly adapt to the dimly lit passageways. He gropes along in comical fashion. Hunched one moment, squinting beneath cubicle doors, on his toes the next, looking over the doors for tell-tale flickering light. Most of the cubicles along this section appear to be full, even the one he lost his money in yesterday. He turns the corner to try another row, spots the booth entrance to the dancing girls and frenziedly tears at the five-dollar wrap.

Tommy slides in and turns the twist lock, hooks his coat and settles down on a pull-down stool. With a coin choked fist, he dabs a bead of sweat that has rolled into his eye. Slowly easing off the stool, he unzips his fly and begins to coolly feed the meter-box. There isn't the same urgency as yesterday, he knows his five bucks will convey him through at least fifteen minutes of pure heaven. POW! The shutter lifts. The music begins: Hot Chocolate's, 'You Sexy Thing', beats the chamber. The stage lit before him, Tommy stands statue like for a second, then begins to pant and shake in his own Garden of Eden.

His eyes dart for movement. Where are the dancers? Then right below him, a naked chiquita writhes on the floor. She's young, can't be more than eighteen years of age. So close, he can almost touch her through the glass. Sweat trickles down his cheeks. She spreads her legs wide for Tommy. He drools into her hairy bush. Her hand reaches up and squeezes her small tit, then it slithers downward to play in her furry belly.

Tommy leans forward, his drenched forehead caressing the glass partition.

'C'mon, baby, open wide for Tommy.'

He jerks back his foreskin, settles into a steady rhythm. The

175

girl snakes backwards, colliding with a paper palm tree. Tommy watches the tree fall across her and slows his stroke in anticipation. The girl doesn't bat an eyelid as she sucks on a branch like it's Tommy's cock, then slowly straddles the tree. Tommy fixes on her outspread arse, begins to lick at her outline on the glass. He lengthens his stroke, feels his balls exploding and arches his back.

It's over. The meter shows a non-returnable two-dollars-twenty. Tommy shakes his head and thinks one day he'll get his fuckin' timing right. The next minutes are spent cleaning up and watching the girl try her best to upright the palm tree.

Kenny entered the parlour, Hicky followed two minutes later. Hicky said it was best this way; two guys walking in together would arouse suspicion, might even think they were a couple of queers. Kenny agreed wholeheartedly on that score, and volunteered to go in first. Kenny swapped a one-dollar bill for tokens and threaded his way into the abyss. It was his first time in such a place. The only time he'd been this close to tunnel darkness was on a ghost train at a funfair back home.

He wandered around in circles, thinking, should he try a quarter's worth? Then remembered Hicky's fury with his eggs over easy breakfast, and kept on walking. In the strange surroundings, Kenny thought he'd been in here forever, when a hand fell on his shoulder. Kenny was so shocked, he began to topple through a swing door. Hicky pulled him back.

'You dumb son-of-a-bitch! Keep it down, you're gonna empty every fuckin' cubicle in the joint,' hissed Hicky.

'Jeez, Hicky! You scared me shitless,' gasped Kenny.

Hicky grips Kenny firmly by the collar and pulls him centre of the passageway.

'You seen the fat guy?'

'I ain't seen a livin' soul. This place is kinda spooky.'

'Spooky, my fuckin' ass. You still got the dollar's worth of tokens?'

'Right here,' whispered Kenny.

Hicky held out his hand, 'Give 'em here.'

Tommy adjusts his clothing and opens the door. He's about to step out, recognises the kid who bummed the light, sees his friend and sneaks back inside the cubicle. He doesn't lock the door, thinks they'll walk on by.

BOOM! The door bursts open. Tommy sucks air and back-pedals into the far corner. Hicky levels the bowie knife and hurls himself across the cubicle at Tommy. In darkness, such a move could be hit and miss, but Hicky sticks him good. Tommy feels him coming at him like an express train, covers his head, draws his knees up tight. It's no use – the blade plunges with jackhammer speed.

'What the fuck!' hollered Kenny, scrambling in and falling against Hicky.

There's an eerie silence as Hicky throws the bowie to one side and goes through Tommy's pockets. Kenny watches on in bewilderment. It all happened so fast.

'Why didn't you ask him–' Kenny cries, fighting for breath.

Hicky pushes past, knocking Kenny sideways.

'You want I should ask for a receipt! Let's get the fuck outta here,' shouts Hicky, dashing down the passageway.

'Central to Six Delta?'

'Six Delta?'

'Six Delta, we got one dead Caucasian male at the front of the Flamingo. What's your location? Over.'

'2435 Fremont. Checking out suspected perpetrators from last night's incident. Nobody's home, over.'

'Central Six Delta, please respond, over.'

Driscol smiles into the police radio.

'Roger, over.'

Normally it'd be, 'Driscol, we got a body over at the Flamingo. Get your ass over there,' so he reckons the dispatcher must have someone of weight looking over her shoulder.

By the time Driscol had gunned across town and hit the yellow cordon tape, the body had already been shipped to the morgue. Apart from tape and chalk line, there's only a few goggle-eyed bystanders and a fresh-faced patrolman. It's like nothing of consequence had happened.

Driscol negotiates the tape.

'What we got?'

'Some guy took a dive off the fourth floor. Wenkle's inside taking the details. Some balls, eh?' said the patrolman, looking up.

Driscol looks back along the roadway, wondering if the ambulance had taken another route back to the morgue, he hadn't seen it on his way over.

'Ain't that somethin'? I just got the call, clipped across town an' already the stiff is on the slab,' said Driscol, shaking his head.

The patrolman winks an eye at Driscol.

'The management called 'em out pronto. You know how it is? They want people inside – not on the outside.'

'You got a name for this guy?'

'Naw. Wenkle will have all that shit. Go see him, he'll be in the lobby,' said the patrolman, gathering in the tape.

Driscol can't believe what he's hearing.

'What's your name, son?'

'Larry Parkinson.'

'Listen, Larry. I know for certain that a doctor and photographer ain't been near. You an' Wenkle's ass is in a sling, buddy. *You* go see him, tell him get down here fuckin' sharpish,' snapped Driscol.

Larry reddened, rehooked the tape and took off to find Wenkle. Driscol took shade under a palm and smoked a full cigarette before Wenkle sprang out from the building.

'What the fuck you playin' at, Wenkle? You lost your fuckin' marbles? Who certified the body?'

Wenkle snaps his pad and slices the pencil behind his ear.

'C'mon, Driscol. What's the beef? You know how it is?'

Driscol knows how it is. It seems the Flamingo has more pull than City Hall these days. He should tear Wenkle off a strip, drill the detective on police procedure, but it would go in one ear and out the other. Wenkle opens his pad and flips the pages.

'A guy from Boston, by the name of Frank Francione. Word has it he'd been heavy at the tables an' there ain't a nickel in his room. The old fuckin' story, Driscol. He musta jumped,' said Wenkle, noting the surprise in Driscol's face when Francione's name was mentioned.

'You know this guy, Driscol?'

'Never heard of him. You checked with the day clerk? Made sure he didn't have any money in the house safe?'

'If he did, they ain't tellin'. Naw. The guy done his money, took a dive, believe me – can we take the fuckin' tape down now?'

'Central to Six Delta.'

Driscol walks towards the Charger. Remembered he'd forgotten to take Lenny's badge number, and turns back.

'Central to Six Delta!'

'Six Delta.'

'Central to Six Delta. We have two black males acting suspiciously at the rear of the Day and Night drug store on Main. Check it out, it could be the guys you're lookin' for, over.'

'Roger, over.'

As Driscol slides into drive, Wenkle pats the roof of the Charger.

'Keepin' yer kinda busy, eh?'

'Yeah, Wenkle. You wanna try it some time,' Driscol shouts, burning rubber.

'Fuck you,' Wenkle called after him.

Ray Dixon saw the two negroes mooching about the Dumpster of the ice cream parlour next door. He didn't like the look of them one bit, and detailed Lois to keep a close eye, while he called 911 from his office. Their faces looked familiar, sure they'd been the store, some time or another. But Ray knows from past experience; in this neighbourhood, you can't be sure about anything!

A store assistant opens the door wide as Driscol strides across the sidewalk. Everyone in here knows the big guy, he's helped them in the past with all manner of low-life. The shop-lifter demanded nothing more than an ordinary patrolman to write the ticket. When junkies tried trading phoney prescriptions or the place was getting cased, Central sent along a heavy-weight.

'How'ya doin', Danny? They're out back.'

Driscol unholsters his .44, and steps outside to sweep the area. If those motherfuckers were here five minutes ago, they sure ain't now.

Driscol looks over to Lois.

'Which way did they head?'

She told him she needed to use the bathroom, came back to the window and they were gone. Ray apologises, sorry he'd wasted Driscol's time. Driscol said it didn't matter, best be on the safe side, and followed Ray into the office to take down particulars.

Driscol adjusts his bifocals on the tip of his nose. These are a new item in Driscol's life. Never thought it would happen, but the old peelers are failing him these days, and he don't like them one bit.

'Give their heights, Ray . . . Five-eleven, maybe six? Big guys, eh? You said one guy was limping. How was it? Like he's – hang on, Ray.'

He peers over the rim of his glasses into the store, sees Susie walking the shelving, picking up bandage and antiseptic cream. Straight away, that old gut feeling tells him he's lucked in. Driscol eyeballs her to the cashier, watches her pay the tab and walk out the door.

'I'll swing by later, Ray. I gotta go!'

Staying alert for prowl cars, Joey dodged along Highland. Once or twice he'd heard their sirens close by and tucked inside a builders' merchant yard. Sneaking along like some bandit, hiding in streets, Joey's never been afraid to walk. So, what's new, ain't it always gonna be this way?

He reached the junction with Sahara and stooped behind a low wall, poking his head over brickwork every so often for signs of Mary's station wagon. This is too exposed, he wished he'd arranged someplace different. He hears the beeping of a car horn, shoots up and peers over the wall. There's no sign of the Woody. From a different direction, he hears the horn again. Susie's pulled in ten feet behind him – what if it had been the cops?

Susie watches Joey make a dash from cover. On the way over, she'd been thinking if she was doing the right thing; should she be getting involved with a man she barely knows, and is wanted by the police? Mary told her, Joey was a little rough around the edges, but kept himself to himself, and would have defended Moe the best he could. So Mary had convinced her, but there were one or two nagging doubts. What was the fight over? Was it a chance mugging? Or was it retaliation, for something Joey had done to the negroes? These were questions that ran through her mind over and over again. Joey makes a beeline for the station wagon, and hurls himself into the passenger seat.

'Anybody followed yer?'

Susie holds fire with the gas and looks at him strangely.

'Follow me? Who'd want to follow me?'

'It don't matter. Let's go, eh?'

Susie pulls away slowly, looking quizzically at Joey for direction, 'Where we goin'?' she askes.

'Dunno. Outside city limits, I guess. I need someplace to straighten out.'

'If you're thinkin' on my place? Forget it, Joey. From where I live, I can see your old work station, plain as day.'

'You live on Fremont?'

Susie wheels the Woody onto Sahara.

'Sure do.'

'Ain't that the story!'

Susie hit Sahara and cruised on for Boulder Highway. Joey asked how Moe was doing, Susie said things looked on the up and quickly changed the subject. He asked how Mary was coping, but got the same cold response. Joey felt awkward. He watched the scenery roll by, glimpsed a cotton-tail break cover and scoot open ground, and thought about his own predicament. Unlike the rabbit, he didn't have a clue where he was heading, but they both had a similar insight for predators. Joey's perception of the rabbit has momentarily dulled his sense of danger. If he'd have been more vigilant, he'd have seen Driscol's Charger 500, tailing them at an adequate distance.

Fifteen minutes later, Susie pulls off the highway and parks up behind a small motel.

Susie glances over at Joey, 'I know these people. You'll be safe here.'

Joey knots his shoulders, and unconsciously paws the small .38 in his jean pocket.

'You got any money, Joey?'

'Yeah, what'd you need?'

'Twenty will cover two nights – is two nights enough?'

'That'll be fine,' said Joey, reaching into his back pocket, drawing a handful of crumpled notes.

Susie takes it and steps out of the station wagon.

'Stay here, while I pay the desk,' said Susie.

Driscol saw the wagon slow, make a left and cut the highway. He pulled over into a service station and shut down the engine, thoughtful in his next move, the radio crackled into life.

'Central to Six Delta.'

Driscol hears the dispatcher echo round the headlining, but he's lost in thought as Joey walks into the Bueno Vista motel.

'Wake up, Driscol!'

Driscol fiddles the tuning knob, pulls a face, annoyed at being disturbed.

'OK, Rosa, what're got?'

'You're gonna love this one, Danny. We have a homicide in the Pleasure Flesh—'

'The one on Industrial?'

'Yeah, you got it.'

Driscol places the flashing light to the roof of his car.

'I'm on my way, over.'

He floored the pedal into town. His thoughts run back to Joey and the Bueno Vista. That guy's gonna stick around a day or two, he reasons. Joey must be fatigued and disorientated by recent happenings, maybe he'll take a drink in his new-found safety and hit the sack, loopy juiced. Driscol will drive by at sunup.

For a full five minutes, Tommy's body lay slumped in the booth; nobody had stepped inside to view the pretty chiquita. It was the girl who raised the alarm. She hadn't seen the booth window light up for ages, which in a way demeaned her star-studded status. After all, she's working tips, like the rest of the town. She'd kicked the canvas back-cloth to alert the manager. His head popped out beside a crudely painted Hawaiian dancer. She'd pointed towards the blank screen.

The panic that erupted was incredible. Within seconds of Tommy's body being found, fluorescent tubes lit the building, burning holes in men dashing blindly up and down passageways. One old-timer cleared the booth without his trousers, and bumped smack bang into two faggots hanging on to each other for dear life. The management had the presence of mind to lock the security turnstile, which created a greater commotion. Men were piling into each other faster than the Indy 500.

Sergeant Wenkle was the first bull on the scene and couldn't believe his eyes. He was soon joined by every available squad car in the area: murder in a porn joint is very big news, and every cop there knew he'd have his face on the TV screen come six o'clock. Cars and trucks stopped to nosy on, and pretty soon there were more than three dozen bystanders waiting for a TV news crew to take up position. With cameras rolling and a cheer from the crowd, Wenkle paraded a string of motley characters out of the Pleasure Flesh. Fingers soon began to point behind gleeful faces. In the line-up was a minister from the Candlelight Wedding Chapel, a local doctor, and a well-known celebrity. The crowd had a field day. This was better than Thanksgiving.

Wenkle was all powerful when Driscol arrived. Giving interviews, correcting reporters on the precise spelling of his name, and lots more that made Driscol sick to his stomach. He stood and watched the show, wished he'd been detailed to take charge instead of Wenkle. He'll fuck it upside down anyways, he thought, as he hopped the Charger and took off for lunch.

The suitcase was light in Angelo's mighty fist. It felt like there was nothing in it, but twice he'd counted out the seven G's in Frankie's room, and twice he'd come up with two grand more than Carlo was expecting. He'll give Carlo five, Carlo would never know what Frankie had skimmed from the house on his final night. What's the guy deserve anyway? Carlo ain't used his funeral services in the past ten months, so fuck him.

Outside the Flamingo, the case went in the trunk of the rented Chrysler and Angelo took off down the Strip for the Starburst. Francione had flown like a bird, it was easy. One more piece of business to deal with, then he'll return to Boston. He'd wondered what O'Sullivan looked like after all these years, whether he'd recognise him straight off the bat. One thing's for certain, O'Sullivan will recognise him. Angelo drew some looks when he'd asked for Tommy at the motel. Nobody seemed to know much about him. He took Tommy's room number, said he'd call by later.

Driscol ate a light lunch in Pete's place, drank a soda pop and played four hands of Chinese patience. There were no messages, the place was half empty. Driscol tipped Maria two bucks, a knowing smile, and left.

His next stop was McCarren airport, he was out of there in fifteen minutes flat. Next stop, the All-Star, south of Tropicana. The manager, Sergy Woolfe, made coffee and small talk. Driscol soon had all the information he needed, and was wheeling the streets of Las Vegas.

16

It had been years since he'd watched TV, but with little else to do till Susie returned, he pushed the button and swung his legs over the arm of a chair.

Every ten minutes or so, the set is telling him Des Arness and Gunsmoke are beating Larry Sanders out of sight for prime time favouritism. Forty minutes go by and he's seen more advertising than he's seen all his life. He walks over to the blinds and looks outside for signs of Susie. She's late, said she'd only be an hour or so at most. Joey's so hungry he could eat his way through a full menu. He flicks the channels for a local station. Perhaps there's news on last night's mêlée?

The news is part through, when something bizarre draws his curiosity. He knows that place, Maurice Turner has a piece of the action. The camera is focused on men parading outside a porno joint, glides into the crowd and settles on a big cop that Joey's seen around the streets. He pricks his ears up – he heard it right – some guy from Boston has been murdered in there. They didn't give a name. He hopes to fuck it's that nosy bastard, Mace. Will that be one off his back? Nah, he couldn't be so lucky, there's a million guys come down from Boston.

Headlights penetrate the blinds, throwing brilliant light around the room. Joey pulls the .38. They dip twice, a signal from Susie.

'Where you been, is everythin' all right? I thought you might have been followed,' said Joey, snapping the door shut.

Susie rests two dolly bags on the table.

'Nobody's followin' nobody. I just made it out of the hospital, there's been a turn in Moe's favour.'

'That's great, Susie. Was Mary with you? Did you speak to him?'

'Speak to him! I couldn't stop him. He was askin' after you, Joey.'

'He did! Ain't that somethin'?'

Joey's taken back a little by the occasion. Moe's on the mend. As they drove out here, Susie had been sharp with him, that he understood. But now, she knows the story.

'He said, watch out for Freddy. Does that mean anything?'

'Freddy's history. Let's get to it, Susie. What're we eatin'?'

Susie dabs her cheeks, smiles at Joey and tosses him a bag.

'You like Chinese?'

'I do.'

'I got you something else in the trunk.'

Joey jumps back, startled. There's a catch. What the fuck is going on?

'No surprises!' said Joey, mockingly.

She steps back and laughs.

'Moe sends his regards – there's a pint of Irish in the trunk, what'd you say we celebrate, Joey?'

The cabby blasted his horn impatiently, cursed his fare had to be Abilene. Ray's schedule was always tight Sunday evenings; every time she kept him waiting. Abilene was adding the finishing touch with sensational cerise lipstick, screwed a finger in Ray's direction and defiantly dabbed perfume on her hot-spots. She was going to knock 'em for dead tonight, and show Charlie he'd done the right thing in keeping her on the casino's payroll.

Ray looked across and sniffed her fragrance.

'You done good tonight, Abilene. Five minutes must be a fuckin' record.'

'Ha, what's eatin' yer. Ray? Grace still got you on ration?'

He locks the cab wheels and makes a U-turn. A gang of negroes step into the courtyard and stare at Abilene menacingly.

'These coloureds are all over the place. I bet it's to do with that shootin' last night.'

'Oh, yeah?'

'Oh, yeah! Word has it on the street they got Joey in the frame. What's the gen, Abilene?'

'I ain't seen him to ask. Step on it, Ray. I'm runnin' late as it is.'

Ray throws a look of despair and glances at the meter.

'Jeez, Abilene, pardon me for breathin'. Like it's all down to me you're fuckin' late?'

The atmosphere inside the Mint is electric. The place is full, the tables lively, cocktail orders coming thick and fast. Karen nudges Masie as they walk out the staff room.

'Look at this lot, Masie. We're gonna make big bucks tonight.'

'I hope so, Karen. I opened my mail-box this mornin' and found the utility bill.'

'On a Sunday? Who's *your* fuckin' postman?'

'I only open the darn thing once a week, figure there ain't no way I can pay bills on a Sunday!'

They both giggle and face up to Mike.

'Hey, you girls, how'ya doin'? What's the joke?'

'You're the joke, Mike, gimmie a tray,' said Masie.

Mike sighs, passes over the trays and looks over Masie's shoulder.

'Hey, Masie! Look what the cat dragged in.'

Masie turns and can't believe her eyes. Abilene swans in like she just bought the place, and is about to make some changes.

The last hour had been hell for Masie. She'd looked for

Jimmy Jinks, he'd been called to another casino. Mike had heard and seen enough, and told them several times to shape up, their constant bitching was no good for business. He watches Abilene cut through gamblers with another order.

'Make it snappy, Mike. I got a break comin' up,' said Abilene.

'You two girls better be gettin' your act together, I've already had two complaints from Marrante since you came on shift.'

'Fuck Marrante, and just do the order.'

'Any more an' I'm gonna let you loose on him,' replied Mike, making ready the order.

'Yeah, yeah. I got it covered, Mike. Don't you know the rules by now? It ain't what you know, it's who you know,' said Abilene, tapping her nose.

Mike glances sideways as Karen and Masie approach the bar.

'Make me next, Mike. I gotta a Texan tipping big time,' said Masie.

'Maybe your luck's gonna ride tonight, hey, Masie?' said Karen.

Abilene lifts her tray, shoots a look at Mike, 'He must be tippin' big, Mike. You seen the price of a face-lift these days?'

'Cut it out, will ya?' said Mike, sternly, turning his attention to Masie and Karen.

Abilene throws her head in the air, 'See you after my break, Mike.' Then evaporates amongst the players to dispense drinks.

The staff lounge is almost as busy as the casino itself. Off-duty croupiers mingle and gossip on the night's play, each story more exaggerated than the last. Abilene joins the line for the coffee station. With all the activity around her, Abilene didn't see Masie enter the lounge, didn't notice Masie at her shoulder until the last minute.

'What're doin' on your break? Oh, I get it. You come for advice on beauty treatment?' sneered Abilene.

'Off you! You gotta be jokin'. You're past it, bitch,' scoffs Masie, reaching for the cappuccino machine's handle.

'Yeah, right. There's a few more years left in me yet.'

'You wanna bet,' shrieks Masie, grabbing Abilene's hair, forcing her face into the jet of steam. With all her strength, she holds her there, the steam spluttering, scalding the flesh from Abilene's cheeks. Abilene screams with agony, her arms flaying, sending crockery smashing to the floor. Croupiers rush from all directions, strong hands grab at Masie, propelling her back, pinning her to the floor. Others run to Abilene's aid with saturated dishcloths.

'You crazy bitch!' screams Abilene, tears stinging as they stream down her blistered face. She knows she's finished in this business, who will employ her now with a disfigured face? Not even Charlie Powell could bring that off. Masie's finished too. This Fall she'll watch the leaves turn golden brown in Deadsville, Kentucky.

Several autos, a string of dusty pickups and four police cruisers park the front rank of Pete's All-Night-Diner. In shadow, to the side of the building, sit a Lincoln Continental and a blue rented Chrysler.

Driscol bellies the ramp and pulls tight to the Lincoln. Ain't I seen this baby before? He takes a closer look, it belongs to Mitch Griffin. What the fuck is Mitch doin' here? Pete's diner is a far cry from his usual eating haunts. He doesn't want to see Mitch tonight, there'd be too many questions and too few answers.

The juke box is murdering Angelo's ears. A kid behind him is popping bubble gum and he's wondering why the hell Jerry has brought him here. All these cops at the far end of the diner aren't helping his digestive system. His chilli-cheeseburger lies cold on the table.

'What the fuck we doin' in a dump like this, Jerry?'

Jerry snaps round and stabs a finger into the kid's bubble, turns back and faces Angelo.

'I got someone I want you to meet tonight. He'll be here any second, an' after that we'll make the Dunes, OK?'

'Who's the guy?'

'A cop. A real jerk. We'll have some fun, pull him about some in front of his home team,' said Jerry.

Angelo grunts. He knows he's been brought along as back-up, there's no way Jerry would attempt a one man show in a room full of night-sticks.

Driscol walks in the door and acknowledges patrolmen sat at the far end of the diner. Normally he'd walk straight through to Pete's office, but Pete's behind the counter taking the ice-machine apart.

'Would you fuckin' believe it, Danny? Twice last week I had Roberto's crew out here to fix this goddamn thing. Tomorrow, it's goin' back!'

Driscol leans over the counter and shakes his head.

'Buy a new one, why don't ya? You're makin' a bundle here.'

Pete tosses the wrench along the tiled floor and makes for the espresso machine.

'Business! I'm tellin' yer, Danny – sometimes I wish I was back on the job. You want coffee?'

'Yeah, I'll take coffee. Then I got to be goin'. You got anything for me?'

'Nah. Sweet FA. Milk or cream?'

'Cream – ain't that Mitch's Lincoln outside?'

Pete steadies the cup on the counter and glances to the top tables.

'Sure is. His kid Jerry's in with some bozo. Take a look.'

Driscol lifts the cup to his lips, stares straight ahead.

'Naw, fuck it, Pete. They'd be trouble, an' you don't need it.'

A young kid and his moll punch buttons on the juke. They take each other's hands, waiting on the music.

'50 Ways To Leave Your Lover' breaks melodically over the young couple. The kid pulls her in close and they sway in each other's arms. A cop whistles, another claps his hands, the atmosphere easy as Paul Simon bows out and makes way for another.

Jerry leans back in his chair as the music stops.

'Hey! Driscol! I see the zoo keeper give yer the night off. Pete, tell him, go buy his monkey nuts some other fuckin' joint. This place is strictly for the human variety.'

'Help Me Make It Through The Night' beats out of the speakers, but no one's listening to John Holt.

'This one's for you, Driscol. *You* ain't gonna make it through the night!'

Pete shoots Driscol a troubled look. Driscol stays fixed on the *Playboy* calendar behind the ex-cop.

'C'mon! Driscol. I got somethin' for yer. It's here – look – right under the table. You wanna play with it?'

Kenny props Pete's diner wall, rocking his head in time with John Holt. Hicky moves swiftly between parked vehicles, peering through side-windows for an easy hot-wire. A couple of minutes ago an old Dodge Charger had nearly picked him out with its headlights. That had been a close call, Hicky had dived under a pickup's differential and waited for the Dodge's shocks to settle, and its occupant to stroll into the diner. It was no good, parking lot brightness was keeping him on his toes.

'What the fuck are you playin' at, Kenny? Didn't I tell yer to keep your eyes skinned?'

Kenny hooks his foot to the wall and takes no notice. John Holt is one of his favourites, he's heard enough of Hicky's bad mouthing and grand schemes to last him a lifetime. He knew this trip wouldn't be a picnic, but to stick some poor guy for the sake of a few hundred bucks has turned his stomach. His first thoughts when he saw the string of cop cars outside the diner was to run inside and give himself up. One thing was for sure; Hicky wouldn't have followed him in, and he'd finish up

taking the rap for both of them. That would have been good-
bye to Wisconsin forever.

Hicky drags Kenny off the wall.

'Let's go see what's around the corner. It's too fuckin' bright
out there.'

The cops down the far end watch mesmerised as Driscol
takes shit from this young kid.

'Where's Julie tonight, Driscol? Makin' out with her pimp?
Perhaps she needs some of this, you fuckin' asshole.'

Driscol slowly turns his head, sees Jerry's hand stroking
something underneath the table.

The tablecloth rises as Jerry's Colt automatic comes into
view. The weapon snags the edge of the table, Pete moves back
and ducks behind the counter. Angelo distances himself from
Jerry as the young blood frees the Colt. For a second, the lone
figure at the counter appears isolated and vulnerable – like
quick silver – Driscol's on the turn, levelling his .44.

PAKOOOSH! PAKOOOSH! Five times the .44 barks
rapid fire. The diner explodes into screams and activity. Cops,
kids and Japanese tourists hit the deck and scramble for cover.
Ruby crashes to the floor with a tray full of spaghetti, hears the
clatter of Jerry's automatic as it impacts floor tiles and smells
cordite as .44 shell casings dance the floor around her.

Driscol pierced Jerry and Angelo twice with upper body
shots. The fifth smashes the front of the juke-box clean away.
As the music and echo of gunfire fade, one cop makes a lunge at
Driscol, but is thrown aside as people scrambled for the exit.
Another cop clambers unsteadily to his feet and makes an
effort to control the door. It's no use, most of the customers
just barrel through and scarper in every direction.

Pete chances a terrified eye over the counter and sees Driscol
still standing in the fire position. Cops are on their feet but
keeping a respectable distance. Angelo is slumped face down in
his hamburger. Jerry lies on his side, crimson blood seeping on
to Pete's newly tiled floor.

'Gimmie the piece, Danny. C'mon, buddy, lay it on the counter – please,' said Pete, nervously.

Driscol relaxed his arms, held the shooter loose for a moment, then passed it up. There was no indication of remorse on his face. He'd drawn the quicker, made it tell. Who wouldn't have done the same?

Once Pete had the .44 safely out of Driscol's reach, police radios broke the eerie silence, cops rushed over to the bodies.

Kenny fell to one knee as the shots rang out. He thought they were meant for him and wrapped his hands tight around his head. He broke out in a cold sweat, his heart beating so fast it almost left his chest. He looked along paint-washed block-work for Hicky and saw him lifting a brick out of the dirt.

Hicky was on top of the Chrysler when the gun fire errupted. He'd dismissed the Lincoln; too fancy scamansky. The cops would stop it before it reached the county line. The brick burst through the side window, Hicky quickly slipped the door handle and dived beneath the steering column and tugged at wiring. The ignition fired as people stampeded the parking lot. Hicky floored the rented Chrysler's gas pedal, he saw Kenny sprinting after him in the rear view and slowed.

Joey gently lifts Susie's head and frees the arm that has been her pillow for the past hours. His sleep has been broken by a coyote's howl somewhere in the desert. Not wanting to disturb Susie, he carefully rolls away from her warmth. Outside security lighting slips the window blinds, casting bleary shadow over strange surroundings. Susie stirs, Joey waits for her to settle before sliding to the edge of the bed.

Rubbing tiredness from his eyes, he walks around an easy chair and splits the blinds. A shooting star bolts the ink black sky, the howling stops; the coyote has found its mate. Joey soaks in the tranquillity for a while, then tiptoes to the handbasin and dips his face into cold water, washing clean the aftertaste of whisky.

Resting his elbows on his knees, he scans the remnants of the bottle and wonders if that was the reason for his lack of sexual appetite. It wasn't that he didn't find her attractive, her sensuality had aroused him. They had talked easily and laughed freely, but once they were between the sheets he had lost all desire to make love. Every time she made a move, Joey switched off, his thoughts shifting between Fremont Street and the Starburst, to Abilene, and his lost rainy day tucked underneath the apartment floor board. Will Driscol leave no stone unturned to find him?

Wrapping a blanket around him to keep out the early morning chill, he didn't notice Susie watching him.

'It's too cold out there, Joey. Come back to bed.'

There was no hint of sexuality in her voice. She realised they were two people brought together through unfortunate circumstance. With time, she could get to like this tough, yet quiet and unassuming man. She knows he'll have to move along in the next day or two, but who knows, maybe he'll keep in touch with Moe.

Trudy poured freshly percolated coffee and heaped blueberry muffins on the silver Princetown tray. Eddie turned down the volume on the lounge TV and offered to help.

'I'll be right along, honey. Just relax, I'll bring it through.'

She'd smiled inwardly. It's been a while since she and Eddie had enjoyed a quiet evening together, and tonight they were going to make the most of it. As she poured the cream, the telephone rang, they looked at each other in disappointment, both realising its implication. Trudy cautiously lifted the handset.

'It's for you, Eddie.'

'Damn!'

Eddie Drome knew it had to be Central.

Trudy looked on as Eddie turned away and cupped one hand to his ear to shut out the sound of the TV.

'Goddamn it! You absolutely certain about this? . . . keep him in my office. I'm on my way.'

Trudy had heard Driscol's name mentioned several times around the house before, he was a hard cop that worked under the captain, now she heard it cussed as Eddie searched for his car keys.

Two detectives sat the captain's desk keeping watch on Driscol. They'd looked at each other with mild amusement, then back at Driscol. The big fella seemed to be taking it all too good, the cigarette hanging from his lips like he didn't give a shit. Perhaps he didn't. But why? This was surely the end of his police career. They slipped off the desk Marine style as the captain entered the office and dismissed themselves with kind words in Driscol's ear. The captain said but a dozen words as Driscol handed in his badge.

'You're a loose cannon, Driscol. You've blown it, no bastard's gonna cover you any more.'

Driscol was suspended pending further enquiries. He'd blown it. What the fuck. He owns a piece of everybody in this town. Police pay and pension? Shit. There's bigger bucks to be made out there on the streets.

17

Driscol looks down at the gauge, fixes his shades, and sets his eyes on the road ahead. It's an eight-mile drive to the Bueno Vista, and soon he'll have to pull over for gas. A mustard-coloured Mustang shoots out from nowhere and barrels up behind him. Driscol taps the pedal some – the Mustang bites in – sucking chrome from the Charger's fender. His eyes dart into the rear view, can't make a thing through the Mustang's tinted windshield. Easing into the side of the roadway, near-side tyres turning dirt. The Mustang's powerful V8 guns stereo like in his ears. For a moment, Driscol's off guard and nervous. Instinct makes him reach awkwardly for his shoulder-holster and draw the .44 automatic. SHIT! It isn't there no more. The Mustang whips, then swings wide to overtake. Driscol's hand snaps back to the wheel, the Mustang sails by. A Hispanic leans out the Mustang and screws a finger back at Driscol.

'Motherfucker!' screams Driscol into a cloud of dust.

Along the highway, the Mustang dilutes to a tiny dot as Driscol brakes on to the Bueno Vista's frontage.

Susie opens her eyes and turns to look at her wrist watch lying beside the bedside lamp. Her eyes travel the unfamiliar room, to Joey, lying fast asleep, like he had no worries in the world. She recalls how they'd drank the watered whisky and talked freely. Their clumsy foreplay, and awkward love making when Joey had come back to bed. How she'd initiated the first moves, and felt the tenseness in his body, and knew it was a mistake. He held her in his arms for a long time afterwards. No words were needed, they both knew their clumsiness was down to outside pressure.

Susie gently shakes his shoulder, 'I got to be goin',' she said.

Joey stirs and looks into her eyes, 'Stay a while,' said Joey, reaching beneath the mattress, making sure the .38 is at hand's reach.

'I need to call the hospital, I got plenty to do.'

'Call 'em from the desk, why don't ya? Save you runnin' back into town.'

'I could do–'

'Do it,' Joey cuts in, 'an while you're there, see if they can't rustle a coupla coffees,' he said, jokingly, a twinkle in his eye.

Hooking the phone, Susie's pleased with the recovery Moe's making. She smiles as she makes her way to the reception.

'How'ya doing this beautiful morning, Bob?'

'Just fine, honey, yourself?' said Bob, pencilling in a crossword.

'I'm feelin' good. That was the hospital, daddy's comin' on great.'

Bob folds the newspaper, looks at her surprised, 'Old Moe? What's he been doin' with himself?'

'He got stabbed on Fremont two nights ago, it was all over the news.'

'Jeez! I read it in the paper. Who'da thought – you tell him, Bob sends his best – be sure you do that for me, Susie.'

'I will. What's the chances of two coffees, Bob?'

A deep voice rumbles behind her, 'Make it three, Susie.'

Startled by the familiar voice, she turns and confirms who it belongs to. Her blood rushes, a cold shiver runs her back.

'Let's step to one side, Susie,' said Driscol.

Susie's panicking, she's got to play it cool for Joey's sake.

'You followed me out here? I've told you all I know, which ain't a lot,' she said, defensively.

'I know your father's on the mend. I've been there this mornin'–'

'You been hassling a sick man?' said Susie, trying to throw him off track.

Smart ass! thinks Driscol, looking at her, 'Your old man was concerned over this Joey fella. Tell him Joey ain't around no more. His ID tallied at the Greyhound terminal. He checked out for Los Angeles at six o'clock this mornin'.'

Driscol turns and walks out of the building.

'Your coffee's about ready, honey,' Bob shouted, from the kitchen. Susie stood bewildered.

18

'C'mon in, Jack.'

Jack Bones removes his trilby and closes the door quietly behind him. He takes an apprehensive step, his eyes combing the gloomy room to a table at the far end. Jack doesn't recognise the caller's voice and shuffles diagonally, the linoleum's chill beneath his feet. Trembling hands clutching his steel-blue trilby tight to his stomach, he stops, cocks his head, trying to make out a familiar face.

'What the fuck's the matter with you?'

The voice this time belonged to Carlo Grasano, and Jack breathes a sigh of relief as he treads softly to the chair that has been reserved for him.

He'd received a telephone call earlier in the day. The caller spoke with a heavy Italian accent, told him to be at Angelo's Funeral Parlour at two o'clock prompt. Jack was flabbergasted.

'Ain't that Persaci's place?' he'd uttered nervously. The caller hung up.

'That's the ticket, Jack. Sit yourself down, relax,' said Carlo.

Three men sit around the table with Carlo. One is old and paunchy, the other middle-aged and tanned. Jack recognises the third as Carlo's right-hand man, Vincent Riboco. Carlo waves a cigar between the three men.

'Let me introduce you. To my right, my old friend Stefano

Marfeo from Chicago. To my left, Michael Napolitano from Miami. Vincent, you know already.'

'What am I doin' here, Carlo?'

Carlo turns his head to the door marked Chapel of Rest.

'Go take a look inside, Jack.'

'Take a look at what?' said Jack, blinking nervously at the polished mahogany door.

Carlo leans back in the chair, the cigar clenched between uneven teeth.

'Be a gentleman, Vincent. Open the door for Jack.'

Candle light flickers serenely on rich oak and the heavy brass handles of two opened coffins. Jack's blood runs cold as he takes fearful steps into the centre of the chapel. First he sees white sheen folds that line the coffins, then the waxen faces of Frankie Francione and Angelo Persaci. Jack's stomach sinks, he crosses his chest, pledging atonement to God, Grasano, or anyone who can save him from his fate. Riboco looks on impassively, he's seen and heard enough and shakes the garrotte free from his overcoat pocket. Through reddened eyes, Jack must have seen the candles flutter, shadows dance, as Riboco slid in behind him and snapped the piano wire around his neck.

Carlo acknowledges Riboco with a nod. Yesterday's business has been settled.

'So, Michael. You got yourself a bookmakin' business. Remember to look after me when you're makin' the odds, eh?'

Napolitano smiles and bows his assurances. Carlo turns to Marfeo.

'My dear friend Stefano is now an undertaker, an' two minutes into the business and he gets his first customer. Can't be bad.'

Marfoe gives an icy smile of appreciation, but Carlo's not there to receive it, he's busy talking into Vincent's ear.

'Dump Jack out on Suffolk Downs – seems only right. Send Driscol the fifteen grand, tell him I'll be in touch later.'

Riboco makes to leave, Carlo pulls him back into his seat.

'Put a box of Havanas in the package for Driscol. He done a good job, I appreciate that.'

Thirty-eight miles east of Tucson, Arizona, two pickup trucks trail dust as they head east into the small town of Benson. Both vehicles carry construction workers from a nearby timber-frame housing project. It's early evening, the boys riding the tail-boards in good spirits, looking forward to tomorrow's Fourth of July celebrations. Six-packs and a bag of ice had been purchased at a roadside filling station for the run home, and those not shooting the breeze catch the wind and watch the sun dip west into purple mountains.

Slumped on the bed of the rear truck, Harlan Arrowsmith rests the Bud between his boots and reckons his ma makes the meanest honey roast turkey this side of Twin Buttes. Tucker Middleton reckons that can't be so, while Willie Rael mutters he couldn't give a shit, and tosses an empty over the side.

'Aw, shit, Willie. You just scored a jack-rabbit,' shouts Tucker, handing a fresh can to Willie, and a guy they've grown to like, but know very little.

'What're doin' tomorrow, Joey? You gonna join us over at the Union? Grindstaff'll be there an' he's bound to pitch in a box of beer,' said Tucker.

Grindstaff owns the construction company, and every Fourth he throws down a box like it's one big deal.

'Thanks, Tucker. Maybe I will.'

'Fuck Grindstaff. You come our place an' ma will slice you–'

'You're full of bullshit, Harlan,' shouts Willie, hanging on to the gate as they hit a hole in the road.

Ten minutes later, the truck pulls up outside the Stop 'n' Go grocery store on Larkenburg. They pile out into the street, Harlan heads off home to ma, the rest sling their tool-belts over their shoulders and decide their next move.

'C'mon, guys. Let's make it Annie's place, we can watch the game on the big screen TV,' said Willie.

The crew didn't take a lot of convincing. All agreed, they wait on a school bus to pass and cross the road. Joey walks in the opposite direction.

'Where you goin', Joey?'

'Over to the Landmark,' Joey calls back.

'See you tomorrow. Make sure you're there, Joey,' Willie shouts.

Apart from Budweiser neon and pool table light, the Landmark is as cool and dark as a cave. Stetson hats and baseball caps line the bar. The booths are full, Marty Robbins booms 'El Paso' from the juke box, couples two-step on the small dance area. The Landmark is humming with the laughter. A few heads turn as Joey lets in daylight, then back to their entertainment when they see it's a regular face. The brunette behind the bar signals she'll be with him any second.

'Make it a beer, honey,' said Joey, finding room for his tool-belt on the floor.

'You had a good day, Joey?' said the brunette.

'Yeh. Yourself?'

'I had a letter today from Moe. They've just got back from vacation, it's done him a world of good. He's doin' real fine, sends his love.'

'What else did he say?'

'You'll love this one. He said to watch out for Freddy,' said Susie, laughingly.

'I'll bet,' said Joey, smiling

'There's an envelope inside for you,' said Susie, handing over the mail.

She leaves Joey to open his mail, and gets busy serving customers. Joey walks to pool table lighting and slowly reveals the contents in the envelope. A social security card in the name of Joseph Riley rests in the palm of his hand. Looking into the envelope for clues to who would have sent him this, he pulls out a newspaper clipping and a handwritten note. He lays the clipping on the pool table and smoothes out the creases to read the headlines.

LAS VEGAS JOURNAL June 25th 1976
HEADLESS BODIES FOUND ON STATE LINE

The bodies of two negro males were discovered yesterday on the California Nevada state line. Police believe the two men were from the Las Vegas area . . .

Joey reads no further. What's the connection between the card, the clipping and himself? He reaches in for the typewritten note.

I owed you one. This is a payback.
DD

Susie watches Joey as he scrutinises the papers at the pool table.
'Everything OK, Joey?' she calls over the noise.
Joey tucks everything in the envelope and keeps a tight grip. He motions her to go to the end of the bar.
'You sure Moe didn't have anything else to say?'
'Why, what's the problem?'
'Where did Moe get the envelope from?'
Susie frowns, 'Dunno, but he said he had a visit from that cop, Driscol. Why? It ain't got nothin' to do with him, has it?'
'I think it has. It all makes sense now.'
Joey turns and smiles inwardly. Clutching the paperwork, making a fist, he raises it in the air in triumph. Who'd a thought it? Fifteen years of hide and seek, and finally, a cop bought back his ticket to freedom.